A SAIGON PARTY

(And Other Vietnam War Short Stories)

A SAIGON PARTY

(And Other Vietnam War Short Stories)

Diana Dell

Copyright © 1998 by Diana Dell.

Library of Congress Number: 98-89471
ISBN #:   Hardcover   0-7388-0285-9
          Softcover   0-7388-0286-7

All rights reserved. No part of this book may be reproduced or transmitted in any form or by any means, electronic or mechanical, including photocopying, recording, or by any information storage and retrieval system, without permission in writing from the copyright owner.

Most of the people in these stories are imaginary; any resemblance to persons living or dead are wholly coincidental. If anyone thinks he/she sees himself/herself in any of the characters and feels libeled, please be informed that Diana's sister Barbara, one of the people to whom this book is dedicated, is a 30-year, take-no-prisoners' attorney.

This book was printed in the United States of America.

To order additional copies of this book, contact:
Xlibris Corporation   1-888-7-XLIBRIS
PO Box 2199   1-609-278-0075
Princeton, NJ 08543-2199   www.Xlibris.com
USA   Orders@Xlibris.com

CONTENTS

INTRODUCTION 11

BARBIE AND KEN EXPERIENCE THE WAR 55
A PEDICAB DRIVER PEDDLES THROUGH HISTORY .. 58
SUNNING ON THE DECK 78
A CIA HIRED WIFE BARES HER SOUL 81
THE 4TH OF JULY 90
MAJOR HOLLOWAY, LIFER 92
THE VIETNAMESE ROCK STAR
    INTERVIEW ON AFVN 99
YOLANDA'S FAVORITE BEGGAR 105
SAIGON RUMORS 108
BARBIE'S COMBAT ZONE DIARY 110
GENERAL WESTMORELAND'S HOUSEBOY
    (AND VC SPY) TALKS 115
THE LIBRARY CARD 120
THE GLAZED DONUT DOLLY REMINISCES 122
A SAIGON PARTY 131
THE PHILANTHROPIC EXECUTIVES 137
THE WAR THROUGH PAMELA ROSE'S EYES 140
A SAIGON WARRIOR'S JOURNAL 157
ROB CLAWSON, SOLDIER OF FORTUNE 161
THE VC COLONEL, A.K.A. HANNAH 167
THE AMERICAN JOURNALIST'S
    DEATHBED CONFESSION 188
DAN QUAYLE'S DOUBLE 211

ACKNOWLEDGMENTS 226

DEDICATED TO
BARBARA McPHERSON, CAROL DINGLE,
AND DAVID McPHERSON

Persons attempting to find a motive in this narrative will be prosecuted; persons attempting to find a moral in it will be banished; persons attempting to find a plot in it will be shot.
—Mark Twain

INTRODUCTION

From October 1970 to May 1972, during that period of gradual U.S. troop withdrawal, I lived and worked in Vietnam.

For the first six months, I was a program director at the USO Aloha Club at 22nd Replacement Battalion in Cam Ranh Bay, then the civilian organization's in-country director of public relations and the host of a daily radio show, "USO Showtime," on American Forces Vietnam Network (AFVN), the military station in Saigon.

As an eyewitness to the most significant event of the coming-of-age Baby Boom Generation, I probably will be telling war stories until my final moment on this earth.

However, my tales—some exaggerated, many true—are not about battles, blood, gore, or angst. They are usually about participants of the war other than grunts: CIA agents, bar girls, war profiteers, missionaries, donut dollies, strippers, civilian contractors, pilots, cooks, telephone operators, disc jockeys, rock stars, landladies, pedicab drivers, generals, Buddhist monks, movie stars, pickpockets, politicians, prostitutes, prisoners, beggars, nightclub owners, drug counselors, Montagnard tribesmen, foreign correspondents, ambassadors, doctors, humanitarians, celebrity tourists, and other REMFs (rear echelon mother f_ _kers), civilian as well as military.

Kenny, my younger brother, who died in the Mekong Delta on November 5, 1968, a date forever etched in my memory, was the reason I went to Vietnam.

While walking point on his last day alive, he moved a platoon through a heavily mined area and disarmed several booby traps. His scout dog tripped a well-concealed land mine, killing Kenny instantly, or so the Army claimed, obviously, to lessen our family's pain.

Before flying off to war, he talked into the long nights, while at home on leave, of wanting to return as a hero from combat with a chest full of medals to prove it. And he did.

Kenny came back home with numerous decorations, including the Bronze Star for, as the citation stated, "exceptional heroism in connection with ground operations against an armed hostile force while assigned to the 199th Light Infantry Brigade."

It is still painful to remember the funeral. I stared in a daze as the seven uniformed Army Reservists, safe from combat but not its destruction, stood ramrod straight, aimed their rifles at Heaven, and fired three times with precision. The 21-gun salute sounded like three single shots. Taps drifted throughout the cemetery and seemed to touch the souls of those congregated, even the people who did not know Kenny, 21 for eternity, lying in the flag-draped coffin.

The young men cried the hardest. Many openly wept for perhaps the first time in their adult lives. They seemed to grieve for themselves more than for my younger brother, for their own generation, for their own useless war. The remaining tearless women could not hold back any longer when they heard the angry boys sobbing uncontrollably. Exhausted with sorrow, I could not shed a tear and resented the obvious response taps was meant to evoke.

We buried Kenny next to Daddy, a World War II veteran, who had died two years earlier of a heart attack. Then, you would assume, the healing process for the survivors began. Not so. None of us—my mother, sister Barbara, brothers Jimmy and Ricky, sister-in-law Ruth, and I—ever got over Kenny's death.

Initially, my family and I tried to put Vietnam out of our minds; but for some reason, I had a burning desire to go "over there" and see what the hell was going on. But how and in what capacity? I certainly did not want to join the military. During Kenny's tour of duty, I did my bit for the antiwar movement, volunteering with the Eugene McCarthy for President campaign.

The only other Americans besides soldiers in Vietnam that I saw in magazines, newspapers, and on television were reporters and politicians on fact-finding missions. So many events. So many stories. So many facts. Every day, for years, the media barraged the public with information, much of it contradictory.

"If you can't convince us, confuse us," my father frequently quipped about the government and the press.

During the year and a half after Kenny's death, I went from feelings of grief to sorrow to hopelessness to not giving a shit to finding absurdity all around me. I skipped acceptance. Everything was a joke. A cosmic joke.

After the funeral, I was depressed and did nothing but sleep for three months, taught second grade for the next four, then went to Florida to teach in a newly desegregated middle school.

When another summer arrived, I headed back home to East Vandergrift, a small Pennsylvania town. Besides visiting childhood chums, I attended plenty of weddings, the town's main social events. Sophie Zabinski, one of my neighborhood pals, had quite a shindig. At the reception, I met her roommate from Washington, Caryn Hart, a secretary for National Alliance of Businessmen (NAB), who was sorry to lose Sophie as a roomy.

Caryn and I hit it off the moment we met at the PNA (Polish National Alliance) bar during the gala wedding party. She suggested that I try looking for a job in D.C. and stay with her. There was plenty of room since Sophie's departure and another three months left on the lease.

I arrived in Washington the first week of July 1970, when Nixon and Agnew were running the world. A few days later, I was perusing the classifieds in the Sunday *Washington Post* for any job that sounded remotely interesting: Private Detective Trainee, Photographer's Assistant, Movie Extra. After a while, at the bottom of a page, I spotted: "Social/Recreation Worker, college grad, U.S. citizen, over 24, for position in Thailand, Korea, the Philippines, Vietnam."

Vietnam! This, I had to check out. The ad was placed by National Catholic Community Service (NCCS). The religious connection gave me pause, but the word "Vietnam" peaked my interest.

The next morning, bright and early, I was primly perched in the executive director's office on H Street. A very dignified Dr. Helm (Ph.D., not M.D.) explained that NCCS was one of the six agencies that formed USO. The others were Young Men's Christian Association (YMCA), Young Women's Christian Association (YWCA), Salvation Army, Traveler's Aid, and National Jewish Welfare Board. Hence, the name United Service Organizations; and I always assumed that USO was primarily celebrity shows—Bob Hope, Martha Raye—and Hollywood-type canteens that I had seen in World War II movies on television.

After chatting with me for over an hour, Dr. Helm introduced me to Mr. Horn and Mr. Honeycomb, the other administrators. The three H's ran NCCS on H Street. I never could remember who was who, what their roles were, or what their respective responsibilities were supposed to be. They sort of blended into one person, like the Stepford Executives.

I fit all the qualifications they were seeking in an applicant for a social/recreation position in Vietnam: a citizen of the United States, Roman Catholic, 24 years old, college graduate (I didn't mention by the skin of my teeth), and a practicing member of the faithful. Well, okay, I fibbed. I had not seen the inside of a church for well over five years, except for Kenny's funeral; yet I boldly informed the H's on H Street that not only did I attend Mass every Sunday, but I also received Holy Communion each week as well.

Hitler—another H—said, if you are going to lie, tell a whopper to be believed. Or was it (H)immler who made that comment? I felt that God, who I was fairly sure had a bizarre sense of humor, would understand. At any rate, what did going to church every Sunday have to do with going to Vietnam?

I didn't know then, but found out later, that USO and its six agencies were having one hell of a time recruiting volunteers for

Vietnam. When I say "volunteer," I don't mean to imply that I was not going to be paid. In fact, I didn't know anything about salary negotiating. The H guys matter-of-factly told me what the wages were, and I accepted. Gee, they sounded honest when they claimed every new employee received $7200. So busy convincing them of my honesty, integrity, and veracity, to name but three traits I assumed they possessed, I never dreamed they would lie to me about money.

When I got to Vietnam, I soon discovered that I was the lowest paid of all the staff from the six agencies.

The standard, incredulous question I heard more than once was, "Didn't you even try to haggle for a higher salary?"

The holier-than-thou H's on H Street casually reported, "Oh, regarding wages, everybody starts at the same level of pay."

I suppose I should have become suspicious when they cautioned, "we think it prudent that you not discuss your earnings with anyone at all in the organization," as though this information were top secret crypto or something.

"You're hired as far as we're concerned," one of the H's said, "but you have to be approved by USO headquarters in New York. It's merely a formality."

Believing that I must have really impressed them, I strolled into another office while they placed a call to USO's home office in New York to arrange an immediate interview.

Sitting smugly in the adjoining room out of earshot, I imagined they were notifying the USO bigwigs in the Big Apple, "She's wonderful! She's charming! She's perfect!"

Now, after these many years, I'm reasonably sure that the words spoken into the phone by Dr. Helm (Ph.D., not M.D., as he pointed out each and every time he introduced himself) went more like this, "We caught one. Yeah, she'll do. She won't embarrass us, and she didn't even dicker about money. That makes three to Vietnam for us this month. How about the other agencies? How are the Jews doing? What about the Protestants at the Y's? No, don't worry, we won't lose her. We won't give her a chance to even think about it. She will be at the airport in an hour. Play with her a little before you accept her. We do not want her to think we are too anxious. And, Jack, try not to drink too much over lunch and apprise her anything she does not need to know, such as wages."

Jack Daniels, director of personnel, met me at the airport and escorted me to USO headquarters. We didn't actually go in. Instead, we drove by; he pointed at a building and said, "There's USO. Let's go to lunch."

While he did all the talking during the interview, I got the impression that he was getting a little drunk. Well, it was more than my imagination, because lunch lasted from 11:30 till 4:00, during which time he ate no food and downed at least 10 scotch and waters. No wonder he was as skinny as a rail.

Jack Daniels was excited about me (I don't know how he could have been, since I barely got a word in edgewise), hired me (for the second time) on the spot, offered an immediate expense account, and arranged for training at the Portsmouth, Virginia USO while the paper work was processed for Vietnam. I had to get a passport, series of shots, and security clearances. The job title was assistant director.

"When can you start?" the looped personnel director asked.

In a split second I decided to play tourist in D.C. for a few weeks. "The end of July would be good."

"That's three (hiccup) weeks from now. Owkaay," Jack slurred.

I was getting almost a month of paid vacation even before beginning employment. Nice job.

Riding back to D.C. from New York on the Metroliner after accepting the civilian position with USO, I met a film producer who had gone to West Point for two years. After I informed him that I was off to Vietnam, he told me about a general who took potshots at Vietnamese peasants from his helicopter. I was appalled. So was he, but for a different reason.

"If the general wasted two gooks, he bragged about bagging six." The former plebe shook his head in disgust at the dishonesty of embellishing kills.

The documentary creator explained that he had transferred out of West Point when it dawned on him that he might have to play soldier in a war and enrolled at the University of Miami. All the while waiting out the draft, he picked up a master's degree, got married, had a child, and taught for two years.

"Just to be on the safe side, I also became a Quaker," he added. "I sure as hell wasn't going to be mistaken for a dink by some trigger-happy, nearsighted two-star in a low-flying chopper."

On the way to get drinks, Shane enlightened me about his friends who had faked medical exams, acquired law and MBA degrees, married quickly, and were lucky enough, or connected enough, to obtain slots in the Reserves and National Guard. Because of my drinking companion's loud voice and friendliness, the bar car was soon abuzz with conversations of ways the men in suits had avoided the draft. It was a shared camaraderie, and each person was enjoying reciting his tale.

Only two minority members were present—the Black man serving drinks and me. I could see in his tired brown eyes that he knew boys who were drafted or had enlisted. Silently, the weary bartender and I listened to the young men boasting about how smart they were. As far as they were concerned, serving in Vietnam was the penalty for those who lacked the wherewithal to avoid it. The word "sucker" was used more than a few times that evening to describe soldiers fighting and dying in Vietnam, not smart enough to get one over on Uncle Sam.

Not one of them expressed any outrage at the war. They didn't give a hoot about its nobility or immorality or care about the Vietnamese on either side. Their primary concerns were lying, cheating, faking, conniving, defrauding, and pulling a fast one on the military.

Two Columbia University grads, leaning against the bar, chortled about going to peace rallies to pick up girls, to get laid, to smoke some pot, and to get on television.

"At one rally my buddies and I went to there was a crowd of about 2000. Of that throng, I'd estimate that, tops, there were 10 asshole do-gooders, and the rest of us were there to party. Jesus, those fag pinkos are so f_ _king serious. If they don't like this country, we should ship their sorry asses to Moscow where they belong. Thank God there are so few of them, or they'd put a damper on all the fun," one of the Ivy Leaguers firmly stated with patriotic passion.

Remember those persistent TV images of masses and masses of well-intentioned students against the war? Hmmm? The media has some 'splaining to do, Lucy, about inflated numbers and other inaccuracies.

"It's a badge of honor to avoid military service," bragged a husky guy displaying the American flag in his dark blue suit lapel. "I've got more important things to do with my time than play soldier."

Boys who served in Vietnam, like my brother, were called "saps" and "losers" and "chumps" by the well-dressed, briefcase-toting draft dodgers in that smoky, boisterous bar car, rocking and rolling to Washington, D.C., our nation's capital, that hot July night in 1970.

The next three weeks in D.C. was one big party. Convinced I was off to my doom, Caryn, my temporary roommate, insisted that we go out every night to bars and house parties with her friends.

One of her co-workers had founded an organization called "Zero Population." I asked him, "But don't you want to have kids?"

"Oh, yeah, I plan on having five," he answered, surprised at my question.

"You're kidding, right?" Surely he was joking.

"No, I'm not. The fundamental objective of Zero Population is for the wrong people not to procreate."

"Oh, I understand." I certainly did. It was clear: he was one of the bright guys. I had to know, "How did you stay out of going to Vietnam?"

"A very, very high lottery number. My uncle's the head of the draft board in my home town and made sure it was," snickered the fellow who felt that he was the right kind of person to populate this planet.

Caryn's boss at National Alliance of Businessmen, a chap named Winston Windsor, a dead ringer for Michael Caine, squired me around the capital during those three weeks. Veddy British and in his thirties, he perceived the war as no big deal in the scheme of things.

"Your country is flush with cash, not only because of Vietnam, but also because of the huge military budgets lining the pockets of every company doing business with the military around the world," explained the Alfie look-alike.

Winston believed that my going to Southeast Asia would be a marvelous adventure. "The romantic Orient. Kiplingian characters. Gin and tonics. Oh, how I wish we British still had our empire that the sun never set on. You Yanks are so bloody lucky."

The next step was informing my mother, brothers, sister, and sister-in-law about my new adventure. Lordy, the reaction to the news was overwhelmingly negative, much more so than I had assumed it would be. It had been less than two years since Kenny was killed, and everyone's, except Winston's, perception of Vietnam was one big battlefield. Mine was too.

After a week at home filling out all sorts of paperwork for the FBI and other security agencies, I flew to Virginia while everything was being processed and it was determined if I was or was not a subversive, radical, or Bolshevik spy.

I swear to God, I did not have a clue what I was getting into or even what to expect. I just wanted to see Vietnam, where Kenny had died. I wanted to be an observer. Also, to be honest, I began regarding the journey to the war zone as a once-in-a-lifetime experience, recalling Winston's quixotic monologues about the exotic Far East.

The training in Portsmouth consisted mostly of sunning by the pool, similar to that tan-crazed Doonsebury character, at my temporary abode at the Holiday Inn. The executive director at the

USO in the Hampton Roads' area, Randy Foreman, adamantly insisted that personnel destined for Vietnam should not work.

Following the boss's orders, I checked into the USO a few hours a week and the rest of the time relaxed on the deck and read like crazy. During this time, I also kept Randy at bay, because he felt that before traveling to the war zone and my ultimate death, I should have the privilege of sleeping with him.

Showing up at the motel during odd hours, he relentlessly tried everything to seduce me, to no avail. He composed poems. (Remember those Rod McKuen books? Like those.) Randy sent flowers and daily invited me out to breakfast, lunch, and dinner. I couldn't complain to anyone, because he was the person who wrote my progress reports, had been with USO for 10 years to my one month, and was a man in an organization headed by men.

The moment that I realized he was a harmless flirt, Randy—Hugh Hefner's double, down to the trademark pipe—made me laugh. He was quite amusing and fun to be with, when not verbally lunging at me; and he was married, so had to behave himself in front of witnesses.

Within a short time, Randy and I became pals. Often we would be lounging by the pool, and I'd glance up from my book to comment about a moving or thought-provoking passage I had just read.

As he intently listened, nodding his head in understanding, he would say something such as, "God, I would give my life just to see one of your breasts."

His shocking remarks, which rolled off me like water off a duck's back, to use one of his favorite phrases, were becoming as innocuous as he was. Either Randy needed to impersonate Casanova, or he was preparing me for the lewd comments he believed that I would hear from female-deprived GIs in Vietnam.

Oh, incidentally, the males at USO headquarters and the three H's at NCCS thought Randy was a prince and a great executive—a family man, a pillar of the community, and a hell of a swell fellow. A man's man.

When I sporadically showed up at the USO recreation center for a dance or other program, I heard all about Consuelo O'Keefe, who had been in training a few months before I arrived and was now in Vietnam. Not of Irish descent, Consuelo was full-blooded Latina, and O'Keefe was her adopted name.

The sailors, particularly the Blacks and Hispanics, thought the world of her. Randy appreciated her, too, and implied that they had a hot, intensely steamy affair during her training. (In his dreams.)

Sandy Snob (not her real name, but one that suits her), the program director at the USO and a woman my age, did not have one kind word to say about Consuelo. Sandy was so square that, compared to her, Tricia Nixon appeared to be a drugged hippie. I mean, that gal wore white gloves to teas and on dates, while women her age were burning their bras.

The sailors who volunteered at the USO admired Consuelo, who was like a big sister to them. Encouraging them to read, she created lists of books and talked them into going to college after their military obligations were complete. All this, mind you, without the support of her Maidenform.

Consuelo O'Keefe, I quickly discovered, was one of those characters that others either loved or hated. She either pissed you off or amused you. I couldn't wait to meet her in Vietnam and rake Sandy Stupid over the coals.

Consuelo had organized a project to clean up the poor section of Portsmouth, the south side, where the Blacks of the city lived. After Senorita O'Keefe left, the weekly activity was dropped until I came along and started it up again. It was a blast for me and the many sailors who contributed their Saturdays. The townspeople began perceiving the sailors in a new light, not solely as bar-hopping rowdies about to defile their virginal teenage daughters.

Sandy Shithead (not her real name, but one that suits her), for some unknown incentive, maybe jealousy of Consuelo and at this time me, contacted the members of the local USO board of directors (entirely white) and informed them of the rubbish detail (in her words), declaring it unseemly and unfitting for a Caucasian girl (Consuelo, now me) to ride in the back of a trash truck in the Black section of town with Black sailors. The august group of pale officials must have shuddered at the thought.

There actually were USO clubs in the Southern states, at the time, that were segregated, and snow-white Sandy felt it was a shame that Portsmouth didn't have two separate ones for whites and for Blacks. Dear, sweet Sandy Sanctimonious (not her real name, but...) is now married to a minister. And people insist that priests should wed.

The clean-up undertaking came to an end soon after that, even though Randy loved it. The horny wimp could not take my side of the garbage debate because Sandy's family was very influential in the (white) community, and she was a little old-fashioned about Black folks.

No skin off my bronze back. I just spent more time sunning at the pool, reading, and fending off Randy's burlesque advances.

While soaking up the rays, I used to admire the boats moored at the dock just beyond the swimming pool. One day, a young girl sitting on an oddly shaped craft waved, and I waved back. After that initial, neighborly gesture from the oldest of three children, the Goodwin folks, owners of the three-hulled 35-foot sailboat, the Wild Whale, were soon constant guests of mine at the swimming pool.

They were docked at the Marina for a few months before continuing their around-the-world trip, which they expected would take three or four years. They had already been at it for two when I met them and, among other things, had missed being struck by a passing freighter at night, almost lost their 40-foot mast in a storm off the coast of Venezuela, gouged the bottom of the boat on a reef in Puerto Rico, and had the auxiliary motor conk out off the coast of Mexico and sailed 1500 miles to Panama for a new one. Brave them.

Cowardly I bawled like a baby every time I got a shot—small pox, typhoid-paratyphoid, tetanus-diphtheria, poliomyelitis, influenza, typhus, yellow fever, cholera, and plague. After each one, I became either sore, sick, or exhausted and had to take to my bed for a day or two, similar to one of those frail women in a Victorian novel. When I weakly emerged from seclusion and headed to the pool, the kids spotted me, ran over, and inquired about which shot I had gotten.

Whichever one it was, they chimed in, "Oh, we had that one, too." Then they conferred with each other about how it was "no big deal" and none of them experienced any side effects, implying, I am sure, what a chicken I was. The little show-offs. And me, so nice to them.

A few weeks before I left Portsmouth, a new trainee breezed into town. Peter Dickerman had been in the Navy in Vietnam and afterwards joined USO through YMCA. His assignment after his training period was to be a USO director in Thailand. (Men started as directors; women, as assistant directors.) Tall, blonde, and Paul Newman-handsome, Peter figured out extremely early (the first five minutes) that training under Randy's command meant basking at the pool at the motel.

Peter Dickerman loved to tweak noses. When his girlfriend from D.C. wasn't visiting and staying with him at the Holiday Inn on weekends, he was lavishing attention on me in front of Randy in order to "bust his balls," as he put it. Randy was livid whenever he saw Peter and me together.

Whenever I questioned Peter about his experiences in Vietnam, what he related were mostly escapades during R & R's in Hong Kong. The incident involving the prostitute named Parrot, Pussy a Pekinese, a rope, molasses, and him must have been his favorite war-time yarn, because I heard that one at least 25 times. The more nonchalantly I reacted to his feats in the Far East, the more outlandish they became. More props, more characters, more bedroom aerobatics.

Before my training was finished, Peter and I had turned the Holiday Inn into our private party place. After the USO closed, sailors, junior volunteers (young women of high moral character who were hostesses at USO activities), and guys from the Coast Guard showed up with cases of beer and guitars and frolicked until three in my room, Peter's, or at the pool. The Holiday Inn waitresses, desk people, maids, janitors, bartenders, and the organist in the lounge were also part of this merriment entourage.

Shortly after Peter dropped anchor in Portsmouth, he suggested that I fly home to pick up my car, so that we could trek to Virginia Beach whenever we became bored at the Holiday Inn pool. During the flight home, there was a stopover in Philadelphia; and in the terminal I shook hands with Huey Newton, who was surrounded by TV camera crews. In town for a conference at Temple University, he was quite the star. Handsome, charismatic, charming, debonair.

It was a heady time for activists in the antiwar and civil rights movements. Plenty of people who otherwise would not have had their day in the sun, shone brightly back then. And the media, a pack of lemmings, trailed each other and interviewed the same people and events over and over and over again. Still do, as far as I can ascertain.

The reason I even mentioned encountering Huey Newton was because it was so Forrest Gumpish. He was cute, though, in that long leather coat and beret, appearing so, so, I don't know, so revolutionary.

Speaking of activists. A number of years ago on a plane to Paris, I sat next to a woman who had been a leader in the Black Panthers and had been Huey Newton's lover. What was she doing on the jet to Paris? She was on her way back home with her French multimillionaire lover after touring the States promoting her recent book about her time in the Movement. What were her current concerns? Shopping and being seen in the chic places in the City of Lights were on the top of her priority list. As far as I could determine, the Black Power Movement just bumped into her, she joined, and fell in love with the media attention, stardom, power, and celebrityhood that came with the territory.

Whatever happened to the activists of the sixties? I suppose the answer is, they wrote their books, landed their movie deals, made tons of money, and now don't give a shit. Why did the caring about their fellow man disappear? I am not so sure that was their motivation in the first place.

But then, who am I to cast aspersions? When the women's memorial was dedicated in Washington in 1993 and I was summoned to be honored along with other females—military and civilian—who served in Vietnam, I went. What's more, even though laughing at myself, I marched in the parade and accepted thank yous and other forms of adulation from Vietnam Vets lining the streets. Maybe Mother Theresa was the only honest soul out there. Then again, what do we really know about her motives for all that exemplary work she supposedly did?

Whoa! I'm digressing and getting way ahead of the story. Let's return to Portsmouth, before I courageously served my country in Vietnam.

For two weeks, I had a roommate of sorts. Flaming liberal Gary Angel (not his real name), the other assistant director besides Sandy Satan, had rescued one of the junior volunteers who had been thrown out of her house by her abusive mother. Lolita, who was part Cherokee and part Filipino, had nowhere to stay. She also had an illegitimate child that she kept secret from Sandy. Mother and baby moved in with me for two weeks, until Gary and I could raise enough money from beer keg parties thrown in my room to buy her a ticket to her aunt's place in California. We also wanted to raise enough cash for her to have a small nest egg to help begin a new life out in L.A.

During parties, the night desk clerk, as part of his contribution to the Lolita-fundraising kitty, loaned us another room where the young mother and her infant could sleep. When Lolita wanted to join the fun, there were volunteer baby-sitters from the pool of waitresses and sailors who took turns changing diapers.

Almost $1000 was collected. When we put the happy Lolita and her kid on the plane to California, there was a mob at the airport to say good-bye. Many of them were young men that she had dated.

Sandy had fired one of the junior volunteers before I arrived because she had worn a miniskirt to a USO dance. God, she would have had a stroke if she had found out about Lolita's out-of-wedlock baby, Sid, whose father was a sea dog, part Eskimo, part Japanese.

Oh, I forgot to mention, I was sort of engaged to be married (very unofficial, no ring, no announcement) to Robin Rogers, whom I had met when I was a junior in college and he was in law school. He asked me to marry him on our first date, a blind date, when he picked me up wearing a priest's uniform. Proposing continuously for four years, whether we were seeing anyone else or not, he finally wore me down, and I at last said "yes." Yes, as soon as I go to Vietnam, see what it's like there, and then return. The only reason I said "yes" was because he was so damn much fun to be with.

Robin wanted to visit me in Portsmouth, but I declined his offer, remarking in my best Greta Garbo impersonation that I needed and "vahnted" to be alone. Patiently, he said he understood and would wait for me until I came back from Vietnam. He even promised that he would send me cookies and write often.

Yep. Robin was the man for me, despite the fact that I wasn't in love with him. Understanding, loose, sweet, but most of all, he was fun to be with. What more could a girl ask for in a mate for life? No pressure, no hassles, as we boomers spouted in those days in the sixties, which extended into the seventies. No hassles. Nobody wanted any hassle or bullshit. A nation of cynics was being hatched back then, even though we never realized it at the time. So many of us wanted to float along and be constantly amused and entertained while drifting.

During the stay in Portsmouth, I saw loads of movies, read every Pulitzer prize-winning book (fiction, nonfiction, and plays), partied each night, and slept till noon or beyond. I dated a reporter for the local newspaper, who had a student deferment then high blood pressure that mysteriously went away when he turned

26, and a teacher, who left education when he turned 26 and started a career with IBM. There were lunch dates, dinner dates, movie dates, and barhopping. The training was exhausting. I could not wait to go to Vietnam, where I could get some rest.

Now, I know I'm sounding flip about going to Vietnam; but to confess the truth, I was scared silly. And in the back of my mind, I had this assurance that I could chuck the idea and renege. I mean, what were the honchos at USO and NCCS going to do, force me to go? Hence, whenever I had a moment of sanity, I just thought, oh, well, I won't go; instead, I'll call Robin, get married, and live happily ever after, after a whimsical paid vacation in Portsmouth. Plus, I knew that if I did go to Vietnam and changed my mind once I got there, I could easily quit and return home. I would not be shot for desertion or anything. Would I? A civilian woman?

After fond farewells to and from the Portsmouth gang at the USO and the Holiday Inn, I was on my way back to East Vandergrift and then the flight to Southeast Asia. Following three months of exhausting employment by USO, I still did not know much about what I would be doing as far as the job was concerned in Vietnam.

Upon arriving home, I phoned everyone I ever knew to say adieu, knowing that I might not see them again. After writing out my will, I tried to make each moment with my family as precious as I could.

I did get cold feet a few times and thought seriously about changing my mind and not going. I kept visualizing the hardship, the danger. Was I brave enough? Strong enough? Stupid enough?

Soon afterward, while composing a resignation letter to Jack Daniels, the USO personnel director, with cc's to the three H's at NCCS on H Street in D.C., I received a packet of information from USO headquarters with a cover letter from Polly Ann Sweet, former director of public relations in Vietnam.

It began, "So you're going to Vietnam!" and continued in a cheerleaderly tone of excitement. The letter included four pages of suggestions about what I should take with me to war. "Keep in mind that you will need nylons for evening and special affairs, plus your R & R trips...I do recommend colored lingerie...The girls wear dressier clothing for dinner engagements...I did bring a black chiffon dress to Vietnam...Don't forget a mantilla for church..." And when I read the line, "Do include at least two cocktail dresses," I was assured that maybe, just possibly, it would not be the dreaded hardship I had envisioned.

There were plenty of tears—my family's and mine—at the Pittsburgh airport as I boarded the plane en route to the war. By then, inertia had taken over, and my trajectory was hurling me 9000 miles away to I did not know what. I was, however, prepared to face the unknown, secure in the fact that three cocktail dresses were folded neatly in one of the two suitcases I was taking along.

The first leg of the trip had a layover in San Francisco before leaving the United States. Bivouacked at the Hilton, I stayed up all night watching television—nine hours of 18 Superman shows with the original Man of Steel, George Reeve—believing that it was the last TV I would see for a long time, maybe forever. I had visions of being killed in a foxhole in some rice paddy during a rocket attack while wearing one of my cocktail dresses.

This was nuts. I was insane. How could I do such a stupid thing? I kept questioning myself, "What idiot would go to Vietnam if she did not have to?" Boys my age were doing everything they could to stay away from that place. Talking myself out of going, I then talked myself back into going throughout the night and into the morning. By noon, I was so sleep deprived that I put myself on automatic pilot and caught a cab for the three o'clock flight to Tokyo, the next short visit of my odyssey.

Sitting in the San Francisco airport, waiting for that flight across the Pacific, there was only one thing on my mind. "Faster than a speeding bullet. More powerful than a locomotive. Able to leap tall buildings with a single bound. Look! Up in the sky! It's a bird! It's a plane! No! It's Superman. Yes, it's Superman. Strange visitor from another planet who came to Earth with powers and abilities far beyond those of mortal men. Superman! Who can change the course of mighty rivers, bend steel with his bare hands, and who, disguised as Clark Kent, a mild mannered reporter for a great metropolitan newspaper, fights the never-ending battle for truth, justice, and the American way," kept being repeated in my thoughts over and over and over and over again like some broken record that I was powerless to change.

That flight, which passed through a zillion time zones and took 16 hours, really turned my body clock upside down. It made one stop—Anchorage, Alaska. The only reason I mention that stop is whenever anyone asks if I had ever been to Alaska, I say yes. Well, it's the truth.

Chatterbox me, I talked with almost everyone on the plane and especially became chummy with Caroline, Max, and Steve, members of a Berkeley and Columbia left-wing student delegation headed to Vietnam on an antiwar fact-finding mission. By the time the Pan Am jet landed in Tokyo, we seemed like lifelong friends. But, except for the flight, two days in Tokyo, and part of the five I spent with them in Saigon, I never saw them again these many years; and except for one or two letters after they left Vietnam armed to the teeth with facts, I never heard from them again either. We all seemed to live in the present and were too busy going forward in our daily lives to look back. At least I know I was, even though I thought about that trio often over the years and still have warm memories of that brief time with them.

For some reason, my Berkeley/Columbia buddies and I had been booked for two overnights in Tokyo. Wow! We painted the town red, me and my pinko friends. None of us had slept on the plane over the Pacific, nor had I snoozed the night before in San Francisco. A little afraid of going to Vietnam, we were practicing that old adage, "Eat, drink, and be merry, because tomorrow you may die."

Ed and Vivian, two hippie-looking (long dirty hair, peace symbols, bell bottoms) college students from Harvard and Radcliffe, traveling around the world, also on our flight, joined our group in taking in the sights. The six of us went to a Japanese bathhouse, even though public baths were outlawed since the American occupation after World War II. Satosan, a bartender we met our first night, arranged for us to go to one exclusively for Japanese. We missed the tea ceremony, but crammed plenty of other touristy stuff into those 48 hours—shopping on the Ginza, Takarazuka (a Radio City Rockettes-type show), and plenty of saki and sushi. We snapped pictures of each other standing in front of everything. There was one of Caroline being shoved into the subway during rush hour by a person whose job it is to push passengers into the cars.

It was such a blast, the first time out of the U.S. for each of us, that their group decided to stay another day, before heading to Hong Kong, and tried to talk me into sticking around too. I decided against it, because I didn't know who to call in Saigon to report that I was delayed in Tokyo. And anyway, I didn't think USO officials in Vietnam would buy the excuse that there were only three bars left out of 4000 that we had not visited and wanted to hit those before leaving Tokyo.

Caroline, Max, Steve, Ed, Vivian, and Satosan accompanied me to the airport and waved good-bye as my next plane headed for Saigon with a three-hour stopover in Taiwan. Yes, I answer, I have been to Taiwan.

Flying Air Vietnam, I was thankful I never ate breakfast, because the morning meal was raw fish mixed with raw eggs. On top of a hangover. The Vietnamese businessman who was heading home, sitting beside me, was pleased when I gave him my meal and spent the entire trip lighting my cigarettes with his gold Dunhill lighter. Hmmm? I thought Vietnamese were poor and here was this guy, no older than 30, who appeared rather prosperous. His English, with a trace of a British accent, was excellent. He had learned English in Hong Kong while at boarding school as a boy, he told me. I had never met anyone as sophisticated as he seemed. Books, movies, plays, travel, the chap could converse about anything.

When I told him about my new job, he said he knew many people who worked for the USO in Saigon.

"No kidding?" I assumed he meant Vietnamese.

"No, I am a friend and business associate with many Chinese as well as Americans."

Just before landing in Saigon, passengers were required to fill out cards divulging how much currency they were carrying into Vietnam. Mr. Urbane whispered that I should not declare the 300 in greenbacks and instead double it on the black market money exchange. I didn't know much about Vietnam, but I did understand that what he had just suggested was illegal. Peter Dickerman had recommended the same thing and wanted me to hide money in my shoe and then swap it on the black market. I decided against it. I did not want to get caught and land in a dingy Vietnamese prison.

Many thoughts were swimming through my head as the plane approached Saigon's Tan Son Nhut airport, including: Why would a stranger tell another stranger about committing a crime? And what kind of business did Mr. Smooth as Silk do with Americans working at the USO in Saigon? It was a fleeting thought that did not re-enter my mind again for many months, and when it did, I was pretty sure I knew who he not only knew, but also who he did business with at the USO.

The plane landed, and I was expecting a representative from USO to welcome me to the war zone. Walking down the steps of the plane, everyone gasped from the heat. Not me. Back then, before menopause, I loved the heat. The hotter, the better. It was the strange smell that had me puzzled, and just about everybody else who spent time in Vietnam during the war talks about it. Jet fuel? Garbage? Car fumes? I didn't know then, and I don't now, but I never again smelled it anywhere else.

Waiting for hours, I kept checking the Air Vietnam counter to see if I had any messages. None. I waited and waited and waited. Lots and lots of soldiers came up to me and asked where I was from and what I was doing in Vietnam. Before long, I learned that Saigon had a daily eleven o'clock curfew and a one o'clock on weekends, and I had to be where I was going by then or else sleep in the airport overnight until 5:00 a.m. when the curfew lifted.

I repeatedly stopped civilian men and asked if they were from USO and searching for me. I must have looked like Little Orphan Annie. Finally, a middle-aged USAID (United States Agency for International Development) civilian offered to give me a lift into downtown Saigon and suggested that I check into a hotel then go to the USO in the morning, since he was certain it closed at 10:00 p.m. By now it was 10:30.

After dropping me off at the Eden Roc Hotel, a third-rate establishment, and helping with my two suitcases, he sped home. Before leaving, he assured me that I would be safe and there was nothing to be afraid of. Right. I was terrified and felt very lonely and tired.

Before going to bed, I went to the bar in the lobby for a Coke and met a group of pilots from Cam Ranh Bay on their way to Hong Kong on R & R the next day. The one who was a spitting image of Lt. Calley of My Lai fame bought me a drink and, before I had taken two sips, asked if I would like to go to bed with him.

I wanted to clobber him, but instead heard someone saying, and realized the words were coming from me, "No thank you. But thanks for the drink."

Each room in the hotel had a Vietnamese woman assigned to it who stayed outside the door throughout the night in case the guests desired anything. I kept waking up during the night, because mine was gregarious and either singing at the top of her lungs or having loud conversations with the other Vietnamese women squatting near the other doors in the hallway.

I did go out one time to ask my congenial guard (in English— Ugly American that I was) for a towel. I went through an elaborate pantomime for 15 minutes. Puzzled for the longest time, she at last squealed and shook her head, disappeared down the hall, and an hour later returned with a Coke on a tray. I signed the tab and tipped her a dollar bill. You would have thought that I had just given her a diamond. Crying with joy, she kept patting my head and kissing my hand. It dawned on me that I might have over-tipped.

The next morning, I woke up not knowing where I was. When it hit me that I was in a hotel room in Saigon, Vietnam, I screamed out loud, "Oh, shit!"

The room was like an icebox from the air-conditioner. I turned it off before proceeding into the bathroom, which had a bidet (the first one I had ever seen) and a toilet with a pull chain, which I kept yanking like some two-year-old with a new toy.

While I lounged in a shampoo bubble bath, a giant, and I do indeed mean humongous, cockroach raced across the floor. My blood ran cold. I hated them then and still abhor them now. Those repulsive critters. If I were a spy in possession of America's greatest secrets, the only thing an enemy would have to do is threaten to lock me in a room with one cockroach and I would spill my guts.

I threw a bar of soap in the direction of where I saw the cockroach go. It appeared, glared at me, and then scurried to a corner and disappeared into a hairline crack. I'm lousy with measurements and am still amazed that my son is an engineer, but I did notice that that cockroach was as big as the bar of soap. How is it possible for an insect the size of a pack of cigarettes to crawl into a crack in a wall that is barely noticeable?

While I was in training, and I do use that word loosely, in Portsmouth, I read so many books that I was on a first-name basis with everybody at the local library, including the cleaning staff. One of the books that I read three times was Franz Kafka's *Metamorphosis*, about a fellow who turns into a cockroach.

And the only reason I'm rattling on and on about cockroaches is that when people find out that I lived and worked in Vietnam, they invariably inquire, "Were you afraid?"

"Yes," I reply. "Of cocky cockroaches."

After I finished bathing, I tiptoed into the bedroom, which by then was as hot as an oven. The ceiling fan was circulating sweltering air. The air-conditioner had two settings—on and off. So the ritual of 10 minutes on and 10 minutes off began. After drying off with the sheet, I put on something that was not too wrinkled and set off to find the USO.

I would have asked Lt. Calley's twin for directions the night before, but I never had the chance after his crude proposition at the bar. He had scared me so much my first evening in Vietnam that I took the elevator up a floor past mine then quietly walked down in case he was following my movements in order to rape me while I slept. Little did I know then that all he had to do was bribe the desk clerk. After witnessing the maid's reaction to American greenbacks, I venture to guess $5 would have sufficed and he would have been slipped a key to my room.

That first day none of the Vietnamese in the hotel knew what the hell I was babbling about when I asked where the USO was, even the ones who did speak English. I asked to see a phone book. Nobody knew what that was either. Not to worry, I thought. I'll just find a GI and ask him. I did not have to look far. As soon as I walked outside, there were hundreds of American men in military uniforms. To the left was the Saigon River. I headed right. I had not taken a few steps before I spotted two MPs not far ahead. They escorted me to the USO Saigon a few blocks away.

My initial impressions of Saigon? Let me just state that for a girl from small-town East Vandergrift, Pennsylvania, who thought Pittsburgh was a big and exotic place, this place was surreal. Salvador Dali would not have stood out in that setting. I stuck out like a sore thumb, though, especially when my two burly chaperons and I passed the bars and brothels on Tu Do Street. The bar girls and prostitutes gave me the once-over, sized up what they probably regarded as the competition, and threw some rather rough language my way. No man (let alone any woman) had ever in my life told me to "f_ _k off." And for those few blocks, I was instructed to "f_ _k off" at least 50 times. I had the sneaking suspicion that those Vietnamese professionals did not like American women very much.

"Don't pay them no mind," Sgt. Alabama advised me.

Oh, sure, easy for him to say. He didn't have everyone on the street, Vietnamese men, women, and children, as well as throngs of soldiers—Americans, Vietnamese, and Koreans— staring at him and giggling.

I tried to enjoy the scenery as we neared the end of the bar part of Tu Do Street. As we turned the corner heading to Nguyen Hue (pronounced Win Way), I observed an American soldier leaning down, whispering in a bar girl's ear and fanning money in front of her nose. I smiled knowingly and just at that moment our eyes met.

The very young working girl smirked and yelled, "American c_ _t!"

I was warned about coarse language from the GIs but nobody cautioned me about the Vietnamese bar babes. Without thinking, I threw her the finger. The MPs, walking protectively on either side of me, roared with laughter at the gesture.

My first daylight glimpse of Saigon will forever stand out in my memory, exactly as the first of anything usually does: Blaring rock music assaulted pedestrians from bars. Teenage prostitutes strutted their stuff in size-one miniskirts. Teenage boys rode double on Honda motorcycles. Miniature blue and yellow cabs barely missed the scooters. Old women squatted on the sidewalk over steaming pots. Signs advertised dress makers, massages, and quick marriages. American soldiers towered over elderly Vietnamese women, who wore conical hats and carried parasols.

Black market stalls lined the sidewalks. For sale were boonies (boondocks, bush) hats, flight jackets, Crest toothpaste, cartons of Marlboro cigarettes, Hershey candy bars, Tampax, cameras, Prell shampoo, and hundreds of other items that were shipped from America to PX's in Vietnam but somehow never made it to the intended final destination. The consumer products were either stolen from the docks or bought from GIs who made a little extra money on the side, the MPs explained.

"How come nobody does anything about all this stealing and black market stuff?" Miss Innocent I wanted to know.

The burly, Southern MP, who had been patrolling the streets

of Saigon for eight months explained, "Every once in a blue moon the Saigon police, the 'White Mice,' as we call them, arrest a handful of the merchants who are selling goods on the street. It's a symbolic gesture meant to show that corruption will not be tolerated. The next day, the same shopkeeper is back on the same spot selling the same products and the same White Mice pass them without a second look. Shit, whenever the PX is out of something, I just come here and buy it. Everybody does. Need anything yourself?"

There were beggars every few feet and throngs of kids with hands outstretched asking for P (piasters), the South Vietnamese money. Buddhist monks with shaved heads strolled by, stopping occasionally to buy an item from the black market stands. The air was filled with odors of cooking food and automobile fumes. Petite girls were selling sweet-smelling garlands of flowers.

During our walk, the Black MP, not the one from Alabama, said that he had met a really neat (his word, I swear) USO girl in Danang a month earlier while he was on in-country R & R at China Beach. "I'm fairly sure her name was Consuelo O'Keefe."

Talk about a small world. Not that she and I were friends, but I felt as though I knew her before meeting. And what I knew of her I liked. In my mind, the pro- and anti- Consuelo camps had been formed. So far, I preferred the people who belonged to the pro faction.

Finally! The USO was in sight.

There was a guard at the entrance checking identification. Nonchalantly, he waved my escorts and me through without even a glimpse at any of my documents. Before going in the club, I stopped to smile at the little boy, not more than six, who was peddling plastic bags in front of the USO. The MPs howled when I paid him his asking price of 50 piasters. They claimed I lost face because I did not bargain. I certainly did not need the plastic bag, but the kid looked so cute that I just wanted to stare at him for a moment while the transaction took place.

Sitting down next to him was a tiny girl about four years old, his sister, he told me in pidgin English. The little bag seller had on gray Bermuda shorts and sandals. She had on a cute yellow dress, tattered but clean. I wanted to hug them, but the boy seemed so serious that I didn't want to embarrass him.

I stooped down when I gave the kid the 50 piasters, which I borrowed from Sgt. Alabama, and he insisted that I take two bags. When the MPs saw the boy give me the extra bag, they each shelled out 50 piasters, with no haggling, and the three of us strolled into the USO holding our plastic bags.

The place was enormous. To the right, when we entered, there was an information desk. The sign on the wall behind it announced, "USO Saigon, Your Home Away From Home. Ping Pong. Letter Tapes. Snack Bar. Pool Tables. Piaster Exchange. Flowers By Air. R & R Information. Stateside Telephones. Saigon Camera Tours. Musical Instruments. Concession Arcade. Checking Facilities. Writing Material. Air-Conditioned Lounge. Open Daily 8:00 a.m. to 9:00 p.m." Farther down, there were leather couches, a bunch of tables near the snack bar, the booth for money exchange, and at the very end of this cavernous room a band was performing on a stage.

The band members were Vietnamese. The musicians were wearing tie-dyed shirts, jeans, and love beads and peace symbols on chains around their necks. Each of them had long hair. The lead singer, a female, was sporting a miniskirt and white boots. The Vietnamese Nancy Sinatra was just finishing singing "These Boots Are Made For Walking" and was a hell of a lot better than Frank's daughter.

There was nobody behind the information desk, and I just stood there taking in the scene as the female singer started belting out "Me and Bobby McGee" in a fairly good imitation of Janis Joplin.

"May I help you?" a male voice inquired.

When I turned to the person speaking, I gazed into the face of a very attractive Oriental man. It was obvious that he wasn't Vietnamese.

His name was Danny and he was Chinese, he proudly blurted out. From Cholon, the Chinese section of Saigon. The guy oozed charm from every unblemished pore.

Before long, I was behind the desk looking at his autograph book of famous people who had come into the USO—movie stars, reporters, politicians, singers, writers, as well as baseball, football, tennis, hockey, and basketball players. I glanced at the signatures of Bob Hope, Gypsy Rose Lee, James Stewart, John Steinbeck, Martha Raye, Sam Yorty, and a couple of Miss Americas.

"You met all these people?" I asked, impressed and somewhat puzzled. "What were they all doing here?"

Danny, from Cholon, smiled a charming smile. "Best hamburgers in town!" My Chinese companion obviously took great pride in the USO. "Besides, Miss Diana, have you ever seen the movie *Casablanca*?" he asked.

"Sure. Lots of times. Why?" I did not have a clue where the conversation was going.

"Well, the Saigon USO is the same as Rick's Cafe Americain. Everybody makes it to the USO when they come to Saigon, just like Rick's place in *Casablanca*."

I had to laugh. But upon doing so, I could tell he thought that I was laughing at him. Quickly, I assured him that I was not making fun of him. It was just that I did not expect all of what I had seen and heard so far. I do not know what I anticipated, but it was not what I had experienced so far. He looked perplexed at what I was trying to express.

Before I had a chance to explain to him why I was there and to ask if he would help me find a USO official to let him or her know that I had arrived, Danny was explaining to me the similarities between Rick's Cafe Americain and the Saigon USO. He, of course, fancied himself as Humphrey Bogart.

Waving his arm to survey the club, he whispered, "There is lots of gambling at the pool tables and the joint is crawling with an abundance of spies—CIA and VC disguised as kitchen help, no doubt. There is plenty of illegal deals and transactions being carried out all around us," he confided.

The young man had a wonderful imagination and I really could have, and probably would have, spent hours listening to his stories; but in the middle of one of them, a middle-aged woman approached us and demanded to know, "Who are you and what are you doing behind *my* information counter?"

Priscilla "Prissy" Powers was the honcho of "the American women volunteers at the USO and president of the Saigon American Women's Club," she quickly enlightened me.

Danny had already snapped shut his autograph book and was standing at West Point attention as though in the presence of a four-star general.

You know how sometimes things pop out of your mouth and you do not have the faintest idea where they came from? Well, it was one of those moments for me.

"Do you know Consuelo O'Keefe?" I asked her.

In spite of the "yes, she is a nice girl" answer, I could deduce by the grimace she made at the mention of Consuelo's name that Prissy Powers did not like my soon-to-be and, as far as I was concerned, present good friend. Danny's beaming face at the mention of Consuelo told me that he was one of the good guys.

With the litmus test out of the way, I was escorted upstairs past the musicians, who now were singing "My Girl" and waving at me from the bandstand. Two GIs shooting pool whistled; and the Vietnamese snack bar workers stared at me, huddled together whispering to each other, and then giggled while the band started throwing me kisses.

Prissy softened a bit and asked obligatory questions. "Where are you from in the States?" "Where did you do your training?" "What does your father do?" In other words, she really wanted to know if I was rich and worth her time.

I told her my father played the harp, forgetting to mention that he was dead. Then, I quickly turned the tables and asked her some dumb questions. I learned that she had belonged to a sorority in college. Restricted—no Jews. Natch. She was so stupid that she did not even try to hide her bigotry.

Prissy's better half (anyone had to be better than this crow), Nathan Powers, was the owner of Powers Construction. As we reached the last step upstairs, I was briefed that they knew, and were "dear, dear friends of Ambassador Ellsworth Bunker," a Yaley like Nate. The Powers duo had been in Saigon doing construction business since 1961 and also owned a travel agency that catered to affluent Vietnamese and foreign business owners like themselves.

Holy Cow! They had been in Vietnam for nine years! Business had to be booming. It did not take a rocket scientist or a seasoned Asian hand to sum up that there was a ton of money to be made from the Vietnam War. Danny's autograph book alone could someday be worth a bloody fortune.

On the second floor, there was a counter of souvenirs, postcards, paintings on black velvet, and ceramic statues of heroes from Vietnam's ancient history. A beautiful Vietnamese woman was behind the counter speaking French to her young female helper.

There were six phone booths, where GIs were standing in line, waiting to call home. A gold-plated sign that announced "USO Executive Office" was attached to the double doors across from the phone booths.

The Queen of Saigon ushered me in; and the American receptionist, with the biggest beehive hairdo I had ever seen in my life, glanced up and saw Mrs. Powers, snapped to attention, and practically curtsied. Prissy Powers, who could have easily passed as the mother of Sandy, the oh-so-prim-and-proper program director from the Portsmouth USO, made the introductions and left.

Mrs. Beehive's courteous tone changed to near hostility as soon as the middle-aged war profiteer was out the door.

"We weren't expecting you," the office worker snarled at me.

Then, out walked an American man, a few years older than I and partially bald. He saw me, smiled, and stretched out his hand to shake mine. Richie Smith, the treasurer, laughed when I told him I was a new program director. He was not surprised in the least that the personnel director from New York headquarters had forgotten to send a telegram about my arrival.

Guiding me into his office, in a stage whisper, he confided, "Jack Daniels is a great guy, but he drinks a tad too much. He'll remember you eventually and send a telegram before your 18-month tour is complete."

Within a short time, Richie introduced me to the Vietnamese and Chinese secretaries in the executive office, helped me with all the paperwork (forms for this and forms for that), and gave me a brief rundown of the USO clubs in Vietnam.

I was sent out in the hallway to the gift shop where that lovely Vietnamese woman had one of those photo machines that motor vehicle offices use, and I was photographed for various identification cards I would need to travel around Vietnam. I had to exchange my American greenbacks for piasters and MPC (Military Payment Certificates), the funny money used in military establishments, such as the PX and movie theaters.

Consuelo O'Keefe, I found out, was in Danang, but Richie wasn't sure how long she would be there since she did not get along with Rob Clawson, the USO coordinator up north.

Richie, who only had nice things to say about everybody, said he liked them both, but Rob did not think Consuelo represented USO well by showing up at her club wearing Indian saris with a dot on her forehead and meditating with the Vietnamese kitchen help. Before going on an R & R to India, she had converted to Buddhism. Since her return, she toyed with the idea of becoming a Hindu, but could not imagine giving up hamburgers and steaks. That made perfect sense to me.

All new USO employees in Vietnam were given a five- to seven-day orientation in Saigon upon their arrival. A time of unsupervised exploration. Talk to people at the USO. Take tours. Walk the streets and mingle with the Vietnamese. Investigate. Sleep off the jet lag. Look, listen, and learn.

Richie guided me into the office next to his. Two American women, one talking on the phone and the other listening to the conversation and grinning, were sitting at desks facing each other. The older one, maybe mid- to late-forties, with bluish hair, was trying to calm down the person at the other end of the line.

"Now, now, take it easy. Yes, yes, I understand. No, no, he can't fire you. What? Please, Consuelo, speak English. I don't understand a word of Spanish, except adios. No, no. That's better. No, no, I wasn't going to hang up. Listen, Darling, I'll fly up there tomorrow and try to straighten it all out. And, in the meantime, if you see Rob coming your way, cross the street and pretend you don't see him."

A throw-your-head-back belly laugh erupted from the blue-haired peacemaker. She looked at me, waved Richie and me into the office, and continued.

"Listen, Consuelo, it appears that a new assistant director has arrived without New York letting us know. I really must go, but don't worry. I'll see you tomorrow." Pause. "Yes, yes, peace to you too, Pumpkin."

"Don't you just love her?" This comment from the younger woman, the one with the short blonde pixie, maybe late twenties or early thirties, Molly Dew, the assistant director of public relations and Margo Flame's (the one who just hung up the phone) right-hand woman.

Hand shakes all around. And an explanation to Molly about the hearty laugh. When Margo advised Consuelo to pretend not to see Rob coming her way, Consuelo replied, "Amiga, that would be impossible since Rob is so fat that if he were in a before and after diet plan advertisement with a sumo wrestler, everyone would assume the picture of the wrestler was the after photo."

Oh, yeah, I forgot to mention that Margo was wearing a hat. The kind Hedda Hopper always wore. She even looked like Hedda Hopper. When I asked her if anyone had ever remarked that she resembled the famous Hollywood gossip writer, you could tell from her beaming face that the answer was "affirmative," as I soon discovered was the military lingo for "yes."

Affirmative. Negative. That became another way of telling

whether I would like or dislike someone. If a person could not say a simple yes or no, I really felt there was no way I could give someone like that my trust. I guess I am exaggerating a bit. But, if an individual said, "affirmative" and "negative" instead of "yes" and "no" and did not like Consuelo O'Keefe, well, you can figure out the rest.

Next, we—Margo, Molly and I—went to lunch downstairs.

"The best hamburgers in Saigon," Molly gushed. "And the safest to eat, as long as you don't use mayonnaise on them. The kitchen staff always forgets to put away the mayonnaise."

Molly Dew, former high school teacher from New Mexico and current assistant PR director, also hosted the 30-minute radio show, "USO Showtime," at 12:30 and left for the military radio station, AFVN, after wolfing down one of the best hamburgers in Saigon.

The band on stage was finishing a rousing rendition of "Proud Mary" to a packed lunch crowd of GIs, who were either stationed in Saigon or on their way to or from R & R's. R & R stands for Rest and Recreation or Rest and Relaxation, in other words, a week's vacation from whatever war job they had.

USO employees were entitled to one R & R every three months. And if there was space available, we could hop on military flights for free heading to Hong Kong, Bangkok, Australia, and Hawaii. Wow! Talk about falling into a great job.

Hold on a minute. You're probably saying to yourself, "Is this the same young woman whose main reason for going to Vietnam was to see the place where her brother had been killed? Is she the one who wanted to be an observer to a war she felt was wrong? Where's the angst? Where's the war?"

In defense of my Oh Wow attitude about my first full day in Vietnam, I was tired, didn't know what was expected of me, and felt like Alice in Wonderland with a great tan from my training period in Portsmouth. My eyes and ears were wide open and, except for all the soldiers and the sign at the information desk requesting men to check their weapons, it was hard for me to believe I was in a war zone.

Everybody in Saigon seemed to be waiting. Waiting to go on R & R. Waiting to make a phone call back to the States. Waiting for a burger. Danny was waiting for a celebrity to saunter in and sign his autograph book. Prissy and Nate Powers were waiting for another lucrative military construction contract for their bulging coffers. Foul-mouthed streetwalkers were waiting for the next customer. I was waiting to find out where I was going to be assigned and when I was going to see the war, the one I saw nightly on television news in the States.

The USO Vietnam personnel director, Averell Van Buren, was on R & R (didn't anybody work around here?) and the executive director, Charlie Stonewall, the main man, was in Bangkok on USO business, so Margo was in charge. The PR director ordered me to hang out in Saigon for a week, get over my jet lag, and relax. After checking me out of the Eden Roc Hotel, she helped me to get settled into the penthouse apartment USO rented for staffers traveling through Saigon.

Penthouse? Well, it was really a sparsely furnished, top floor apartment in a building across from the USO. It was cheaper, in fact, than booking people into hotels. Directors and assistant directors were continually flying into Saigon either as new arrivals or from clubs around Vietnam for meetings, or for new assignments, or for pep talks, or to complain about some other co-worker.

Consuelo O'Keefe and her boss, Rob Clawson, from Danang were frequent guests at the penthouse, since they were regularly soaring in to complain about each other.

I bunked in the room that Consuelo usually stayed in. The walls were decorated with "Che Guevara" and "War Is Not Healthy For Children And Other Living Things" posters. The bedroom that tubby Rob Clawson frequented had a framed photo of Richard Nixon, the guy who proclaimed in October 1969, "I'm not going to be the first American president who loses a war." Need I say more about their individual personalities?

That first week in Saigon was packed with multifarious activities: I dined at Caruso's, an elegant French restaurant, with Jacques, a French photographer who lived in the same building as the penthouse; took a bus tour of Saigon and visited the zoo, Botanical Gardens, Quang Trung Judo School, and the Central Market, where Saigonese shopped for fresh fruits and vegetables, live ducks, and skinned rabbits, and foreigners haggled over flea market treasures from the Japanese occupation during World War II, French trinkets, and American military junk; smoked grass for the first time with the Berkeley/Columbia crowd from the plane and an AP stringer they met in Vung Tau, working out of Hawaii, in Saigon on vacation; gave candy, gum, and money to every 10th beggar I passed; said a prayer at Our Lady's Basilica on my brother Kenny's 23rd birthday; shopped with Margo Flame, the PR director, at the PX and bought a 35 mm camera for a fraction of what I would have paid in the States (Margo bought perfume, nylons, two ice cube trays, cosmetics and booze, at ridiculously low prices); declined numerous times to exchange money illegally, sell my new Nikon, or buy drugs, a monkey, a snake, or a machine gun; was interviewed on Molly's radio show at AFVN (American Forces Vietnam Network) and met Martha Raye in one of the studios telling war stories to a bunch of DJ's; took hundreds of pictures of beggars, bar girls, street urchins, pedicab drivers, children with no pants defecating in the street, a man peeing against a wall, a woman breast-feeding an infant next to her husband who was cutting his toenails beside their black market stall overflowing with products stolen from American ships at the docks; lunched at an Italian eatery with Richie, the USO treasurer, and his Vietnamese wife; supped with a *New York Times* reporter (who claimed Vietnam was becoming boring and Cambodia and Laos were the places to go for action) and my antiwar delegation buddies on the rooftop restaurant of the Caravelle Hotel, where we watched DC-3's drop flares on the far side of the Saigon River; had drinks at the Continental Palace outdoor verandah, where Graham Green jotted notes for *The Quiet American* and Somerset Maugham once held court; talked to hundreds of GIs ("Where you from?" "Where you stationed?"); befriended Mitzy, the Nancy Sinatra wannabe singer, who along with the band escorted me to a nightclub to catch the show of one of their rivals; stayed up till three every night reading USO literature, brochures, pamphlets, and flyers, as well as Saigon tour books, magazines, and English-language newspapers with ads for massage parlors and escort services featuring comely Swedish girls; spent a day with the director of the USO in Dian (where Nixon visited in 1969), during which time she showed me her club, took me to a party at the base and, driving back to Saigon in her pink jeep with a bumper sticker that read, "Vietnam: Love it or Leave it," we were shot at by a sniper hiding along the road; feasted with Danny, from the USO Saigon information desk, owner of the autograph book, and his mother, father, six brothers and sisters on a 16-course dinner in Cholon, the Chinese section, where he asked for my signature just in case I ever became famous; ate escargot, onion soup, steak tartar, froglegs, Baked Alaska, and lychees for the first time; had my future told by a sidewalk fortune teller; cocktailed at Margo's garden apartment, where I chatted with Sebastian Cabot, who was in-country on a handshaking tour; danced with 45 GIs at a sock hop put on by the staff at the Tan Son Nhut USO near the air base and at one time a fabulous villa used by a plantation owner from the Delta for weekend trysts with his mistress; sent scads of postcards to family and friends back home; authorized my pay to be sent to my mother in the event that I was "interned by an alien force" during my employment with USO; and got very little sleep, due to the sounds of mortars in the distance.

The noise I heard was called "outgoing," which was our side shooting out somewhere. "Incoming," which was the enemy firing toward us, did not occur during my first week in Vietnam. Once I was told that the frightening sound was actually outgoing, it started to lull me to sleep and would do so for my entire stay in Vietnam.

Averell Van Buren, the personnel director, returned from R & R and decided that I would be sent to Cam Ranh Bay, where there were three clubs. The directors there could decide what to do with me. Mmmm? I did not detect any long-term planning here in Vietnam, but then again, what could I expect? Still no telegram had been sent from New York that I was on my way, and it had been a week since I had arrived.

Off I was sent to the airport with one of the USO drivers, who, when he wasn't driving people from the executive office all over Saigon, hung out with the owners of the black market stands outside the USO, sort of like a permanent sidewalk sale.

By the way, I did not meet one American who did not buy something from illegal vendors. I bought a hairdryer for the 220 current, because the PX didn't have any and had not for months, even though the item was listed on its manifest sheets of goods delivered.

Armed with all the necessary documents needed to get on military flights, we passengers took a bus from the terminal to the plane on one of the runways. Metal mesh covered the windows of the bus to protect us from grenades that might be tossed our way. Remember, this was a war zone, after all.

When the bus stopped, one of the pilots jumped in and matter-of-factly reported, "This will be the last plane out of Saigon before Typhoon Louise, which is minutes away, strikes. Anyone who doesn't want to take the chance can get off now and take the bus parked alongside that plane over there back to the terminal."

Half of the soldiers got up, gathered their belongings, and left. The other half and I decided to beat the storm. Well, why not? I was eager to get to Cam Ranh Bay and besides, I knew the pilot was bullshitting about Louise being "minutes away."

While sitting in the airport with me, he and his copilot asked if I would like to ride in the cockpit with them during the flight and joked about giving the GIs a chance and a good excuse to spend another day in Saigon before they had to report back to work. I was starting to see how loose things were around here.

Finally onboard, I waited, securely strapped in the navigator's seat, for the C-130 to take off for Cam Ranh Bay, and I did not have an inkling of what else. Maybe I would finally see the war, the one Kenny had died in.

Off we flew, into the wild blue yonder, with me, who has to

pretend I'm writing to distinguish between right and left, perched in the navigator's seat. From the cockpit the view was panoramic: Gleaming white villas and thousands of shanties. The muddy-brown Mekong Delta. Boats and ships crowded on the Saigon River.

The flight took the coastal route north to Cam Ranh Bay. The blue-green water of the South China Sea came into view. The scenery of isolated beaches and pounding surf was truly breathtaking, until it started to rain. And rain, and rain, and rain. Visibility was zero as the rain pelted the cockpit window. Typhoon Louise was closer than the flyboys had anticipated. All conversation with me stopped as the pilots concentrated completely on the lighted instruments on the dashboard (I know it's not called that in a plane, but that's what they told me it was) in front of them. I had never sat in a cockpit before and did not realize how much work was involved in flying a plane. I was impressed.

The rain started to let up as we got closer to Cam Ranh Bay. Ole Louise was behind us, I was informed, and it would be an easy landing. As the plane approached the airfield, the pilot handed me the microphone and I did what they said to do.

I pressed the button and spoke, "Pilot to tower. Pilot to tower. Request landing instructions. Do you read me? Request landing instructions." Then I let go of the button.

The pilots were chuckling. No answer. The copilot said that I forgot the last line to let them know I was finished transmitting.

I did it again. "Pilot to tower. Pilot to tower. Request permission to land. Do you read me? Repeat. Do you read me? Over and out."

This time I got an answer.

The voice through the copilot's earphones, which he was sharing with me, barked, "Roger. I hear you. Now who the f_ _k am I talking to? Over and out."

As the plane circled, the pilots were beside themselves with laughter. I was getting a little nervous at this point. I always heard that taking off and landing were the most dangerous parts of the flight. When I expressed this fear, the pranksters assured me that circling was safe, and that's what we were doing.

So again I took the microphone, pressed the button, and said, "This is flight two-two-niner. Request landing instructions. Over and out."

The voice from the earphones responded, "Flight two-two-niner. There better not be a girl flying that plane or you guys are in a heap of shit. Over and out."

The joke had gone on long enough, and the rain started to pick up. Louise got closer as we circled. The pilots got dead serious and there were lots of "Rogers," "Affirmatives," and "Over and Outs," and they landed the plane.

What a view I had! It was so exciting to watch from the cockpit as the airfield got closer and closer. My adrenaline was pumping; but the pilots, who were so loose playing around with the tower seconds ago, were sitting straight up, fiddling with this button and that knob, and in monotone voices smoothly touched down.

My heart was in my throat; and I kept thinking, "this plane is going so fast it will never stop and we're definitely going to crash into something and I'll be blamed because the tower thought I was flying the plane. If I live through the crash, USO will surely fire me. The Air Force might make me pay for the plane. Jesus, how much could one of these things cost?"

Oh God, I prayed, eyes shut, and only opened them when the pilot said, "Well, how did you enjoy flying a plane?" We had not crashed before I could see the war.

Oh, I must mention, when pilots are in the process of landing a plane and they use "affirmative" or "negative," that doesn't bother me; but when you ask someone if he would care for a drink or another cookie and the answer is "affirmative" or "negative," now that annoys the crap out of me. Especially if that someone is a civilian woman sounding more like a military person than a military person. Like Ruby McGillacutty, my soon to be new boss.

I wish someone in Saigon had warned me about her, but new people in Vietnam—military and civilian—had to go through a sort of initiation or baptism. Nobody already there and feeling like an old-timer wanted to make the first few days in Vietnam easy for the new person or FNG (military slang for f_ _king new guy). The rule of thumb was to learn how things worked as you went along.

A blue bus with metal mesh protection took us to the terminal. Inside waiting for me was a middle aged woman—I thought about 48, but later found out she was actually 39 and intending to stay that age for many, many years—wearing a yellow slicker, yellow boots, and a yellow fisherman's hat. Her yellow hair was plastered down from the rain. Years later when I saw my first Paddington Bear, I instantly thought of that initial meeting with Ruby McGillacutty.

At that point, I was just happy to have been met at the airport and quite pleased to see a smiling face greeting me warmly. She was even holding a piece of cardboard with my name spelled out in large red letters. I looked around the terminal and noticed that we were the only two women there.

While Ruby and I stood there chitchatting, the pilots came up to us to shake my hand good-bye. Ruby lit up like a Christmas tree.

"You guys want to go have a drink?" she purred.

They quickly answered in unison, "No!"

I was surprised, because on the plane they said that when we landed we would go find Lynn Willowbrook, the director of the USO Coffee Bar at the airport, and have a drink at the officers' club on the air base.

As they quickly walked away, Ruby shouted at their backs, "You pilots don't know how to have a good time. Whatsa matter? Don't you like girls?" Talk about guts. Ruby, nonplused at their response, stared at me, grunted, "f_ _k 'em," picked up both of my suitcases, ordered, "Let's go find Lynn and see if she wants to go have a drink," and started marching in what I assumed was the direction of the USO Coffee Bar.

Lynn Willowbrook was tall, had long brown hair, and was

wearing a flight suit that she had made in Hong Kong, just like the pilots wore. She was slim enough to get away with the outfit. Ruby gushed about how great it looked on Lynn and said she wanted to have one made for herself.

Lynn glanced at me at the same time I glanced at her, and then we both looked at Ruby, at least 50 pounds overweight and appearing even heavier in the yellow slicker, yellow boots, yellow rain hat barely hiding her yellow slicked-down hair.

Our eyes revealed our silent screams, "Don't, Ruby. Don't! For the love of God, don't embarrass yourself."

Instead, Lynn sweetly said, "That's nice."

Ruby batted her eyelashes and, trying to imitate Lynn's sweetness, asked, "Can I have the name and address of your tailor in Hong Kong?"

Tripping all over her tongue and lying through her teeth, Lynn told her, "Oh, darn. I think I lost the receipt when I was shipping some boxes home. But as soon as I remember the name, I'll let you know."

"Liar, liar, pants on fire," my eyes silently revealed as Lynn made eye contact with me.

Lynn was closing the USO early, because the airport, which was now deserted, would be shut down until Typhoon Louise had come and gone. Since Ruby had decided to go back to her club, USO Aloha at 22nd Replacement Battalion, about 10 miles away, Lynn offered to drive me to the trailer park where I would be living, with a stop at the USO Cam Ranh Bay Club to meet Jolly Jackson, the director, and Bertha Bombeck, the assistant director.

Off Ruby went in a pickup truck. Lynn and I waved good-bye as we drove in the opposite direction in an uncovered jeep. Someone had stolen the canvas top a few weeks after Lynn had traded a case of steaks for the jeep from a supply sergeant at the air base, who had gotten the jeep in a trade he made with some guy from the motor pool at the Army base. The supply sergeant gave the motor pool guy an AK-47, the Chinese-made gun used by the NVA (North Vietnamese Army) and VC (Viet Cong)—the enemy. The AK-47 was given to the supply sergeant by a truck driver GI passing through on a convoy, who had swapped a case of whiskey (part of his cargo) for the weapon, whose third owner was a GI loading-dock clerk in Saigon. The first owner was an enemy soldier, who was killed by a grunt in the Mekong Delta. The combat GI brought the weapon to Saigon and traded it with the clerk for a typewriter, so that he could write the definitive Vietnam War novel. WOW!!! I was truly impressed.

The rain was pouring and Lynn was grinding the gears.

"Could you please reach back and get the umbrella?" she politely asked me as the MPs at the front gate of the airport waved us out. Turning around, I reached for a blue-and-gold-striped beach umbrella. "Open it up and hold it. It won't be much help, but at least it'll keep the rain out of my eyes so I can see where I'm going."

She was swerving all over the narrow, muddy road and concentrating intently on keeping to the middle. On each side were steep embankments. The right side ended in water, and the left led to what looked like woods.

"I'm so tired, "she moaned, not realizing that I was quite worried because of the road conditions. Her driving was so lousy that I could not imagine how she had ever passed a driving test. I wished I had packed a rosary as my mother had suggested.

Lynn continued, "I didn't get a wink of sleep last night." Oh, great! Then she announced more to herself than to me, "I think we just lost the brakes." We were going downhill.

As she pumped that pedal, I cursed myself for not listening to my mother about those Catholic beads. Lynn pumped furiously and bingo, the saints be preserved, the brakes were working again. Slowing down a bit, she repeated how tired she was. By now, I was holding the umbrella completely over her head and decided to strike up a conversation so she would not fall asleep.

"Nice umbrella," I started the conversation rolling. "Where'd you get it?"

I should have known. It was gotten through a convoluted barter transaction that she made with some supply sergeant, who got it from a cook, who got it from a nurse, who got it from a pilot, who got it in Hawaii on an R & R to meet his wife. The nurse was the pilot's in-country girlfriend.

Lynn was now wide awake telling me about other possessions she had acquired through barter; and I wasn't so frightened anymore, since on the left of the now wider road was level ground, wet sand, and on the right was the same. The "Welcome To Cam Ranh Army Depot" sign was straight ahead, and again the MP at another gate waved us through.

"Doesn't anybody check identification around here? I mean, it looks like security is too lax with VC planting satchel charges and all that stuff I read in the papers back home," I, the FNG, wanted to know.

"Do you really think two white American women could be mistaken for VC terrorists?" was the answer I got from the driver whose head was being protected from the pouring rain by an umbrella stolen from the Hilton Hotel on Waikiki.

After only eight of the over 600 days I spent in Vietnam, I could plainly see that there was a whole other side of the war that the media did not report. I wonder why.

BARBIE AND KEN EXPERIENCE THE WAR

Barbie arrived at the Continental Palace a tad past six. Immediately, she spotted Ken, seated at a table on the outdoor verandah with a bottle of Ba me Ba (33), the local beer, in front of him.

"God, this tastes like formaldehyde," he complained, then stood up and pulled out a wicker chair. "Give me good ole American brew, any day."

Instantly, the waiter rushed over to take Barbie's order.

While waiting for Ken to sit back down, she glimpsed around the fashionable terrace, the let's-meet-for-drinks' place since French Colonial days.

At the same table where Graham Greene drank while jotting notes for *The Quiet American*, four reporters, recently back from what they considered the "real war" up north, were sipping gin and tonics. The dashing correspondents waved hello.

In another corner, partially hidden by a giant potted plant, two Eurasians sat like mannequins, beaming at their companions, a pair of middle-aged civilians old enough to be the girls' fathers. The cut of the men's Sears and Roebuck catalogue clothes and their deeply tanned, muscular bodies were a dead giveaway that they were construction workers for the American cartel RMK-BRJ.

Rumor had it that LBJ was profitably connected to the corporation through his Texan friends, Brown and Root, two of the six wealthy initials.

The highly paid manual laborers, similar to many of their peers in the war zone with nagging wives and bratty kids Stateside, lavishly spent most of their paychecks on the eager-to-please mistresses meekly sitting across from them.

Barbie glanced back at Ken and frowned.

"Yeah, I know," he responded, interpreting her silent outrage, "the Ugly Americans can buy anything."

The waiter stood by patiently, pencil and pad in hand.

"I will have a Coca Cola," Barbie, who handled protocol at the American Embassy, ordered the old man without looking up at him. She smoothed an imaginary wrinkle from her lap. "And please, do make sure the glass is clean."

A beggar on Tu Do Street thrust a hand toward Ken. He reached into the pant's pocket of his khakis and gave 20 piasters to the old woman in black pajamas leaning on a cane. The mamasan grinned, revealing brown teeth from years of chewing beetle nuts, and mumbled her gratitude, "*Come un um*," before hobbling down the street.

Ken examined the label on the beer bottle, searching for a clue to its contents, and asked, "How was your day?"

Barbie described her visits to the Cathedral and the zoo. "Afterwards, a group of us gals shopped and shopped. I swear, I've been in more stores today than in the entire five months since arriving in Vietnam."

Ken smiled. He enjoyed hearing her voice, no matter what she was discussing. Barbie adored his smile. Taking a slight breath, she rattled on about being measured at Cat Minh Tailors for an ao dai, the traditional Vietnamese dress, and a correspondent's suit, the foreign journalist's combat zone attire. At the overpriced Than Ly gallery, she and her friend Madge bought ceramic elephants, lacquerware, and "those fabulous egg-shell paintings" that every American in Saigon was so mad about.

Balancing a silver tray above his right shoulder, the waiter returned with a chilled six-ounce bottle of Coca Cola and a twist of lime perched on an iceless glass.

Barbie reached into her leather shoulder bag for a Kool. Ken leaned forward with the gold Dunhill lighter he had bought for a song in Hong Kong a month earlier, while they were on R & R.

Still fumbling for a book of matches in his spotless white jacket, the waiter grunted his disappointment at not reacting quickly enough to accommodate the tall, blonde lady.

The beautiful couple laughed as the old man shuffled away in embarrassment, exactly as his grandfather had, long ago when Somerset Maugham, holding court a few tables away and downing one aperitif after another, loudly called him "my favorite boy" after patting his ass.

Under the center ceiling fan slowly stirring the tropical air, a group of Japanese businessmen were admiring Barbie's good looks.

Ken reached for her hand across the table, squeezed it lightly, and quietly said, "Let's go. I have to get back to the base. The old man's throwing a cocktail party for a group of visiting Congressmen. Duty calls."

Strolling back to her place, they bumped into a friend, a Red Cross executive, getting out of a cab in front of the apartment complex. The women chatted for a few minutes as Ken lingered at the door of the tiny yellow and blue vehicle and listened.

"I'll phone you tomorrow," he whispered in her ear after softly kissing her goodnight.

As he closed the car's door, the Vietnamese driver charged into traffic. Suddenly, Ken's taxi became part of the chaotic motorized scene of rich Saigonese with well-maintained Peugeots and shining Citroens, surging ahead of their less connected countrymen on Honda and Lambretta motor scooters.

Ken stared through the taxi's back window until Barbie and her friend became white specks among the hundreds of yellow ones. Sitting up straight, he patted the ribbons ("fruit salad," the General called the decorations) adorning his starched captain's uniform and smiled. Ever since meeting Barbie, he seemed to do that a lot.

Closing his eyes for a moment, he thought of his classmates from West Point, strategically placed throughout Vietnam, also acquiring medals and promotions. Smiling broadly, he could not help wondering, though, if they were enjoying the war quite as much as he was.

A PEDICAB DRIVER PEDDLES THROUGH HISTORY

I am originally from North Vietnam and descend from a long line of pedicab drivers. As a matter of historical fact, my family had been in the business three generations before Gia Long became emperor in 1802 and unified Vietnam.

From family stories passed down from generation to generation, I understand that we did quite well driving around the various mandarins and other court officials and hangers-on.

When the French gained power in the late 1800s, the business still flourished. The only problems were that the French were notoriously lousy tippers and extremely rude.

My father was apolitical. Dad did not care who was in the government's driver's seat as long as he owned his pedicab business and could support his family.

Then, one day in 1929, the year I was born, a certain French general hired my father to pull him around Hanoi for a whole day. At the end of the allotted time, my father was sure he would receive a big tip besides the fare. But alas, the general stiffed him, fare and tip, and my father was extremely angry, to say the least, but knew he had no recourse. For that reason, he joined the underground movement to oust the French.

His clandestine duty was to drive French officers to brothels where Vietnamese whores, also laboring for the underground, had venereal diseases. He would peddle them to restaurants where they were served poisoned food. He would take them to hotels with rooms with bedbugs. Anything to make the officers miserable.

By the time the Japanese assumed authority over us in 1940, I was in charge of my own pedicab, helping my father harass the French.

At first, we thought that since the Japanese were fellow Orientals, they would be nice to us and rotten to the French. Wrong. The Japs were pleasant to the French and mean to us Vietnamese.

A year after the Nips stormed on the scene, Ho Chi Minh returned from his wanderings to Vietnam and formed the Viet Minh to fight both the French and the Japanese. The Viet Minh is the shortened name for the Viet Nam Doc Lap Dong Minh Hoi, or League for the Independence of Vietnam. My father and I were among the first to sign up for the battle.

If it had not been for the American spies from the Office of Strategic Services (OSS), who paid us to fight the Japanese, we would have starved. The Japanese never paid for a ride anywhere. Can you believe that? As if Trung and Son Pedicab Service was some form of public transportation.

My father was sure that the Americans would win the war and help us get our country back from both the Japanese and the French. But, as you are well aware, after the American victory that did not happen.

After World War II, the French—cocky as all get out—decided that Vietnam was still theirs, and the British helped them take back control.

What could we do? The French were bleeding us dry. We had no choice but to continue fighting them.

It was 1946 when the French Vietnam War began. The money from the OSS had stopped. The French were back in power.

My father and I merely wanted to work in our pedicab business; but as fate would have it, we became soldiers for the cause. Dad and I both figured that once we beat the Frogs, we could resume our career. Oh, how destiny rules our lives.

My father and I became actual Communists after we attended

a luncheon in honor of the original Viet Minh. Ho Chi Minh gave each of us a medal and had his picture taken with us. Even after all these years, I can still remember how excited my father and I were to be congratulated by Uncle Ho.

Talk about charisma. That guy had it in spades. Quite frankly, we became Communists because we wanted to hang on to Ho's coattails. Any fool could see that the fellow was really going places. His picture was everywhere! Brothels, restaurants, flea markets, train stations, bars, cinemas, shops. Everywhere you looked, there was Ho's photo hanging on a wall.

What are my memories of our jobs during the war with the French? Primarily, my father and I engaged in the same activities as we did before that war. We drove French officers to infected prostitutes, made sure they acquired food poisoning, and—please remember this was war—we also rolled them after our bartender agents slipped them Mickey Finns.

Pop and I stole reports, military maps, battle plans. As a matter of historical fact, General Vo Nguyen Giap, the military leader of the Viet Minh, personally congratulated my father and me for our courageous accomplishments.

I spent the entire war years in Hanoi, despite the fact that I begged my father to see if he could pull strings and get me into the battle at Dien Bien Phu.

His answer was always, "We should each serve our country in the best way we can. We each have special talents."

With all humility, you can say I peddled my way through the war. Be that as it may, at the time I desperately desired to be firing a gun, or charging a hill, or something else as romantic and heroic. On the bright side, being in Hanoi during the war kept me in contact with all the important figures running the show. I networked like a son of a gun.

Let me see, that war ended in 1954. The Geneva Convention was signed that year, dividing the country at the 17th Parallel. Ho was our leader in the North, and Diem was chosen by his American puppeteers to rule the South.

I will never forget that year, 1954. That was the year my father died of heat stroke. It was during the time that the Catholics were frantically trying to leave North Vietnam for the South. The American Navy was assisting with the evacuation.

Allow me to deviate. When the war finally ended, my dad and I were back in the pedicab business. Best of all, the U.S. government needed all the pedicabs they could get their wealthy hands on to transport people to the docks. Spectacular! Money was flowing like water during that exodus.

Permit me to backtrack and elucidate why people were fleeing. The American newspapers reported that our populace in the North were rejecting Ho and his Communist government for Diem's anti-Communist regime in the South. Newsreels revealed tens of thousands of folks on the move, ostensibly running from Communism to Democracy.

Tsk! Tsk! The sheer power of film is extraordinary.

Would you care to learn the true explanation why people were fleeing the North for the South? I will tell you. Incredibly, a certain rumor had begun to circulate that the Virgin Mary was moving South, so a lot of stupid people decided to follow her.

Believe me, I am aware for a fact that a bunch of CIA—formerly OSS—agents started that one. As a joke, I later learned. They thought they were smart, but our side pulled a fast one. Untold numbers of the refugees were actually Communists heading toward Saigon in order to be in place when Ho decided to unite the country by fighting Diem, either at the voting booth or on the battlefield.

My father, a real go-getter, peddled and peddled and peddled and smoked and smoked and smoked so very much during the exodus that he worked and smoked himself to death. From the waist down, he resembled Arnold Schwarzenegger; but from the waist up, he was a chain-smoking Barney Fife.

I became the head of the family, which comprised of my mother and six sisters. I had a lot of mouths to feed. Quite frankly, I thought that 1954 was the end of my soldiering for the cause. Was I ever wrong.

Learning of my father's demise, Ho summoned me to his headquarters in a mountain cave. Dear God, that man was a romantic! Ho pleaded with me to work full-time for the Revolution. I had no choice when I saw his tears. I accepted, and he thanked me profusely.

He arranged for my sisters and mothers to work in government offices, thereby setting me free to labor completely for the unification of Vietnam. I essentially became Ho's surrogate son and number-one troubleshooter, so to speak.

He knew of my splendid exploits against the French and Japanese, working with the OSS. Ho was well aware of how ingenious I could be. Accordingly, Ho decided to give me full reign to formulate ideas to help maximize efficiency. You have to understand, he had spent many years in the Communist party and saw far too many goldbrickers and conformists and yes-men.

My first administrative task was to set up secret roads for travel to the South, after the official exodus, in order to carry supplies and send troops for future needs.

The South was being supplied by the United States and we were being equipped by China and the Soviet Union. Yet, Ho did not want to merely march across the 17th Parallel and start a massive war. He did not want Chinese troops showing up and never leaving. Are you aware that the Chinks were our constant enemy for a thousand years before the French paraded in? They most certainly were. And enough was enough.

With great patience, he wanted to slowly supply our agents in the South and have them do the fighting. The only way we could get weapons and new agents southward was to use the mountain trails that went from North Vietnam through Laos and Cambodia to South Vietnam. Actually, and with complete modesty, I was the one who named these mountain paths the "Ho Chi Minh Trail."

Traveling that route was a rugged trip, but we had no other

option. I myself made the trip many times with teams of cadres hauling supplies on their backs.

Yes, the journey was arduous, and yet, very few weapons were getting through. At that speed, it would have taken decades to supply our brothers in the South.

Then one day, while I was gliding around Hanoi in my pedicab, which at that time I only used for pleasure or to take my mother for a ride on Sundays, an idea came to me. Why not use bikes to haul supplies? Bingo!

Ho loved the idea and put me to work devising the right type of bike that a cadre could push. This way, one man or woman could transport three times the load using my bicycle. Within a short time, we were heaving thousands of supplies to South Vietnam.

After I solved that problem, Ho then begged me to focus my attention on the tunnel systems in the South. He hoped that I could perform another miracle and make them more efficient. Mind you, at that juncture in history, the tunnel systems were no better than gopher holes.

I dreaded another arduous trip down the Trail—not that I carried anything, including my briefcase. Quite frankly, I was overworked and emphatically informed Daddy Ho that I needed a certain amount of time off to rest. I required a breather to recharge my brain cells.

Can you possibly guess what that lovable character did? He begged me to go to Paris for a week's R & R.

Not one to let my leader down, I hurriedly departed Hanoi for the City of Lights. The return ticket was to Saigon, so that I would not have to take that dreadful and time-consuming journey down the Ho Chi Minh Trail. Rank has its privilege.

Paris was marvelous. However, you know me, Mr. Idea Man, invariably thinking up something new. For instance, while I was bicycling down the Champs Elysees, I met a French soldier, an enlisted guy from the French Vietnam War, and he remembered me.

He kept thanking me copiously for introducing him to his wife. Please be aware that I only did naughty things to officers, not enlisted men.

This particular ex-soldier reminded me that I had directed him to a brothel where he met the girl who later became his spouse. Be that as it may, he was biking along with me, and for sport we had a race down the Champs Elysees. Before we knew it, a crowd formed. Two handsome young men in tip-top form and all that. Efficiently, to make a long story short, he and I—mostly I—invented the Tour de France bike race. True story.

While originating the Tour de France bike race, I realized how much I missed peddling. It was such great exercise, for the body as well as for the spirit.

After a glorious week of food, biking, touring, I flew off to Saigon. On the plane, I met the most beautiful girl I had ever seen in my life. She was headed for Saigon and her freshman year at Saigon University.

I could not take my eyes off her the whole flight. Spectacular legs! When we landed in Saigon, I was despondent, realizing that our paths would never cross again. Alas, if they ever did, we would be fighting on opposite sides. I deduced by all the shopping bags she was toting that she surely must have been a Capitalist.

With a heavy heart, I checked into Communist headquarters, which at the time in the late 1950s was located in the basement of a dress boutique.

Madam Nhu shopped there, as well as all the other well-heeled Saigonese women. Not only did I charm Madam Nhu, but I also befriended wives of generals and cabinet ministers there.

Madam Nhu, as any idiot well knows, was President Diem's sister-in-law. Since Diem was a bachelor, she acted as first lady. Mamie Eisenhower, she was not.

Madam Nhu was more anti-Communist than Joseph McCarthy. That woman was so bad and mean and bitchy and vain and corrupt that she made our side appear good in comparison. Not that we were not, mind you.

While I was bivouacked at Headquarters, before starting the tunnel inspection, I helped in the emporium. To be factual, I redecorated the entire place and expanded business threefold. The money earned from the frock shop went for the Revolution.

Saigon at that time was still known as the "Paris of the Orient" with its French architecture, outdoor cafes, and beautiful tree-lined boulevards. Ah, yes, I knew that someday, after our side had won, I would own a pedicab business in Saigon. Little did I perceive that it would be sooner than I dreamed.

Oh, incidentally, one day I was waiting on Madam Nhu and chatting about Paris, a city we both loved. I was informing her about an extraordinary Left Bank restaurant I dined in that was owned by an American. It was the first time I had tasted barbecued food. The chef-owner, an old Negro by the name of Amos, gave me his barbecue recipe, and I graciously copied it for Madam Nhu. Thenceforth, she became a huge fan of barbecues.

At any rate, do you happen to remember when the Buddhists started burning themselves in protest to the Diem-Nhu regime? Madam Nhu was interviewed and said that it was only a "Buddhist barbecue."

Yes indeed, I am the reason she made that comment. It is comical how history is made, is it not? That one quote, headlined all over the world, helped topple the Diem regime, which caused coup after coup in South Vietnam, which helped our cadres gain power. Amazing! Who would have ever thought that my speaking about spareribs could change the course of history?

My tour of inspecting tunnels in South Vietnam, which I began after choosing the perfect wallpaper for the dress shop/Headquarters, took a year.

Incidentally, the tunnels were built during the French occupation and expanded when Vietnam was partitioned in 1954, that awful year when my father passed away.

Our cadres, known as Viet Minh until Diem gained power, then called Viet Cong, hid in the tunnels and emerged at night to cause havoc. They housed whole families, had schools, hospitals, conference rooms, bunkrooms. The tunnels came in handy, too, when the Americans started sending soldiers to fight.

During my inspection, I observed that the underground passages were lit by kerosene lamps. The places were always so smoky. Mind you, I have never smoked cigarettes, and the odor of smoke makes me nauseated. When someone is smoking in a room I am in, I always insist on opening a window. My kids tease me and say that if they had a nickel for every time I asked aloud, "Is the window open?" when someone lit up a cigarette, they would have more nickels than Fort Knox.

I could plainly see I had to find a way to light the tunnels with something other than kerosene lamps. The smoke was everywhere, not only from the lamps but also from the chain-smoking cadres hunkered down in the tunnels. War would be so much healthier if people did not smoke. Nasty habit. Sorry, it is one of my pet peeves.

Firstly, I posted "no smoking" signs in the tunnels. Secondly, to get rid of the kerosene lamps and replace them with electric light bulbs, I contemplated acquiring very long extension cords and plugging them into outlets at sundry Green Beret camps that were set up all over Vietnam before America formally got into fighting the war. But, I soon discovered, the Green Berets did not have electricity because they liked to rough it.

When I reported this intelligence to the VC general in charge of the tunnel system, he merely stared at me and inquired, "Why in the world would they want to 'rough it' if they do not have to?"

"Beats the hell out of me," I retorted. "I imagine they presume that is how they are supposed to live while at war."

Obviously, the extension cord idea was out of the question. Without any apparent solution to the kerosene dilemma, I decided to return to Saigon and get in a bit of exercise. That invariably assisted me in solving problems.

I borrowed a bike from one of my comrades, whose cover in Saigon was as a public relations consultant to President Diem. As a side note, the guy ended up being the second most highly decorated VC of the whole war. (Modesty does not permit me to boast about who was first.) Brilliant man. Absolutely top drawer at styling Diem to appear worse than he actually was.

As I peddled around Saigon visiting the typical tourist sites, I pondered and pondered. Still nothing came to mind. Then I decided to trek over to the zoo. I recollect this as though it were yesterday. I was standing near the monkey cage. With a blink of an eye, I was surrounded by 30 screaming, jumping, and running third-graders and their teacher, a very frazzled middle-aged woman.

Those tykes were climbing the bars, imitating almost everything the monkeys were doing, chasing each other, and merely being kids. I had to chuckle. Then, I turned to the teacher and proclaimed, "If only we could harness their energy, we could illuminate all of Saigon for weeks."

Like a bolt of lightning, it dawned on me: I could get a treadmill and have children run on it day and night, thereby generating electricity for the tunnels. However, the more I regarded that idea, the more I realized it could bankrupt the cause. You know how much kids eat. It was not feasible.

While I scratched my head, one of the miniature monsters knocked over my bike. The idea evolved. That is precisely how the stationery bike being peddled, thereby generating electricity in the tunnels was invented.

After phoning Daddy Ho and reporting to him of my latest concept, I launched the bike-peddling strategy in all the tunnels. Being merely one man, however, it immediately became clear to me that I required assistance. Therefore, I ordered the underground general to find me a team of engineers, mechanics, and students to aid me with the tactics and installation. It was a gigantic undertaking, and I required all the support I could muster.

The initial rendezvous with my underlings was held at the Rotary Club, after hours, where one of our agents was the club manager. Nice place and the perfect cover for a VC planning session.

The club manager had an intimate cocktail hour before the

meeting was to commence. I was standing around, chitchatting with a group of engineers, when in walked some students who had volunteered from Saigon University. And there she was. The girl from the plane from Paris, the one toting all those shopping bags. You could have knocked me over with a feather. I knew at that moment, when I discovered she also was a VC, that she would one day be my spouse.

I, of course, made her my personal assistant for the complete project, which meant that we would tour the tunnels together, setting up teams of riders for the bikes.

I held her hand in the smoke-free tunnel around the U.S. Embassy in Saigon.

I kissed her for the first time in the tunnel at Cu Chi, which, as our luck would have it, became a big American base.

I told her I loved her in the tunnel in Danang, which, as luck would have it again, became an immense American base.

I proposed to her in the tunnel at Bien Hoa, which, as luck would have it, became a large American base.

We were wed in a tunnel at An Loc.

We spent our romantic honeymoon in a tunnel at Tay Ninh.

Our first child was born in a tunnel at Xuan Loc.

As any fool can imagine, the tunnels have very special memories for me. I was young, handsome, virile, madly in love, and accomplishing grand feats for the Revolution by generating more clean energy for the tunnels than Ho and I had ever hypothesized.

Since I was one of Ho's favorites, if not his favorite, my spouse and I owned our own annex at the tunnel at Danang. When the Americans arrived, as luck would have it, they built their PX right over our abode.

Indeed, you are probably thinking: How could those SOB's be so darn lucky with their tunnel systems being at the right places before the Americans started building? Here and now, I am aware that I am going to appear as though I am taking much of the credit for historical events, but here is how it happened.

As I related previously, my wife was a student at Saigon University. An engineering student, to be precise. She graduated with honors after our initial tour of the tunnels and desired to do something meaningful for the cause, in her own right.

Ho arranged a position for her in The South Vietnamese Office of Building Permits. The administrator of that organization was a friend of his from the early days. Ho's crony, incidentally, was one of the top-ranking VC's planted in the South Vietnamese government. There were so many, so very many.

My spouse began her position there shortly after our first born began kindergarten in 1962, the same year that the U.S. Military Assistance Command, Vietnam (MACV) was established in Saigon under the command of General Paul Harkins.

Ho sensed that the office of building permits would be a direfully indispensable office in which to toil.

The South Vietnamese government, terribly afraid of losing any control and being referred to as a puppet of the Americans, demanded that it should and would decide where American military bases would be constructed. My suspicion has always been that some of those wise guys, or maybe double agents, at the CIA had their fingers in on that decision. In my humble opinion, it was either totally stupid or absolutely brilliant, depending on whose side you were on.

My wife, through her strategic and important post at the permit office, arranged for the bases to be assembled over our tunnels, thereby allowing us easy inside access without being detected by the American military.

Additionally, I have to elucidate, the permits—devised by my spouse—spelled out quite clearly that the American engineers could not, under any circumstances, construct basements. The purpose for that clause was absolutely simple: Quite a few U.S. generals fought tooth and nail for the right to have them built, with the idea, I assume, that they could have their own private rumpus rooms underground, away from prying enlisted eyes. Nonetheless, the South Vietnamese permit office held its ground. No basements. Period.

Meanwhile, I spent most of my time visiting tunnel systems, developing better bikes, setting up more efficient generators, nailing up the "no smoking" signs that the VC smokers had torn down.

Quickly, oh so quickly, the years rolled by. Our family was getting larger. By the time our tenth child was born, I was overworked and grossly out of shape.

At the end of 1967, I made a trip to Hanoi, via the Ho Chi Minh Trail, which by then was a 10-lane highway with stop lights, school crossing guards, R & R centers, toll booths, restaurants, motels. I desperately desired to see Uncle Ho and spend some quality time with him.

I remember it so vividly. It was around Halloween. I was bringing him a present, an assortment of candy I appropriated one night after the PX in Danang had closed. Ho had such a sweet tooth. He just loved candy corn and all that other orange and brown sugary candy shaped like pumpkins and turkeys and goblins.

After arriving in Hanoi, I perceived immediately that Ho was tired and somewhat bored. Desolately, he talked about the war dragging on and on, with no end in view. Ho was fed up to his back teeth with it all and merely wanted this war to disappear.

With a heavy heart, I briefed him, "The Americans are not going away, and we are not going to surrender. Maybe the solution lies somewhere in the middle."

Then and there, I realized that his staff was enormously stale. Maybe, I thought, he required a fresh idea from a brilliant person. As I began speaking about striving for something unique and novel, I was also attempting to choose the right moment to lead him into the next room, where I had arranged a celebration in honor of his half-birthday party.

Ho's birthday was in April and he had a party then, but he also liked to celebrate in October. You know how kids will answer that they are three-and-a-half when you ask them how old they are. Imagine a grown man telling a journalist from *The New York Times* that he is 65-and-a-half. Indeed, we each have our quirks.

This half-birthday was, I felt, important because everyone in

Hanoi was so busy that everyone forgot to celebrate Ho's halves in years. I believed it was about time we began re-celebrating this marvelous tradition, Ho's Half.

While chatting about bombs and bridges and Brigitte Bardot, I slowly guided him toward the door, flung it open, and bellowed, "Surprise!" Joining me was a chorus of voices belonging to General Giap and his staff, Premier Pham and his staff, and Ho's whole household staff and their families.

Ho was truly overwhelmed and turned to me with tears in his eyes. I stared into those baby-browns and conveyed, "Uncle Ho, you and our glorious Revolution require more surprises to keep us going."

I will never forget the look on his face that split second before he gave me the biggest bear hug I have ever received in my life.

After releasing me, he swiftly turned to the other leaders of our great cause and asserted, "Comrades, I have a wonderful idea, given to me by my brilliant surrogate son. I wish to discuss my surrogate son's excellent inspiration with you after we finish the cake and ice cream."

The idea, in case you have not already surmised, turned out to be the Tet Offensive.

I was a major part, if not *the* major part of the high-level planning of the biggest military surprise since Pearl Harbor. At that point, Ho wanted to confer upon me the rank of a four-star general in charge of the attack of the Saigon area, but I declined.

Quite frankly, I personally knew far too many generals—South and North Vietnamese, French and American—who were all, to put it bluntly, paper-pushers. Not for me, thank you. I wanted to be useful and keep those ideas flowing for my country and for my leader. No desk job for this clever kid, no thank you.

Ho understood completely—he was most mindful that I would stagnate and die if I had to sit behind a desk—and promptly gave me my next important assignment. I was ordered to set up a pedicab business in Saigon and gather information from the Americans. A very, very consequential responsibility, I might add.

Astounding! I thought I died and went to Heaven. My own pedicab business in the Paris of the Orient. Indeed, a very, very dangerous mission. Too marvelous for words!

My spouse and youngsters and I rarely sojourned to Saigon since she had a government job that required her to travel quite a bit, helping to set up American bases over our tunnels.

As a side note, my wife was a dedicated worker, but not her co-workers. She confided to me many times that the Saigon bureaucrats never went to work. They merely had their paychecks sent to their banks and—maybe—showed up once a year for the annual office Tet party.

On the other hand, she, as well as other VC agents, indeed toiled at the job. Why? Because by doing her job in our enemy's government, she—as well as the other VC plants—helped the Revolution.

Enough about those South Vietnamese slackers. I was explaining about my new mission, to own a pedicab business, a chain of them, and reside in Saigon. Moreover, and best of all: Spy on the Americans!

Things had changed since the first time I spent any time in Saigon in the late 1950s. Diem had been assassinated, Kennedy had been assassinated, the Marines had landed, Johnson was President, business was booming, and American troops were everywhere. Indeed, I do mean every place!

My sisters, by this time, were all married, and my mother was not getting any younger. I arranged with Ho to move the entire family to Saigon to assist me in my new clandestine endeavor, Trung, Jr. and Brothers-in-law Pedicab Service.

Of course, Ho could not merely give me the money from some petty cash box. So, I had to investigate about acquiring a donation from someone who did business with our agents in Saigon.

Hurriedly, I rushed to Saigon to arrange the financing of the pedicabs.

A number of our agents were business owners and also members of the Saigon Chamber of Commerce. As a guest of one of the brothel owners, I went to the weekly luncheon to see what I could arrange. It did not take long to acquire the endowment.

One of our agents, who headed up the illegal money exchange operation in Saigon, introduced me to an American by the name of Guido from Chicago. He made weekly trips to Saigon to launder money from his company's pizza parlors in the United States, which were mainly in business to launder money for various American mob families. Hence, the nickname "dough."

While chewing the fat, I discovered that Guido was a major contributor to Kennedy's campaign as well as to Nixon's in 1960. He also supported any candidate who was anti-drugs and for law and order.

I could not for the life of me determine why this guy was against the businesses he operated. Then, my luncheon host explained that Guido did not want any competition.

"But why support both political parties?" I inquired.

The answer was penetrating: "In order to hedge his bets. He wins no matter who wins an election."

This was one fellow from whom I could learn a thing or two.

Money from Guido in hand for the pedicabs, I phoned the family to pack up and get to Saigon. We had a mountain of work to accomplish.

By January, we were in business, peddling around Saigon, gathering valuable information, and planning tactics for the eventful Tet Offensive at the end of the month. It was a heady time, and we all threw ourselves into our mission.

I devised the system where each of my brothers-in-law kept a quarter of what they made, paid me a fourth, and the other half went for VC activities in South Vietnam. The harder they labored, the more money they made for themselves, for me, and for the Revolution.

Overnight, I became a leading member of the Chamber of Commerce, thereby allowing me to establish deals to drop off customers at establishments that gave us a cut—brothels, restaurants, tourist shops, hotels, bars.

The Tet Offensive of 1968, of course, was a huge surprise to the Americans, and the reporters claimed it was a victory for our side. Indeed, that was hardly the truth. It set us back quite a bit; however, you must be aware of what the old sage once said: When someone hands you lemons, make lemonade. That is exactly what we did.

Tet was the terrible turning point for the Americans, even though they won. In the eyes of the American people, thanks to the American press, the American military was losing. Amazing, is it not? Black is white.

Our official order from the top after Tet was to merely bide our time and wait for the American soldiers to depart. Nevertheless, although there were numerous promises and announcements that the troops would be home by Christmas, it was obvious to just about every Vietnamese that the Americans intended to remain a very long, long time.

Indeed, I am aware that this is sounding like hindsight on my part, but the impression worldwide and in America was that by January 1968, just before the Tet Offensive, America was winning and would be leaving within a short time. That was 1968. The troops finally left in 1973. That is six more years. Count them: 1968, 1969, 1970, 1971, 1972, 1973.

Everything everywhere all through 1968 was building, building, building. My family and I worked hard, saved our share, and gave many piasters to the cause. Then, in 1969, my world turned upside-down.

Ho died that fateful year, and I changed radically within a short time. With the great man's vanishing, the bureaucrats in Hanoi started jockeying for power. The Soviets, who were helping to finance our fight, were getting bossy and pushy. And I realized that I enjoyed what money could buy.

That period of waiting for the Americans to leave created quite a dilemma for the VC who owned businesses in Saigon. They started to become Capitalists. Not like the South Vietnamese, who had everything handed to them from the Americans. Those walruses did not know how to scramble for a buck. No, it was something else.

Indeed, I realized that without Ho the North Vietnamese high command was similar to the South Vietnamese high command—spoiled by handouts. The fellows in the field, hustling and raising money, were the ones who did all the work and received none of the credit.

Then and there, I began to think: Why should I work hard to help support lazy people? My brothers-in-law were grumbling, too. I knew it was all coming to a head.

The turning point for me came sooner than later.

Over dinner (my mother concocted her extraordinary dog stew) one Sunday, I shouted, "I think Communism stinks. Capitalism is number one. If you work hard, you get ahead. It is the rugged individual who makes all the difference."

Talk about a group therapy session. It was unbelievable. We all agreed that we had become Capitalists and absolutely loved the idea.

Indeed, once I realized that I was a Capitalist, I began to view the war in a different way. Right then and there, my family and I decided to cease sending half of our money to assist in financing the Revolution.

After ending our VC deposits, we worried that someone would visit us from Headquarters and demand to learn why. Nothing happened as we waited for a shoe to drop.

Shortly afterwards, I discovered that over half of the VC agents in Saigon had become Capitalists themselves, including the bookkeeper who had been pocketing our donations for well over a year before we stopped contributing.

I was livid, but there was nothing we could do. Well, not exactly. There was one thing: Ask Guido for assistance in the matter!

Alas, the bookkeeper left the country shortly before my brothers-in-law and I hired Mr. Guido to break a few limbs. The number cruncher flew out of Saigon with all our money and all his limbs intact, I am sorry to report.

I am not going to mention any names, but if you, Mr. Bookkeeper, are reading this right now, I would appreciate a cashier's check for the amount you stole plus interest. As an enticement, let me mention that Guido is still a dear, dear friend of mine and a devoted business associate.

Speaking of the conversion to Capitalism. Indeed, I should have figured out my true calling much sooner than I did. Honestly, I loved making money and buying nice things for the home. Furthermore, I noticed that people with money were happier than people without money. Although I am brighter than a rocket scientist, it did not take one to see the writing on the wall.

I quickly comprehended that Communism, as we knew it, was going to fail in the long run as long as the little guy had a shot at making money.

I imagine those think-tank guys had it all figured out: Have a war, drag it on as long as possible, pour money in, make the Communists discover how marvelous it is to have a chunk of the pie, and before you can say "light at the end of the tunnel," you have converted Communists into Capitalists.

There is probably a group of international executives sitting in a room somewhere smugly smiling because they planned the whole thing. They have every reason to be proud. The brilliant plan worked.

Civil War, baloney. It was Capitalism against Communism on a global scale. Vietnam merely happened to be the right place at the right time.

Indeed, smart guys—such as I—seized every money-making moment. Truly, I am damn proud to be a convert to Capitalism.

Allow me to elaborate further. If you think in those terms of Capitalism creating Capitalists and Capitalists making money, spending money, and creating more Capitalists who are happier than Communists, it is not too difficult to discover who the real heroes of the Vietnam War are. The real honest-to-God heroes were the guys making money during the war, those wise men who owned construction companies, ice cream plants, banks, military hardware businesses—tanks, guns, bullets and the like. Those are the heroes for whom America should be building monuments.

In fact, I have a recurring dream: I fantasize of an enormous granite wall—similar to the one I urged Maya Lin to design— etched with the names of companies that did business in Vietnam during the war. But, I am sure I know why they desire to keep a low profile about their colossal involvement. What else but modesty, pure and simple. It almost brings tears to my eyes when I contemplate how humble and full of humility those patriots are.

In closing, only one thought comes to my tired old mind: Long live Capitalism and the captains of industry, my idols!

SUNNING ON THE DECK

When it finally stopped raining after months of downpours and the sun came out full force, Richie Havens was heard, loud and clear, singing all over the place. "Here comes the sun. Do do do waa."

Cheerfully dry and humming along, Millie, the program director at USO Cam Ranh Bay, started planning activities at the beach for the soldiers who frequented her club: touch football games, cook-outs, snorkeling, scuba diving, blanket parties.

And the deck in the trailer park, where Millie and other women civilians lived, was in constant use for dancing at hail and farewell parties, for birthday celebrations, and for sunning before going to work or on days off.

From a diary Millie kept at the time, one of the entries was written while catching some rays: "I am lounging on the deck in the middle of our trailer park with three of the Red Cross trailer gang, Linda, Paige, and Marjie, who also have the day off.

"Paige and Marjie are arguing about the Middle East. Paige feels sorry for the Palestinians; and Marjie, in her own words, 'cannot believe my ears that any woman in 1971 could possibly support, in any way, those lying, cheating, thieving, and woman-hating cutthroat Arabs.'

"Good, there's a moment of silence. In one hour, we have discussed men's sideburns; National Health Insurance; Janis Joplin's death (Marjie to this day wears an armband in the evenings as a tribute); whether the tie-die look is a phase that will go the way of the hula hoop or is here to stay; who's cuter, Huey Newton or Pierre Trudeau; what war, if any, did John Wayne fight in (I knew the answer was 'none' but didn't open my mouth); who's smarter,

Tricia and Julie or Lynda and Luci; and who's more stupid, Barry Goldwater or Governor Ronald Reagan. The four of us agreed that Gloria Steinem and Henry Kissinger would make a great couple; and that if everyone who claimed to be at Woodstock had actually been there, the door count would have been five million. Marjie was there and gets very suspicious if someone claims to have also been there. That I-didn't-see-you-there expression crosses her face.

"Now all is peaceful. Paige is reading *Love Story*. Linda is skimming *The French Lieutenant's Woman* and looking for good parts. Marjie is devouring *Quotations from Chairman Mao Tse-Tung*, which is officially banned in Vietnam.

"We've also been chuckling the entire morning about the woman who lived in the trailer in the back of the park where the movies are shown. She works, well, used to work as of yesterday, with an unnamed construction company. Yeah, sure. The construction adviser was continuously flying around Vietnam where there is no construction going on. The CIA has got to come up with better covers for their agents. None of us know her name, and she stayed clear of everyone here. She was like a ghost or more aptly, a spook.

"Yesterday, the cement expert strolled through the trailer park hand in hand with a Montagnard native in a loincloth, went to her trailer, and a while later came out with four suitcases. The rumor is that she met this fellow in the Highlands, fell in love, and has decided to take him back to America to marry and civilize him.

"Quipped Marjie, 'Tarzan would be better off keeping his loincloth.'

"We sunbathers groaned when Lucinda, another Donut Dolly, who joined us, cheerfully remarked, 'I thought they made a nice couple.' Geez, she is such a nerd.

"Things are rather quiet today. No helicopter landings as of yet. Chopper pilots, breaking the rules, as well as taking a hell of a risk, land quite often on the deck in the middle of the trailer park, just to stop by and say hello or grab a quick lunch. At first, we women were excited, but then it became a nuisance when our magazines, papers, and suntan lotion bottles were tossed all over the place by the whirling blades as the flyboys carefully landed dead center. If not precise, the blades, which at dead center miss the trailers by four feet, could without a doubt shear off the roofs of our aluminum houses as though someone were opening cans of sardines."

A CIA HIRED WIFE BARES HER SOUL

The very first job I had, besides begging when I was a waif, was as a bar girl when I turned 10 years old. I worked on Tu Do Street. My nerves were shot by the time I turned 16. All that caffeine in Saigon Tea was making me sleep-deprived.

My mother was really worried about me and suggested that I look around for another job. Besides, I was getting too old to be a bar girl anymore. I would have been out of work by the time I turned 18, anyway. So, I began scouring the help wanted ads in *The Saigon Post* and sending out resumes to massage parlors around town.

After a few months of interviewing, I was becoming desperate. Oh, do not get me wrong, I received plenty of job offers. It is merely that I was sick of working for someone. I wanted to be my own boss, but I did not know any business owners who made as much money as bar girls and massage workers.

Then, one day I was having lunch with an American girlfriend who worked at the Tan Son Nhut USO. Consuelo O'Keefe was her name. I was one of her junior volunteers, you know, those young women of high moral character who are hostesses at USO activities—dances, holiday parties, stuff like that. The USO can be choosy in America, but in Vietnam there was not a big supply of young women with high moral character. Consuelo was sticking her neck out by using bar girls as junior volunteers and made it very clear to us that there would be no soliciting in her club.

At any rate, Consuelo was chattering on about one of her boyfriends, Max, a Malaysian who sold Oriental rugs to CIA agents.

And how he was so busy because business was booming that he never had time to take a vacation.

My interest was peaked. "Are there a lot of CIA agents in Saigon?" I asked. Consuelo laughed and pointed out 10 sitting in the restaurant that Max had sold carpets to.

"And they have money to burn," she added.

"Do they come from rich families?" I was intrigued.

"Some do, but that's not the source of their wealth," she answered.

Consuelo went on to explain how the CIA was accountable to no one in the United States government. Congress did not have a clue what money they had or how they spent it. That, essentially, the CIA was its own government with its own set of rules, and in wartime the agency had money to burn anyway they chose, no questions asked, national security and all that. Gosh! Consuelo's American civics lessons were always so informative and interesting.

"Now there's an easy job with plenty of free time to yourself," Consuelo said.

"Me, a spy?" I asked.

"No, silly, a hired wife for a CIA agent."

It was the first time that I ever heard of such a position, and was not surprised in the least that Consuelo knew of a class forming titled "How to Be a CIA Hired Wife" that was going to be taught at the Saigon Community College by the language instructor from the USO.

The course was already booked, but since I was the president of the USO junior volunteers, Consuelo believed she could pull some strings and get me in the first class.

The lessons were taught by an elderly Vietnamese woman who had been a hired wife to OSS agents during and after World War II. When the OSS became the CIA, she made the easy transition for a few years, but decided to retire when she saw the writing on the wall.

I learned that the OSS agents were romantic and brave and daring and intelligent. They came from various kinds of professions and backgrounds before World War II and were hand-picked by General Donovan because the United States needed the best agents to win that specific war.

During the McCarthy-era red scare, the CIA became filled with only robots who spouted the party line. The right-wing Republican Party, that is. The agents all thought alike, dressed alike, looked alike. Anyone even remotely dashing was dashed. Anybody remotely romantic or daring was suspected of being a subversive.

Mrs. Trung, the teacher, knew that the glory days were over, so she took the money she had saved and bought apartment buildings in Saigon. She did not come out and say that exactly, but that was a rumor floating around school. Consuelo had an apartment in one of her complexes.

I remember this so vividly, as if there is a recorder in my head. Mrs. Trung began her class with: "Now, in the OSS days things were different. Those were real men who wanted real women. Every one of them was an individual and, oh my, so handsome and fearless. But those days and men are gone. The CIA is a bureaucracy made up of mediocre bureaucrats.

"At the moment, girls, I know you think spies are romantic. Precisely, they used to be. With that in mind, please take plenty of notes and ask any questions that might pop into your pretty little heads.

"I also am aware that some of you may be VC agents. Well, that is fine. If that is the case, I know that you have been trained in complex ideas. Girls, brush all that out of your minds. With the men who spy for the CIA, remember one word: Mediocre. If you remember that, you will get along fine and make lots and lots of easy money.

"Girls, when I was an OSS hired wife, there was not nearly as much money floating around as there is now. What cash there was back then, the agents used to do their jobs. During World War II, they armed and fed and clothed the peasants who were fighting the Japanese. The OSS agents were part of a grand scheme, the big picture. They were fighting on the side of angels, and they were knights in shining armor.

"Oh, they got paid well, but they were generous to their hired wives and even to our relatives. The CIA agents these days have so much more money, none of it accountable. They use some of it to bribe village chiefs, plan assassinations, set up torture chambers, buy votes, rig elections.

"It has been estimated by my friends' daughters, who are highly successful hired wives as their mothers once were, that the CIA agents pocket 10 times what they actually spend for their jobs. Oh, yes, and they are the first ones on the scene after battles are fought around temples and pagodas. They get the first pickings of antiques and precious stones. Yes, these men are fabulously richer than the OSS agents and astonishingly stupid.

"Keep that in mind and you will become rich, too. Just remember, the OSS agents wanted hired wives who were mistresses. The CIA agents want hired wives to be exactly like the wives they have back in the States. Remember, girls, the key word is mediocre."

Breezing through the class, I aced every test. I learned how to nag, how to get what I wanted at all times, and when to hold back my sexual favors. There were stock phrases that I mastered:

"I've given you the best years of my life."

"You don't appreciate me."

"You never take me out."

"Take out the garbage."

"Take your feet off the coffee table."

One of the best phrases was "I am sick and tired of being the only one who picks up around here." Whenever I used that one, my employer husband would hire a new maid. And when I shrilled, "All I do is slave over a hot stove all day," he would recruit another cook.

Skillfully, I acquired the fine art of cooking lousy meatloafs and soupy casseroles. How to put face cream on right before going to bed. How to shop in haircurlers.

Now, I know this sounds all so drastic, but I kept in touch with a number of my classmates and found out that they almost lost their meal tickets because their husbands grumbled that they did not act like wives. One hired wife tried to initiate sex when she knew perfectly well, from class, that it was imperative to always squawk about having a headache at bedtime.

To be on the safe side, and to make sure my husband felt married, I hired a mother-in-law from an agency. These older women were former hired wives during the OSS days.

To be even safer, I employed teenage kids who played rock and roll records very loudly, snapped gum, and broke things around the villa. As more insurance, I purchased a stained bathrobe from a store specializing in items for hired wives, went to Tupperware parties, and even became an Avon lady.

Besides my salary, I made plenty of money on the side. When my husband came back from one of his secret trips to Laos or Cambodia with a Ming vase or an Oriental rug, I would take the original and priceless object to a VC auction house, sell it, pocket the loot, and then buy a replacement from a cousin who sold great imitations.

I would bring girlfriends around the villa for him to find a mistress on the side, which meant guilt-gifts and guilt-money for me. I also got a cut from the gifts he gave the mistresses for birthdays and holidays. Then, too, my hired mother was always "sick" and needed frequent operations.

From the mother-in-law agency, I hired a brother-in-law. His job was to repeatedly hit up my husband for money for new business schemes. I, as usual, took my cut.

Religiously, I wore flannel pajamas to bed. Of course, when he was out of town on business, I would don my silk teddies and lace underwear. He almost caught me one time when he came back unexpectedly. But when I heard the key turning in the lock, I raced to the bathroom and changed, put curlers in my hair and face cream on, and grabbed my stained and tattered bathrobe. Whew! That was a close call.

Incessantly, I would nag about being in the house all day, and he would give me money to go to a movie with my girlfriend. That was good for quite a bit of extra cash.

If he gave me American money, I would exchange it at one of the illegal money exchanges and get four times its value. If he gave me piaster, I would keep my hand outstretched and he kept putting more in it. That nitwit never could get the hang of what piasters were worth.

To keep him happy, I learned to protest loudly about women's libbers. I would just repeat what he always said about how they hated men and that they did not shave their arm pits. During sex I would use one of the stock phrases from class like "I am not doing that!" or "Are you finished yet?"

His CIA friends, who were all interchangeable, would come over for barbecues and, I kid you not, call me his "better half."

Of course, he had PX and commissary privileges. I would give him shopping lists that could have accommodated a hotel. One of my cousins would stop by in the mornings and buy 90 percent of it for resell on the Black Market. He had stands all over Saigon.

My first CIA husband played those damn Elvis Presley records of his. When he was gone, I would put on Chopin and Vivaldi or some jazz. I loved it when he went plundering with the boys and I could have some time to refresh my brain.

By selling secrets to a VC agent who was married to my sister, I also made a few bucks on the side But it was chicken feed, because all the information I heard him discuss when he thought I was out of earshot was already known by the VC or useless because it was not true.

Like a yo-yo, I had to gain weight and then always be on a diet. I joined health clubs and Weight Watchers. Once a week I went to a beauty shop, because that was what his real wife at home did. I was regularly thinking of ways to look more like the hausfrau he had in the States. For instance, I padded my ass when I wore pedal pushers.

Unceasingly, I griped about the hired help, and he would invariably give me money to pay the agency for new ones. Without delay, I would pocket the money and keep the same maids or cooks. The moron never even noticed.

To keep up the charade, I subscribed to movie magazines and *The National Enquirer* and watched the soaps on AFVN when he was home. When he left, I was so culturally deprived that I gorged on Voltaire and Dickens.

When he thought I was at health clubs, beauty shops, and Tupperware parties, in fact, I was attending classes at Saigon University. While employed by all my CIA husbands, I took classes and over the years picked up a law degree, a medical degree, and a Ph.D. in economics.

Two of my girlfriends, who were also hired wives, and I rented an apartment near the university where we studied and kept our books. Moreover, we held NOW meetings there. Actually, the three of us founded the first Saigon chapter.

I would grumble habitually about feeling unfulfilled, and my dimwit hubby would give me money and tell me to take a ceramics class. At the end of eight weeks of the supposed ceramics class, I would buy a cheap ashtray and proudly show it to him. Thank God, he never turned the damn thing over and saw the "Made in Taiwan" label. The class fee was a hundred bucks and the ashtray cost 50 cents. Quite a profit, no?

My fake mate sent his relatives back in the States those tacky ceramic elephants that every American just had to own. Before sending it, he would show it to me and brag how he, in his words, "Jewed them down." In fact, he always got cheated. And I mean big time. So I suggested that I shop for him, and he would give me the money he normally spent. Then, I would spend one tenth of what my bogus betrothed would have spent and just pocketed the change.

During my hired wife days, I was forever whining about something and he, as well as the others who came after him, predictably responded in the same way. He would give me money. It was so damn easy that it was becoming monotonous.

I visited every relative I had in South Vietnam from the Delta to the DMZ and a few in North Vietnam as well. Not often, though, because I detested the traffic jams on the Ho Chi Minh Trail. After one too many fender-benders, I started to fly to Paris and then fly to Hanoi, using a forged passport, of course. One of my cousins was in that line of work. Still and all, the jet lag really got to me. Mostly, I stayed close to home and worked on my degrees and stock portfolio.

Quite frankly, I laughed a lot during those days. Mostly at his expense. Everything he said or did got back to me through the grapevine. Oh, he would tell his mistresses, my girlfriends, that his missus did not understand him or that he was separated. We all got a big hoot when he would answer a bar girl's question with his standard question, "Do I look married?"

The charade never stopped. I would bitch, "Do you have to smoke those smelly cigars in the house?"

And he was so predictable. The lord of the castle sat in his leather recliner and fell asleep watching football games nightly.

My cousin, pretending to be one of our maids, who was actually a VC agent, spent a week at our place, but decided that the information she picked up was not worth shit. She even asked me if my husband and his agent buddies were "for real" or talking in some kind of code, pretending they were imbeciles.

Let me explain. You see, the plan was for me to leave the house while the boys played poker. My husband thought the maid—my VC cousin—did not understand English, so he and his spy pals would speak as though she were invisible. My cousin, by the way, spoke nine languages fluently. Anyway, he and his CIA buddies would speak freely in front of her, as though she were a stick of furniture.

Imagine, if you will, the United States' foreign policy being shaped by information gathered by these men. Let me give you a few sample remarks during one of their poker games:

"I don't want to be a Cassandra, but I think there's some corruption in Vietnam."

"Do you think any of the troops are smoking that marijuana stuff?"

"Do you think any of the Vietnamese elections are fixed, I mean, other than the ones we fix?"

"I've been hearing some talk, not much you understand, but some whispers about there maybe being a black market here."

"No way, Jose. The CIA would certainly be aware of it."

"I haven't seen anyone lately wearing black pajamas, so I think we're finally getting rid of the VC."

"Wasn't the body count the greatest idea since sliced bread. At last, an accurate way to calculate how well we're doing in this war."

"I don't trust that new man from Langley. He speaks Vietnamese for Christ's sake. He's a little too left for me. I told him to get information from the village chiefs but he spoke to the villagers. What the hell does he think he's going to learn from them. He doesn't even own a belted trench coat. He doesn't have a Vietnamese hired wife. And he dates an American civilian woman who works for the Quakers. They must have scraped the bottom of the barrel for him. But mark my words, he won't go far; he just doesn't fit in with the rest of us."

Let me think. What else do I recollect from my hired wife days with my first CIA husband? Oh, yes, his wife in the States and I both sent round-robin letters at Christmas. And he kept a diary for the memoirs he was going to publish someday. No Winston Churchill, he.

But mostly, you know what I found so amusing? How he and the other CIA agents would watch "Mission Impossible" episodes on AFVN and scoff that Hollywood did not get it right by portraying a Black man and a white woman as agents. My husband and his pals never met any working as agents for the Company.

However, they were definitely right about the sleuth show being fantasy. On it, there were intelligent white men. I personally never met any who worked for the CIA in Vietnam.

THE 4TH OF JULY

On the 4th of July, Pamela hung the Vietnamese Declaration of Independence next to a framed copy of the American Declaration of Independence. The new wall decoration in the USO public relations office was a gift from a donut dolly friend who had left for the States that morning, after being fired by Red Cross honchos for taking illegal flights to visit her boyfriend in Cambodia.

When Pamela's boss, Charlie Stonewall, walked in to see what all the banging was about, he quickly glanced at the document and ordered the PR director to immediately take it down.

"That piece of dog manure was written by Ho Chi Minh, a Communist, and it is anti-American," he yelled.

"Actually, it's anti-French and pro-American," Pamela argued.

"Take it down!" the retired Navy captain with a master's degree in political science bellowed. The young female executive quickly did as commanded.

The American Declaration of Independence, as most people know, was written in 1776. It is the historic document in which the American Colonies declared their freedom from British rule. It eloquently expressed the reasons for proclaiming their freedom. The document blamed the British government for many abuses.

The Declaration of Independence of the Democratic Republic of Vietnam was written in 1945, directly after World War II. It declared Vietnam's freedom from French rule and blamed the French government for many abuses.

It begins: "All men are created equal. They are endowed by their Creator with certain inalienable rights, among these are Life, Liberty, and the pursuit of Happiness."

Ho Chi Minh had carefully chosen those words to show his

admiration for the American Declaration of Independence and, hopefully, to win American support for his cause. Instead, the American government chose to aid the French.

Pamela stared at both documents and whispered, "If words could kill."

MAJOR HOLLOWAY, LIFER

I did two tours of duty in Vietnam. In between tours, I was an instructor at West Point. I was sent over the second time because I had such an outstanding fitness report. Roger that!

The second tour I requested was in a combat unit. Where the real action was. I commanded a firebase.

Initially, I observed the men coming back from patrols looking just God-awful. I called the lieutenant in charge on the carpet and demanded to know why those individuals were so filthy and why their boots were so muddy. They were disgusting!

He gave me some lame excuse about them just coming out of the bush after three days on patrol, a search and destroy mission. I told that young officer, in no uncertain terms, that was no excuse. This man's army is built on discipline and order and, most of all, cleanliness.

In fact, I must sadly and emphatically add, their body count was way down. Immediately, I issued an order to the men of how many body counts I wanted. No excuses. Before long, my orders were followed to the exact number. That is the way things get done. It is an indication that a skillful leader is in charge.

I would state with great conviction, "Sons, I command you to go out there and bring back news of 10 enemy killed." Yes sir, before long, I started getting results.

During the first month of my command, the men came back from patrol looking exactly as they did when they went into the bush, clean as a whistle. They also reported the quota I had set for them. Exactly on the mark! Outstanding!

Then to my surprise, and I might add immense pleasure, the body counts started to double and they returned cleaner, as though they had never even left base camp. Sometimes they would march back sooner than anticipated. When that happened, I ordered them to go on another patrol and kill more gooks.

Discipline. That is what gets things done.

Well, I figured that maybe they were making some mistakes. After all, they were not officers. Most of them were uneducated and stupid and from poor families. There were a lot of Negroes and other minorities and they probably did not count right. Not that I am prejudiced or anything. So, I would add a few more body counts for good measure and send the reports posthaste up to battalion headquarters.

I would even have contests for patrols that brought back more than their daily quotas. Oh, I am aware that it sounds as though I was coddling the boys, but you have to bear in mind that these were considerably dumb kids. With that in my military-trained mind, I used the carrot and the stick approach, the same as you would utilize to trick a half-witted donkey into moving forward.

One of the prizes was a hot shower. I know, I know. I sound like a bleeding-heart liberal. In your dreams, certainly not mine. Perish the mere thought of it.

Another reward was a new toothbrush. Well, practically new. When care packages arrived from churches in the States, the general staff at MACV (Military Assistance Command, Vietnam) got first dibs and so on down the line. The parcels rarely made it to firebases, because there were so many soldiers stationed in Saigon who needed their morales boosted.

On an official excursion to Saigon to try to pick up some care packages for myself and my officers, I suggested to a two-star general at a six-course luncheon that "would it not be outstanding to collect everyone's old toothbrushes and recycle them when new ones came in from the States."

Well, sir, the idea caught on like a house on fire. Before you could say Jack Robinson, every month, field commanders received a box of practically new toothbrushes from Saigon, and I would generously reward the men with them.

I am mindful that I am appearing to be as noble as Mother Theresa. In spite of that flattering assumption, the truth is that excellent leaders worry about their inferior underlings. While on this subject, I received a Bronze Star for the toothbrush idea, personally pinned on my immaculate uniform by General Abrams himself. Affirmative that!

Notwithstanding, I presume that the most important and most coveted honor I bestowed on the squads with the highest body count and the cleanest uniforms after returning from patrols was my respect. You cannot merely expect respect. You must earn it. One soldier at a time. This war was not a Boy Scout jamboree. Not that any of these individuals were ever Boy Scouts. It was a real war and war is hell.

As I said earlier, I commanded a firebase. Whenever a USO Show was due, I would order all the enlisted persons and draftees out on patrol. Every last human being, including the clerks. I did not want to spoil them, and secondly, I wanted to make damn sure the perimeter was safe for the show. No matter how much I strived for top-notch security, the soldiers were always complaining about something. I even heard them gripe about the shows and the music. They wanted that rock and roll garbage and did not appreciate the fine and wholesome entertainers one lick.

The other officers and I would watch the production and then have the show business personalities for lunch. After chow, we officers put on a little show ourselves for the professional performers.

I had a small stage set up in the officers' mess, where my officers and I would sing old college drinking songs. There was a well-stocked bar nearby with plenty of my favorite after-breakfast, after-lunch, and after-dinner drink, Napoleon brandy. After consuming a few refreshments, for a finale, we fine officers would fire a howitzer and demonstrate to the thespians what outgoing sounds like. Afterwards, the hoofers and singers flew back to Saigon. Great fun, really. Outstanding good times!

And the men: One trooper was like a son to me. He was white, of course, and he even had some college under his belt. I forget his name. Anyway, the base was attacked one dawn. Oh, yes, I remember that he was the company clerk. No. Maybe he was the chaplain's assistant. Well, no matter. He is not that important.

In any event, the firebase came under attack and the fellow in the watchtower was killed right off. The young soldier, my surrogate son, climbed the watchtower, threw the dead body aside, and manned the machine gun for over an hour. Oh, yes, he also had the field radio and called in an air strike.

At the time, I was running to the command post, which was the officers' bunker, and tripped over a sandbag. I stubbed my toe incredibly hard. The pain was so great that I fainted. When I came to, the battle was over.

Still in excruciating agony, I ordered the entire firebase to attention. And, mind you, this was before I would let the medic even look at my injury. The XO, a fine captain, gave me a report of what happened while I was passed out from my gaping wound.

It seems that the young man, who had operated the machine gun and called in an air strike, also had done hand-to-hand fighting with a number of enemy soldiers who had penetrated the perimeter. He killed 10 VC sappers and defused the explosives strapped to their bodies. When one of the slopes threw a grenade at me while I was passed out (the yellow-bellied coward), my little trooper threw himself on the grenade. It turned out to be a dud, but it certainly is the thought that counts. Roger that!

After the captain finished giving me the report, I summoned the young soldier to step forward. I stared him straight in the eyes, firmly shook his hand, and informed him that he had done his job well. Nevertheless, he had to pull KP duty for getting so dirty. He was as filthy as a pig.

I am not joking when I say that the soldier was so moved by my generous praise that he began to cry.

I received my third Purple Heart that day. The stubbed toe

turned out to be broken one. One of my young West Point officers also put me up for my second Bronze Star.

However, I am no prima donna. I am certainly not the kind of human being who takes all the credit. Accordingly, I recommended that young soldier, the one who got so godawful dirty, for the Good Conduct medal. He deserved it. Affirmative that!

Of course, after that day, I certainly did not want him to sit on his ditty bag and get soft and rest on his laurels; ergo, I regularly sent him out on patrol. I most assuredly did not want any sissies in my unit. No sirree, no softies. Roger that!

Within a few months into my second tour on the firebase, my men, responding to good solid leadership from me, turned in a 10,000 body count. I was awarded a Silver Star for outstanding leadership in combat and for turning in a nice round number, which made it easy on the MACV accounting office that was terribly overburdened with body count reports from outstanding officers, such as I.

Well, let me see, what else is there? Indeed, I recall the time some snot-nosed punk pinko journalist from *The New Jew Times* came for a visit. He had the balls to say that it was amazing how we had accomplished 10,000 enemy dead when the Vietnamese population within a 50-mile radius of base camp was less than 2000, including women and children.

Can you imagine the gall and the nerve of that spineless fairy telling me to my face that our figures were, and this was his exact word, inflated? Well, now sir, if that is not downright un-American, I do not know what is. I honestly must tell you, the man was as soft as a limp dick. Roger that!

The effeminate reporter also pointed out that my men were the cleanest grunts he had ever seen coming out of the bush, cleaner than Boy Scouts on a weekend in a national park. Now that I think about it and to be fair, at least he could and did say some good things about the soldiers under my first-class command.

Notwithstanding, the nattering nincompoop of negativism had to point out that the seats of their pants were soiled. I was livid that my men had let me down and in front of this Commie sympathizer. From that day on, my subordinates had to take with them on patrols inflatable cushions to sit on when they stopped for a rest.

This wimp writer wanted to go out on patrol with my men. I was overjoyed by the request and by the chance to show that feeble snot a thing or two. I attached him to the cleanest squad with the highest enemy killed. Also, then just to prove to him how tough it was to be a soldier, I cut back their water ration by half.

Later, I heard that he wrote a story about the men he went out with and completely disregarded all the press releases I gave him about the officers on base, the backbone, the spine, the spirit, the soul of everything that happened in Vietnam.

It is painful, occasionally, to dredge up memories of my tours in Vietnam; however, when I am filled with sadness, I gaze at the engraved lighter my officers gave me for my birthday. "Though I walk through the shadow of death, I fear no evil, because I'm the meanest son of a bitch in the valley." Affirmative! Roger that! Outstanding!

On a lighter note, there were many fun things I did for the troopers. They got to watch VD films and Army films on how to clean weapons, how to make a bunk, useful things such as that, as well as good movies, plenty of Doris Day ones and, of course, all of the John Wayne movies. A true patriot. My only regret is that I was born too late. I would have loved to have been under his command during World War II.

Visionary that I am, I was always a little before my time as far as race relations was concerned. Even back then, I was sensitive to the Negroes' needs.

For instance, on the firebase on the anniversary of Martin Luther King's death, to show my respect for the colored soldiers, I had my officers plan a day filled with activities. There were watermelon and fried chicken eating contests. Over the loud speaker, I had my company clerk play radio shows that he taped while at AFVN radio station in Saigon. We heard hours of "Amos 'n Andy" and many more hours of Jack Benny and Rochester. I had various films shown continuously. Let's see, there was Shirley Temple and

Bojangles and, of course, the all-time favorite of mine, *Gone With The Wind*. Numerous people have told me that I remind them of Rhett Butler. Outstanding!

I know it was almost as though I spoiled my men and did nothing for myself. But, I must honestly confess, after all these years in the military, I continue to be tough on myself. I cannot show any weakness. Those men on the firebase, and all the young individuals I commanded, looked up to me for leadership and guidance and strength. Roger that!

But oftentimes the mantle of leadership did get to me. I remember one night in my hootch, I decided to be alone and watch the movie *Patton*. Yes sir, one great leader honoring another. (My wife tells me that I am a very sensitive human being.) Remember the scene where Patton slaps the GI in the hospital, the sissy who claimed that he had shell shock or something, and then General Patton gets reprimanded? I have to confide in you, I cried like a baby. Such injustice in this world. It makes you almost lose your faith. By God, I wish I had been by Patton's side when he hit that insignificant milquetoast. Roger that!

During my firebase command, there were lots of guests: Visiting senators and Pentagon analysts there to find out what I was doing right that other commanders could learn from.

Oh, and the Red Cross donut dollies flew in every once in a while. They were the greatest. Wholesome. So many of them were military brats and were so well-mannered. After spending a few minutes playing games with the soldiers, they would spend the rest of the day with the officers, drinking, dining, and dancing. Those gals were a wonderful respite for a tired old war horse, such as I.

Finally, as my most-loved hero lamented, "Old soldiers never die, they just fade away." I, too, must fade away, back to my study to finish my memoirs for all those young plebes at the Point who one day will be leading troops in war. It is vitally important that they learn important lessons from wise old soldiers, such as yours truly. Over and out!

THE VIETNAMESE ROCK STAR INTERVIEW ON AFVN

Announcer: "This is the American Forces Vietnam Network."

Bouncy "Tonight Show"-type music plays for 10 seconds, begins to fade, and a husky-voiced young man speaks over the music in the background.

Nick: "Good morning, all you sleepy heads in Vietnam who are just joining us. My name is Navy Journalist Nick White, your host of 'Dawn Buster,' your rise and shine AFVN show. Today is Wednesday, May 24, and it's almost 9:00 a.m. When the big hand is on the 12 and the little hand is on the nine, I'm outta here.

"But for now, on with the rest of the show. As a special treat for our late-rising morning audience, we have in the studio a very unique guest. His name is Nguyen Long Dong, the popular Saigon singing star. A group of friends and I caught his act last night, and I positively knew that you servicemen and women stationed around Vietnam would be delighted to hear about this major talent.

"Welcome to 'Dawn Buster,' Nguyen."

Rock Star: "Thank you, Nick. It is good to be here."

Nick: "So, tell me, Nguyen, how do you handle all that fame?"

Rock Star: "I love being a celebrity in Saigon during the American Vietnam War. It is a pretty heady time for a guy in his early twenties such as I am."

Nick: "You must get a lot of fan mail."

Rock Star: "Oh, yes, not only from fans in Vietnam but also from people around the world."

Nick: "Really? What do they ask you when they write?"

Rock Star: "People ask me all the time what it is like living in Vietnam during the war and expect to hear about bullets and bombs and blood and bodies. They are always surprised when I tell them that it is not like that at all. Oh, sure, there are battles, but except for a few isolated incidences, it certainly is not going on in Saigon.

"People write and say that they watched television when Saigon was attacked during Tet of 1968, and they could see that there was all that fighting in the streets, and they witnessed the mayor, who by the way is a friend of my family, shooting a VC in the head and all that. Oh, I write them that most of what they saw was the magic of television. I was living and working in Saigon during Tet of 1968 and slept right through it. Oh, sure, I heard lots of fireworks and explosions, but I just assumed it was part of the Tet festivities."

Nick: "That must surprise them to read that. What other things do your fans want to know?"

Rock Star: "They ask me what it was like in the army before I became a singing sensation. I do not know why they would think that every Vietnamese male was or is in the military. As a matter of fact, none of my relatives or friends are or were. I mean, maybe people are getting the two sides confused. North Vietnam is the Communist side, and I am on the South Vietnamese side which is defending our country from the Commies."

Nick: "Do tell our GI audience what those differences are."

Rock Star: "Now in the North, it seems that everybody, and I do mean everybody, is in the military. I believe the draft age is from 15 to 45 and higher and lower when an emergency arises.

"But South Vietnam is a Democratic society, more like the United States. In the U.S. a boy is exempt from the draft if he goes to college. Same as we are. In the U.S. he can get out of serving for a medical problem. Same with us. Guys in America stay out of Vietnam by joining the National Guard or the Reserves. Sadly, we do not have stuff like that in Vietnam, but our country is more sophisticated with its policy of exemptions for non-military essential jobs."

Nick: "And do tell our American soldier audience, Nguyen, how did you stay out of the military?"

Rock Star: "I did not join because I am a rock musician and felt that I would better serve my country by entertaining foreigners in nightclubs in Saigon. Most of my other friends who did not have the talent that I do had to resort to bribing generals to stay out of the military. I mean, what could they do? They could not very well spend their time in the army. They are so much above those peasant boys who are soldiers. Just like the American soldiers. Real lowlifes. Guys like me and my friends have better things to do than march and shoot and boil rice over some campfire."

Nick: "Interesting. Tell us a little about your family."

Rock Star: "I am an only child. My father works for the government and has so much free time that he is my business manager. He really is the guiding force behind my career. My mother designs my band's costumes and her favorite seamstress sews them. 'No off-the-rack stuff for my little star,' she likes to tell everyone within earshot. Mommy is my biggest fan."

Nick: "And how did you get started in show biz?"

Rock Star: "I formed my first band during my senior year in high school. We played a lot of Beatles' songs, then switched over to Rolling Stones' stuff. We played most of the nightclubs in Saigon, but my favorite was and still is the Eve Club. It really rocks and rolls, especially after Tet of 1968 when everyone became so bored with hearing about the war, like that is the only thing that was happening in Vietnam. I feel sorry for my friends who left the country too early. They missed out on some groovy fun. The night life is unbelievable."

Nick: "Describe to the listeners a typical day in the life of a Vietnamese rock star?"

Rock Star: "I wake up about noon, grab a taxicab over to the terrace at the Continental Palace for a bite of lunch and to sign some autographs, shoot the breeze until three with some other singers and musicians who are playing at the Samurai, Baccara, La Cigale, or Nam-Do, go for a facial or manicure at Beautex and sign more autographs for the girls who work there, then head back home for a nap before showtime at nine.

"The audience is always packed—wealthy Vietnamese, the embassy crowd, high-ranking American officers and civilians, and plenty of foreign correspondents and visiting dignitaries and celebrities from the States. I love to wave to other stars sitting in the audience. And when I direct the spotlight on them and ask for them to join me on stage, they do what all celebrities do, blush and act surprised to be singled out."

Nick: "What celebrities have you called on stage?"

Rock Star: "Well, let me think? Martha Raye and I sang a duet of 'Hello Dolly.' George Peppard and I hummed a duet of 'Breakfast at Tiffanies.' Joe DiMaggio and I sang 'Take Me Out To The Ball Game.' But let me continue about my typical day. You rudely interrupted me."

Nick: "I'm truly sorry. Please continue."

Rock Star: "After the show ends at 12:30, the band and I head over to someone's villa, usually an American civilian's, and party till five or six o'clock. Then, I head back home for my beauty sleep before beginning another hectic day."

Nick: "Sounds exciting, yet exhausting. I assume yours is a lucrative job."

Rock Star: "You know the old saying, the people who do not need to make money usually make the most. Well, that is true. My family is quite well-off from inherited wealth on both sides, and I never think about money much. When I started singing in nightclubs the money started rolling in.

"I cut 10 records during 1967-68, when the war was hot, hot, hot and they hit gold within days of being released. My father marketed them all over the Far East—the Philippines, Thailand, Hong Kong, Malaysia—and Australia. The title of the biggest hit was 'The Vietnam Songbook' and subtitled, 'The Soulful Songs from a Man Ravaged by War.'

"My father was certain that war was a big seller, and he was right on the button. After 'Songbook' hit the charts in the Far East, I did guest shots on TV and radio in 20 cities, including Paris. I was interviewed by *Time, Newsweek, Der Spiegal, Hong Kong After Dark*, and hundreds of other publications world-wide. Every reporter asked my opinion on the war.

"I received flowers and telegrams and letters from thousands of well-wishers urging me to keep my chin up and keep fighting for good against evil. Hollywood agents sent scripts, publishers begged me to write my memoirs, and thousands of women sent marriage proposals.

"I guess we waited too long in responding to the requests, because within months of hitting the charts, I was old news; and the media turned its stupid attention to other less exciting matters concerning the war—drug abuse, atrocities, fraggings, corruption, even some battle things. At first I was a little taken aback at the lack of attention, but then realized that I was happiest being a hometown star."

Nick: "Where would you most like to live and sing, other than Saigon?"

Rock Star: "Saigon is my stage. I never once thought of living and singing anywhere else and just hope that the war will go on forever. But, those infantile antiwar activists in America, who do not have a clue what patriotism is, are trying to end my wonderful life and career."

Nick: "What will you do if the war ends and the Communists take over?"

Rock Star: "My father, mother, and I will leave Saigon on the same plane as President Thieu, a family friend, a few days before the Communists take over my country. We will fly to London or Paris and stay with Uncle Thieu for a few weeks, then my family and I will head to Las Vegas."

Nick: "By golly. You seem to be planning ahead."

Rock Star: "Oh yes, I have thought about it, the what-if?, and have come up with many, many scenarios.

"I may decide to switch from rock to easy listening, do a lounge act. I can imagine quite a following of loyal fans. Maybe not girls in school uniforms like I have now, but older women with blue hair will lavish me with much more attention.

"I can see me still waving to celebrities stopping in the lounge. Mr. Frank Sinatra will salute me from his ringside seat after hearing about my war-time past. And Mr. Tony Bennett will nod in my direction as I start singing 'I Left My Heart In San Francisco.' Yeah, Vegas is my kind of town and the place I will head to if, God forbid, the war should end. Perish the thought."

Nick: "My word, I can see by the clock on the wall that our time is up. Thank you for taking time from your busy schedule to come on the show."

Rock Star: "Thank you, Nick. I am glad I had the opportunity to talk about my role in the Vietnam War, and I am sure you will not mind me telling your listeners that I am thinking about doing a rerelease of my big hit, 'The Soulful Songs From a Man Ravaged By War' and then subtitle it with the original title, 'The Vietnam War Songbook.' Look for it in record stores all over Vietnam."

Nick: "Our time is definitely up. Thank you, again."

Rock Star: "My pleasure."

Announcer: "This is the American Forces Vietnam Network."

Nick: "Well, boys and girls, I hope you enjoyed our special guest. And before Edwin Starr sings about your least favorite subject, here's your quote for the day. It's from Lyndon Johnson, who said in 1964, 'We are not about to send American boys nine or ten thousand miles from home to do what Asian boys ought to be doing themselves.'

"This is Nick White signing off for another beautiful day in Vietnam."

Edwin Starr's "War" begins to play.

YOLANDA'S FAVORITE BEGGAR

Yolanda lived in a garden apartment across the boulevard from the Saigon USO. It was a two-minute walk from home to office, but the short distance ordinarily took the recreation center's program director a half an hour. The street people and she enjoyed engaging in neighborly banter.

"How's business?" That customary morning question went to the two teenagers sitting astride a Honda motor scooter, ready to begin cruising the streets to snatch cameras and purses from unsuspecting foreigners.

"Pretty good, Missy." The delinquents, one of hundreds of similar teams nicknamed "cowboys," beamed at the American civilian as though they were innocent altar boys waiting for Mass to start.

Yolanda paused to toss a greeting and 20 piasters to a paraplegic beggar, a former South Vietnamese soldier crippled from a land mine in the Mekong Delta during the Tet Offensive.

"How's twicks, Soul Sistah?" three adolescent prostitutes, wearing miniskirts and false eyelashes over surgically rounded eyes, in unison asked the Ohio native, just as they did every morning since Yolanda arrived in-country 10 months previously. All four laughed at the audacity of the inquiry.

Yolanda bent down to smell the yellow roses in a bucket of water at a flower stall in the middle of Nguyen Hue, known as the "Street of Flowers." Choosing three in full bloom, she paid the squatting vendor, then presented them to the ladies of the night, who were tottering home on four-inch spikes for some much-needed sleep.

The hard-working girls giggled and blushed when Yolanda uttered the standard Vietnam War phrase that grunts used, "Keep your heads down." Smiling mischievously, the tiny American woman stepped onto the sidewalk in front of the USO.

There, stood her favorite street urchins, a five-year-old boy and his younger sister, selling plastic bags. Not one of the black market stalls on either side of the kids had any plastic bags for sale, though anybody could buy practically anything else, including hundreds of products stolen from the PX or ships at the dock to rolled marijuana cigarettes in sealed Marlboro boxes.

The boy and Yolanda had a well-rehearsed ritual every day at eight o'clock. When the youngster spotted her stopping to sniff the roses, he started shouting his salesman's pitch in pidgin English with a dose of GI slang.

"Hey, pretty black lady, me got bag you weally, weally need. Bes' bag in town. Numbah one like you. Me sell you beaucoup cheap. Come on, don' be a cheap Chahlie."

For these past 10 months, he had repeated the same words to Yolanda at exactly the same time in precisely the same spot.

And she delivered the single response every day, "How much?"

Invariably the answer spilled hurriedly from his lips each morning, "One hunwed Pee."

The haggling had begun. Yolanda countered with 20 piasters. The child scoffed at the outrageousness of such a price from, what he was sure to be, a rich American.

More bargaining with elaborate hand gestures followed.

"My final offer is 50 piasters. Take it or leave it," she snapped at the 36-inch businessman, while winking at the old woman stirring noodles in her soup pot a few feet away.

Right on cue, after her final line in her favorite one-act play, Yolanda ambled into the USO. With one foot outside the three-story building and the other in, exactly where she found herself every morning, as though the spots were chalked with a director's

X's, she halted and quickly turned around as he announced her victory. Unfairly, his big brown eyes conveyed.

The MP guarding the club watched the transaction and nonchalantly sipped a Coke.

Yolanda very slowly counted the 50 piasters. She liked to admire the little boy, intently staring at the bills to make sure he was not being cheated, even though he was well aware who was tricking whom. They both knew.

A bag cost about a penny, and every day for nearly a year Yolanda paid him a hundred times what each one was worth.

The serious miniature entrepreneur, constantly clutching his baby sister's hand, never thought of himself as a beggar as Yolanda privately did. After all, his customers paid for products. The prices might have been a bit inflated, as everything else was in Vietnam, from the cost of bar girls' Saigon tea to body counts, but businessmen were businessmen and business was business. This was not child's play.

At five years old, he was the man of the house, supporting his mother and four siblings. He was the breadwinner-boy of the jerry-built shack made of pop cans in one of the larger refugee slums on the outer perimeter of Saigon.

A foul-smelling canal weaved through his neighborhood, providing water for cooking and bathing. It was also the community toilet for his family and the hordes of destitute farmers flooding into the city to escape the bombs as the war dragged on. Abandoned by unresponsive governments, both Yolanda's and the kid's, the displaced villagers and their offspring eked out a meager living as best they could.

Without any thoughts of global bureaucratic apathy or miserable poverty, Yolanda loved haggling over price each morning with the little Vietnamese boy, the one who sold plastic bags in front of the Saigon USO.

SAIGON RUMORS

Trung Trac Nhi, rumor had it, was not the illustrious beauty's real name. Numerous people believed that she had more aliases than Ho Chi Minh did during his entire wandering lifetime.

Some said she was Eurasian, while others were quite sure of her Amerasian roots. But one thing was true: This was a woman of mystery.

One rumor was that the father she never met had been a minor Irish poet, who frequently visited Vietnam to hunt tigers near Dalat.

At one time or another, somebody told someone else, on the best authority, that Trung Trac Nhi was the illegitimate daughter of a Corsican priest, who spent decades proselytizing in Hue; or a wealthy German rubber plantation owner from the Delta; or Clark Gable, who shot a movie in Indochina in the 1930s.

Trung Trac Nhi was one of those ageless women, the type who appears to be 29 at puberty and at menopause.

A handful of Saigonese wags spoke of a Beverly Hills' plastic surgeon falling in love with her at first sight during a Hollywood party that she attended with Peter Lawford while on holiday in California.

Not a living soul knew her exact age or accurate parentage, but it was whispered during cocktail parties at villas that she had been a mistress to countless, notable men.

Innumerable colonels' wives asserted that they were positive, without a doubt, one lover had been a French general killed at Dien Bien Phu, supposedly sent into battle and his ultimate death by another one of her paramours, General Henri Navarre, the commander in chief of French forces in Indochina.

Others alleged that Ngo Dinh Diem became celibate after Trung Trac Nhi left the future president of South Vietnam, who never married, weeping at the altar.

Certain people knew for a fact that her greatest conquest was a Saudi prince she enchanted at the roulette table in Monte Carlo moments after dumping the king of Siam.

Those who bragged of being her closest, dearest friends swore on ancestors' graves that the love of her life was Adlai Stevenson. Her enemies snickered that that glory was bestowed upon Marlene Dietrich.

Since she had traveled the world extensively for decades—no one was quite sure of the exact number—and resided at various times in Paris, Washington, Hanoi, and Rome, to name but a few cities, it was rumored that she had been a hero of the French Resistance during World War II, an OSS spy, a high-ranking Viet Minh official, and/or a procurer of pornographic art for the Vatican, where, it was rumored, she had the apartment next to the Pope's residence.

Trung Trac Nhi, similar to war-time Saigon, thrived on secrets and intrigue.

Flattered and amused by her fame, the enigmatic celebrity personally collected inflated rents once a month from foreigners living in her luxury apartment complexes in the fashionable parts of Saigon. (No one was quite sure exactly how many buildings she did own or by what means they were acquired.) Then, rumor had it, she wired the money directly to her substantial Swiss bank account, personally managed by Guy de Rothschild.

BARBIE'S COMBAT ZONE DIARY

June 2, 1971
11:30 p.m.
Another wonderful day with Ken!

At mid-morning we began the walking tour of Saigon. Ken and I had been discussing it for a few weeks but never seemed to find the time. Last night, though, after a romantic dinner at Caruso's, I persuaded him to take today off. The General was in Bangkok visiting his wife, so there actually was not much for an aid to do during this lull.

"Sure, Honey. Let's do it, but make sure we get an early start before the heat becomes unbearable," he responded, pulling the sheet up to our waists. "Besides, when our grandchildren ask us about our falling in love during a war, we sure as hell can't tell them that we spent most of our time in Vietnam making love, now can we?"

God, I love him! I love when he casually comments about our being together long enough to have grandchildren, I thought as I slid lower down the bed, put my ear against his stomach, and began caressing him.

"Now see what you've done. We'll never get any shut-eye," he teased, rolling me on my back. "Should I inform our grandchildren that their Nana is a nymphomaniac?"

I shook my head "yes" then pulled his head down and kissed him with passion and desire.

There could never be any man as remarkable as he.

I awoke early this morning, brewed coffee, and sat quietly in the papasan chair staring at Ken asleep on his back. How can men find sleeping on their backs comfortable?

His one leg was hanging off the bed and the other was partially covered with the sheet. I was tempted to tiptoe over to the bed and kiss him gently on the cheek, but I did not want to wake him. Such a light sleeper, he could leap out of bed and be dressed and out the door in a matter of minutes. On the other hand, I need at least an hour to drink coffee, shower, and leisurely begin the day.

I am a night person who moves slowly in the morning. In contrast, Ken is constantly full of energy and alert first thing in the morning (lucky me!) and is the last one to leave a party. It seems as though he never requires sleep, or else not as much as other people do. The General notices, too, and admires that in a young officer.

The man I love will someday be a general. In private moments, when we are completely alone and in each other's arms, I address him as "General." Our private little joke, although we both realize with all our hearts that it is not a joke. God, I pray I am able to handle the demanding job of a general's wife. My hat goes off to those incredible women.

Miss An, my friend Pamela's secretary in the USO PR office, acted as our private guide for the walking tour of Saigon. She moonlights as a tour guide to visiting dignitaries. Her English is as flawless as her French. Both Ken and I send customers her way, and she has been eager to reciprocate our kindness by showing us a little of her beloved city.

We began the tour in front of the USO on Nguyen Hue, also referred to as "The Street of Flowers." It is brimming with flower stalls. During Tet, the Chinese New Year in late January or early February, every nook and cranny of the broad avenue overflows with magnificent flower displays.

Not far away is the City Hall, a gray Victorian structure built at the turn of the century. Nguyen Hue ends on the banks of the

Saigon River, which empties into the South China Sea 40 miles away.

Ken's uniform was drenched with perspiration when we arrived at the monument in honor of General Tran Hung Dao, a 13th Century hero and patron saint of the Vietnamese Navy. Its headquarters are located there at the eastern end of the quay.

We paused at the sidewalk cafe at the Majestic Hotel across from the waterfront park. Ken downed two beers in what appeared to be two gulps, I had a Coke with lime, and Miss An sipped green tea.

The heat is quite annoying to most Americans, but it does not really bother me much. What actually distresses me more is the air-conditioning in U.S. facilities. After being outside in 98 degree heat, it is a terrible jolt to one's system to walk into a 65 degree room.

The Majestic Hotel is at the foot of Tu Do Street, and from there one can see the twin spires of Our Lady's Basilica, one of the oldest buildings in Saigon.

The three of us strolled up Tu Do (Freedom Street), formerly known as Rue Catinat. Miss An called Tu Do the "Fifth Avenue of Saigon" because, as she explained, "of its many excellent but expensive curio and souvenir shops."

I could read Ken's mind and was pleased that he did not ask Miss An if she had ever been to New York to make the comparison. Thank God, he was on his best behavior and too hot to have the energy to be caustic.

Lam Son Square, the center of downtown Saigon, is halfway up Tu Do. Miss An shooed away a platoon of little boys who charged at us from nowhere with outstretched hands, pleading for money, candy, cigarettes. They were awfully cute, but Miss An was thoroughly annoyed and jabbered away at them in Vietnamese. I had to laugh when they stuck out their tongues and mimicked her as they walked away backwards.

Ken confided to me later that one of the tiny fellows asked if he would like to meet his sister, "numbah one virgin."

The Caravelle and Continental Palace are in Lam Son Square. Miss An claimed that Somerset Maugham sipped aperitifs at the verandah of the Continental, thus the three of us followed suit. (Note to myself: Must read *The Razor's Edge*. Ken assures me that it is one of those books I will think about for a long time after I finish it.)

Saigon's world passed us by as we silently sipped sherry from Spain in the shade. Ken repeated that phrase 10 times before tripping over his tongue. He is so darling when he acts silly.

Next site we visited was the National Assembly Building where Vietnam's Lower House holds its sessions. Until 1956 it was an opera house, with its white domes bleached by the tropical sun. From its steps one can look down Le Loi Street and see the Vietnamese Marine monument and the illuminated fountain, another preferred haunt for the street children of Saigon. There are so many of them. Where are those folks from Planned Parenthood when one unmistakably needs them?

The Central Market is at the end of Le Loi Street. There is where the Saigonese women or their maids shop for fresh fruits and vegetables, live chickens and ducks, skinned rabbits, as well as bizarre flea market treasures from the Japanese occupation during World War II, French trinkets, and American military junk. We only spent a few minutes there, because the overpowering odors and oppressive heat were making Ken queasy. The place was crammed with shrieking housewives and squawking maids, each one searching for bargains.

Ken's stomach and back are covered with black-and-blue marks from being jabbed by tiny elbows belonging to graceful and demure Vietnamese women, who go bonkers when shopping at the Central Market every day. This is certainly an outlet for them in more ways than one: Get great bargains and release that submissive tension.

I cannot wait to go back there with Madge. They have not seen hard-core shoppers until they see the two of us shop. Look out, little Saigon ladies!

After escaping the Market without too many bruises (important lesson: never go shopping with a man; they tire too easily), we proceeded to John F. Kennedy Square to observe the close-up view of the red-bricked Basilica.

The yellow building to its right is the PTT (Post, Telegrams and Telephone), Saigon's communication center.

Directly behind the church is Thong Nhut, a lovely boulevard where the Independence Palace is located. It is a modern building rebuilt in 1966 and is Vietnam's White House, both office and residence of President Thieu, a charming man with a lovely wife.

Close by is the American Embassy, completed in 1967. My office is on the third floor, two doors away from the Deputy Ambassador's suite. The British Embassy is also on Thong Nhut.

The Saigon Zoo and Botanical Gardens are at the eastern end, but we decided to cut the tour short, so we did not go in.

"Who the hell wants to see skinny elephants?" Ken whispered in my ear. (The heat was making him grumpy.)

Instead, we strolled back to the USO and treated Miss An to a cheeseburger, French fries, and a Coke. She adores American fast food and claims that she is addicted to cheeseburgers. I am addicted to Ken!

Today was marvelous. I am truly getting to know Saigon well. Everywhere I look there is something exotic and remarkable to see. I could not be any happier.

Ken left an hour ago. He has an early meeting in the morning. I miss him already.

GENERAL WESTMORELAND'S HOUSEBOY (AND VC SPY) TALKS

My favorite assignment as a Viet Cong spy was being General Westmoreland's houseboy at his luxurious living quarters in Saigon. I was with the General before, during, and after Tet of 1968.

To tell you the truth, I sort of liked the guy—a great big dumb bear of a man. Be that as it may, no matter how I felt, I had a job to do for my country.

My most difficult assignment was to try to warn him about what was going to happen in late January of 1968.

I am aware that sounds stupid on our part, but Hanoi's high command was terrified that the Tet surprise could be too good and General Westmoreland would be replaced by an individual with some brains.

To remark that General Westmoreland was thick is a gross understatement.

Truly, our high command sent copious signals his way via captured documents that GIs "found" while on patrol. One important set of papers that we purposefully planted was a requisition order for laundry services in over 65 towns all over Vietnam for battalions of NVA (North Vietnamese Army) troops arriving on the eve of Tet. Hanoi also announced that we were going to celebrate Tet early. A press release was even sent to Westmoreland's public relations office. How many more clues could we possibly drop in his lap?

Westmoreland examined the documents and barely peeped at the press release. He merely yawned and continued writing in his diary, "Nothing important happening. The enemy is still afraid to come out and fight."

While he sat in his office jotting in that stupid diary of his, I continued dusting the statue of the Vietnamese Hero, Nguyen Hue, who had surprised the Chinese on Tet in 1789. It was one of the most famous military feats in our history.

All of our VC agents in Saigon had plastic statues of the famous hero on the dashboards of their autos and pedicabs. You could not walk two feet without seeing his likeness.

Perplexed, I urged the General to tell me once again the story of Nguyen Hue, which I had initially related to him.

Westy sighed, "Oh, okay. Once upon a time, many centuries ago, the cruel Chinese—exactly like the Commie ones today—ruled Vietnam. Then in 1789, along came the mighty Tay Son leader by the name of Nguyen Hue. Well, sir, after force marching his troops up the coast into the Red River Delta, he completely surprised a much larger Chinese army near Hanoi. He attacked on the fifth day of Tet, while the Chinese were sleeping off the food and wine from the festivities. And everyone lived happily ever after."

He repeated the story of the 1789 Tet surprise to me, who kept pleading to hear it again, at least 20 times in the week preceding the Tet of 1968 surprise. Still nothing registered in his obtuse skull.

I was at a loss. So, I started talking about the North Vietnamese military leader, General Giap, who was a history teacher, and his favorite all-time hero was Nguyen Hue, the famous Vietnamese general who pulled a big, big, big surprise on Tet. Furthermore, I added, General Giap proclaimed in each his speeches that history repeats itself.

There was silence after the mention of General Giap's name. I thought to myself, he has got it, by, Jove, I believe he has got it.

Nonetheless, he stared at me with those blank eyes and asked, "I wonder why General Giap wants the North to celebrate Tet early? Maybe he's becoming tired of war and plans on surrendering. I wonder what he has in mind, the little yellow Commie devil?"

Wanting to shake him until his teeth rattled, I decided to play word association with him. He loved that game and we played it often.

I yelled, "Surprise!"
Westmoreland shot back, "Birthday!"
I screamed, "Attack!"
He bellowed, "Heart!"
I screeched, "On!"
The General countered, "Off!"
I shrieked and positively wanted to slap him silly, "Tet!"
Westy quickly responded, "Marilyn Monroe!"

The Hanoi high command was unequivocally terrified that our victory would be so huge that President Johnson would send this idiot packing and the Joint Chiefs of Staff would send a bright one in his place, a general who knew what he was doing. It was up to me to try my damnedest to help him out.

I asked him, "If you could pick one holiday that the enemy would attack on, what would it be?"

He smugly responded, "My birthday." Which, by the way, had been a month earlier. Gees, this nincompoop was trying my nerves.

"Pick another day, General."

He guessed December 7, Columbus Day, Valentine's Day, and Ground Hog Day. I knew he would go through every American holiday, so I stopped the game-playing and strolled into the kitchen to dry some dishes and contemplate. After a few thoughtful moments, I put the dishtowel down and walked back into his office.

As bluntly as I could, I rhetorically inquired, "General

Westmoreland, do you think it could be possible that the VC and NVA might attack 65 towns and cities including Saigon during Tet?" Holding my breath, I waited.

To my astonishment, he erupted into laughter until tears rolled down his cheeks. Slapping me on the back, he bragged that he had studied Napoleon, Rommell, and Julius Caesar at West Point.

I probed deeper, "At West Point, do they teach about any Asian military leaders or battles such as the one that Nguyen Hue waged, the Tet surprise of 1789?"

The General was emphatic. "Negative. It is of no importance. Different time, other ignorant people." Without missing a beat, he added, "Everyone, from scum privates to those jackals in the media call the Vietnam War 'Westy's War.' And, by God, everybody has to play it by my rules. You are an uneducated Vietnamese person. Just leave the war games to me and the experts in Military Intelligence."

Stunned into silence, I felt like Comrade Kane on his deathbed, but instead of the word "Rosebud" forming in my mind, the word "oxymoron" flashed through my brain.

That night, after the General got settled down to watch a Three Stooges movie (Moe was his favorite), I rang up my contact, Comrade Mimi who owned a bar, and assured her that the Tet attack was going to be a complete surprise—more than we hoped for—as far as the General was concerned. It would go down in history as the biggest military surprise against the Americans since Pearl Harbor, only this time the opposite would happen. Pearl Harbor got the Americans into the war and this attack would force them out.

"Gads, what if Westy's replaced before the war's over?" Mimi was frantic. "Oh, well, surely he'll put the blame elsewhere and stay put. I'm crossing all my fingers and all my toes. Ooops, I hear my other phone. Gotta run. Do drop by for a drink real soon. Chou, Darling."

Immediately after Tet, some bozo at military intelligence, one of the West Point men Westmoreland referred to as his "brightest whiz kid," wanted to spread the story that most of the newsmen were on an acid trip during Tet. Because of this, they hallucinated and imagined they saw the VC attack the American embassy, but it was, in reality, a bunch of Korean GIs loaded to the gills who mistook Ambassador Bunker's chancellery for the Kremlin. Besides that, the spinmeisters wanted to leak to the right people that most of the newsreel footage was from some left-wing Commie movie studio in Hollywood.

Trying to calm down a getting-out-of-hand situation, I suggested to the General that he simply confess the truth to President Johnson. "Be honest. Tell LBJ that you were totally surprised by the enemy. And that it won't happen again."

If looks could kill.

The General bellowed at me, "Are you crazy, boy? How do you think I would appear in the history books? Me, who received an A+ at West Point for the course 'How To Turn a Debacle Into a Great Victory.' The first thing my staff will do—after our golf game—is write a 1000-page report using military terms. No one in Congress will read it, but everyone will glance at it and assume by its weight that it is an important document. This will all blow over. I shall return to the States a war hero. I shall become the Army Chief of Staff. I shall conduct the military worldwide. I shall return. In due course, the military community will vehemently blame the press and antiwar movement for any defeats in Vietnam, including Tet. Mark my words, I shall come out of this a war hero. War is a chess game and I am one of the knights."

There is not much more for me to report about my role as VC houseboy. Yes, there is one thing: Simply put, you Americans are damn lucky Westmoreland was not in charge of World War II. If he had been, you would all be speaking German and Japanese right now.

THE LIBRARY CARD

Miss An, one of Pamela's secretaries in the USO PR office, was constantly borrowing books that Pamela had borrowed from the Abraham Lincoln Library run by the United States Information Agency.

USIA managed the Joint United States Public Affairs Office or, as everyone called it, JUSPAO. USIA and JUSPAO were involved in psyops, psychological operations, which were propaganda campaigns aimed at the enemy as well as at the friendly Vietnamese.

It became known years later that between 1965 and 1972, the United States dropped 50 billion leaflets on all of Vietnam, including the Ho Chi Minh Trail, with the goal of winning hearts and minds.

South Vietnam was inundated with posters, banners, newspaper articles, magazines, brochures, comic books, bumper stickers, and matchbook covers, each and every piece of material urging the North Vietnam and Vietcong to stop fighting and come on over to America's side, the good side that was bringing democracy to Vietnam.

Then, of course, the military was spreading the word, too. The Psychological Operations Directorate of MACV, Military Assistance Command, Vietnam, coordinated propaganda campaigns. The U.S. Army had four psyops battalions: the 6th Psychological Operations Battalion in III Corps, the 7th Psychological Operations Battalion in I Corps, the 8th Psychological Operations Battalion in II Corps, and the 10th Psychological Operations Battalion in IV Corps. Each battalion had its own printing plant, photographic and tape recording production equipment, and loudspeaker trucks.

Miss An was reading books faster than Pamela could get to the Abraham Lincoln Library to check them out. So, off they both went one afternoon to get the Vietnamese secretary her own library card.

"May I help you?" the American civilian woman asked in a sugary voice.

Miss An and her boss stood in front of the information desk. Pamela cheerfully informed the American librarian how she could indeed help.

"Oh, I am sorry, but we do not allow Vietnamese to have library cards," she told Pamela. Then, she turned to Miss An—who had just finished reading *Ulysses* by James Joyce—and bellowed, "No allowed books! You understand, Mamasan? You no allowed books!"

THE GLAZED DONUT DOLLY REMINISCES

Golly gee, I just love telling stories about my tour of duty with the Red Cross in Nam. I'll confess one thing, I worked with a great bunch of gals and programmed to a super bunch of boys. Of course, I never dated any of them. The boys, I mean. What in the world would we have in common? Like, you know, I'd be reading Hemingway and they'd be looking at comic books or *Mad Magazine* or something. Spare me! College grads who were officers are the guys I dated.

Gosh! It was like summer camp. Such fun. Oh, don't get me wrong. There were hardships and plenty of inconveniences. But, hey, I'm not complaining. It's just that sometimes, you know, the grunts would ask me out on a date, like I would really go out with them when I had my pick of so many neat officers. But, except for their unmitigated gall of asking me out on a date, some of the GIs were cute when they stayed in their places.

Everyone knows I dated guys from the best fraternities in college. And I just knew that when I got married it would be to someone who was going to make something of himself, like the ROTC guys who planned on going to med school or into investment banking.

Women's lib got its ugly hold on me for a while back in college and I even thought about going to law school. Can you believe that? But, thank God, my Mom, who happens to be my best friend, told me it was unladylike to be a lawyer and much, much better to marry one. What a wise mother I have, don't you think? Bless her soul!

What else? I'm sure you want to hear all about my impressions of Vietnam. I could write a book about my adventures in the Nam!

Though, what instantly pops in my head are pictures of those Vietnamese children with no underwear. Very, very uncivilized and, to tell you the truth, rather embarrassing what with the boys' little pee pees swinging when they walked. Gross! My word!

The soldiers called us donut dollies. It was cute, don't you think? Oh, some of the crude ones made very unkind references to the hole in the donut and all, but I don't want to dignify the insulting metaphor by discussing it. You're not going to repeat that, are you?

Some wisenheimers made fun of our programs, which were cute little games, but hey, we wanted to take the lowly soldiers' minds off their unpleasant surroundings.

I can see Vietnam now. We donut dollies, you know, wore crispy, clean, baby blue uniforms and always had makeup on and perfume. Quite frankly, we were a reminder of why they were fighting and what they left behind at home. Not that most of them were that lucky, but along that line of thinking.

Call me an unabashed patriot and I plead guilty, but hey, I'd do it all over again without a moment's hesitation. I could do without some of the hassling from some of the grunts with bad attitudes, though. For instance, and this is just between you and me, off the record, there was some rumor that went around about the founder of the Red Cross, Clara Barton, that claimed she died of syphilis. Really, I mean, talk about ugly, ugly rumors. Gross!

But, all in all, I loved it, with a capital L. Parties and dances and flying in choppers and playing touch football on the beach. Wow! And we were all, you know, fighting Communism!

I dated mostly captains, a few majors, and one widowed general. You know, it's funny, I never once met an officer who was married while they were in Vietnam. Not once. Can you beat that!

I made it to Saigon once in a while, but I didn't like it too much. There were far too many beggars and little crippled kids constantly bothering you for money. God, they were the biggest pests and so, so oafish. Gross!

I liked the bases where the lonely soldiers were. Saigon had too many American women. I mean, there were so, so many working for USAID, the Embassy, USO, Special Services, you name it, that not once did a GI pass me and yell, "Oh, wow, a roundeye!"

I just adored the surprised looks on the grunts' faces, the ones, you know, just coming out of the bush after a three-day patrol. There I would be behind a Kool Aid stand, being bouncy and positive. Another gal was setting up a bingo game. Another gal, getting the trivia cards ready. And all of us gals standing around just looking gorgeous in our blue uniforms and freshly applied makeup. I bet we were a sight for sore eyes.

I heard more than one GI yell to his buddies, "Is this a war, or what?" Gosh!

Every once in a while I had some trouble with the Black GIs.

Sometimes they'd get smart-alecky with me and say things, you know, in a very rude way, "What in the blank, they used the F word, what in the blank are you girls doing here?" stuff like that. I mean, like it was their war or something.

And there were so many of them! My word! Everywhere you looked you saw big groups of them with combs stuck in their Afros and always shaking hands in a crazy way and the way they strutted. And I didn't appreciate insults from them. I mean, I don't have a prejudiced bone in my body, and I was always nice to Mommy's cleaning lady. But I guess Daddy's right: Give them an inch and, you know, they'll take a foot.

Some of the rear echelon boys could be nasty too.

After turning another GI down for a date, his buddies would shout, "You're only here for the officers." That really hurt a lot.

I mean, all of us gals had grunt friends who were like, you know, little brothers to us. I had a few who I let drive me places, carry things for me. I even was gracious enough to accept presents from them. Diamond pendants, sapphire rings, small stuff. I'm telling you, it gave them such joy. How about that!

One guy used to give me pedicures. Another guy ironed my uniforms after I complained that mamasan left brown stains. Let me explain, and I hope this doesn't gross you out too much. It seems that the gooks who cleaned our hootches and did our laundry used to spit on the clothes while they were ironing. You know, like a steam iron which, by the by, they didn't even have in Vietnam.

I mean, they even beat clothes with a rock at a stream when they washed them. Can you believe how primitive those people are? Gawd! And we actually thought they would embrace Democracy. They deserved what they got, is how I see it. I mean, mamasans chewing beetle nuts and spitting on my lovely uniform. Paleese! Give me a break!

But it was useless arguing with some of the disgruntled GIs. Nothing would have made them happy. I mean, if they weren't happy to see us, what in the world would make them happy?

I mean, come on, the fact is we gals were honest to goodness, you know, all-American true-blue red, white and blue roundeyes. Well, most of us. There were a few malcontents. I hope you don't read anything about them. You won't learn anything worthwhile.

Each Red Cross gal was transferred three times while in-country for our year's tour of duty. The more isolated the base, the more I liked it. Now those boys really treated us like goddesses.

I hated the rear bases. There were too many other American women and I was always sent to clean up some mess created by some of those nonconformist Red Cross gals. The ones who referred to themselves as "women." Well, excuse me, women's libbers. Give me a break!

Some of those troublemakers, who shall remain nameless, but you know who you are if you're reading this, actually, and I know this is going to be hard to believe, but they actually dated enlisted soldiers and draftees. Can you believe that one? Well, I never!

Now, I never actually saw them program or spent any time with them, but I know they did a lousy job. I heard through the grapevine that some of them smoked marijuana. And went to enlisted men's clubs. And at their parties, they invited enlisted persons and Vietnamese people. Like, as if, the war was a joke or something.

Well, I never saw any marijuana the whole year I was there and wouldn't know what a marijuana cigarette looked like if it ran over me.

Speaking of malcontents. Some of the Black boys used to complain that they made up over 25 percent of the combat troops and yet they never saw a Black Red Cross gal. Well, excuse me for speaking, but that was a bold-faced lie. And I want to set the record straight once in for all.

There was so a Black donut dolly. And I knew her. We were practically friends. I don't mean to say that we roomed together or double-dated or anything like that, but I chatted with her in the D.C. headquarters before going to Nam.

She graduated from Radcliffe and her parents lived in Beverly Hills. She had a beautiful face, you know, no Black features or anything unseemly like that. I think her uncle was a famous actor, Stephen Fletcher, or something like that. While in Nam I heard that she didn't go out in the field. I mean, who would she have roomed with and, you know, who could she date? There weren't many Black officers.

Her job most of the time was to go to cocktail parties that generals threw for visiting dignitaries from the States and news reporters, basically to show that the Red Cross did have Blacks. As a matter of fact, she appeared in many Red Cross brochures and posters. Most of them were shot in Manhattan with Nam backdrops, but still.

She was a credit to her race and she was definitely a Black person who knew her place. *Life Magazine* even did a write-up on her. Her hair was long and straightened and she had a little turned-up nose. You had to look real close to see that she was Black, to tell you the truth. She could have gone far, but after her tour in Vietnam she went back to the States and joined the Black Panther Party. What a waste.

Oh, golly whiz, I went on R & R trips to Hong Kong and Australia and Bangkok and traveled through Europe visiting all my parents' friends at military bases on my way home.

I know I'm a little kooky, a regular Auntie Mame. But, you know, when you're young, life is a bowl of cherries. It's what I'd tell the grunts. That the Nam was the best experience of their lives. We all go around just once and you've got to smell the roses.

Back then, I dreamed many nights of marrying someone from West Point. You know, a wedding with everybody in uniforms. The ushers in their dress blues and my bridesmaids in Red Cross blue. And me in a flowing white wedding gown, looking absolutely stunning and pure. By the by, I was a virgin until I was married, not like some of the nonconformist gals in Nam, you know, the ones who dated enlisted boys. Well I never!

Thank God, most of them don't show up at donut dolly reunions that we've held over the years. Oh, those nostalgic reunions with gals like me. We'd talk about our families and how well we married and, yes, even shed a few tears talking about our experiences in Nam, the good times of our service to our country. Incredible!

I didn't have a very good time at the big reunion held in Washington for the unveiling of the women's statue. So many of those rabble-rousers showed up. Even the ones who were fired for taking illegal flights and smoking marijuana cigarettes. How could they even show their faces in polite company? God, and they're the ones who had so much fun. Can you beat that!

I mean, no officers showed up that weekend and D.C. was just mobbed with guys who were enlisted boys and draftees in Nam. It was disgusting how they fawned all over those gals who never, in my humble opinion, represented Red Cross very well.

After leaving a little piece of my heart in Nam, I returned to college, picked up a master's degree in social work, and did some counseling. Call me a do-gooder, I don't care, and I'm not asking for medals or anything, but I wanted to give of myself to help some of the guys suffering from Post Traumatic Stress Disorder. I mean, I know what pain is. I suffer from PMS something awful. Goodness gracious!

But, you'd think that the world owes them a living or something the way those Vietnam Vets carried on about firefights and constantly complaining about seeing their buddies killed, etc., etc., ad nauseam. And then they'd cry.

Finally, I just couldn't take their bellyaching. By gosh, I'd yell at them to stop it and shape up. I'd tell them to look at me. I was there too and I wasn't suffering from flashbacks and all that stuff. I'd tell them that I served in Nam and that I had gone on in my life. I did just fine. I'd say, "It's your life and you can be anything you set your mind to be and, if you had guts, you can do anything you want to do." I showed them who had intestinal fortitude!

You know, I tried to understand the Vietnamese culture and their traditions but sometimes it was just impossible. Like one time, my unit director, who by the way turned out to be one of the nonconformist gals I was talking about earlier, anyway, she told me to go to the off-base massage parlor and see if I could talk the owner into having a ladies' night. You know how great massages make you feel. Really groovy!

Anyway, I went in civvies, a nice pair of hot pants and white boots, and asked to speak to the owner, a Mrs. Trang. When she came out through the beaded curtain, she looked me up and down and asked me if I had any experience. Oh, my Gawd, she thought I was asking for a job. Isn't that a scream? Me, a college graduate, working as a masseuse. Did you ever in your life!

Anywho, when I asked her about having a ladies' night, she said that the massage parlor only had two specials—hand and blow—and they really had no time to do massages.

I protested that her sign said "massages," and she asked me if I'd like to work part-time. She wasn't making any sense, and I could see that she was, you know, as thick as molasses. So, finally, I informed her that I was going to report her to the Federal Trade Association for false advertising.

I mean, I was really psyched about getting a massage regularly, just like Mommy. Mommy even had a masseuse who came to the house once a week. His name was Sven. He came to the house when Daddy was out of town on business. You know, to firm her up. And she used to tell me how nice her complexion was and how good her back felt after his visit.

Like, it was great physical therapy for Mommy. And I knew how great those massages were, because her letters were filled with Sven's name. And Daddy always would write about how great Mommy looked after he returned from his trips.

Anyway, here I was in the Far East and couldn't find one massage parlor that catered to women.

Before I left that establishment, mad as the dickens, Mrs. Trang told me that in the right light I could pass as a double for Marilyn Chambers, whoever she is. That gook woman made no sense at all. And when I got back to the other Red Cross gals to tell them about my bad luck, they wouldn't stop laughing. I guess I'm a born raconteur, don't you think?

Another thing about so-called Vietnamese culture, and this is, like, too, too funny, but true. Vietnamese men used to walk down the street holding hands. The first time I saw it, I blushed. I mean, you know what they looked like, don't you? Totally gross! I mentioned it to some of the enlisted boys, and I asked them if it seemed, you know, strange, wink, wink.

Check this out, you know what those guys said? That it wasn't strange at all. They claimed it was the custom in Vietnam for men to hold hands. Like walking arm in arm with a buddy in the States or like a guy in America with his arm around a friend's shoulder. I couldn't believe my ears! I never realized just how dumb enlisted soldiers were. Goodness gracious!

So I asked some officers and they confirmed what I already knew.

They'd say, "You're damn right, excuse my French, little lady, but if I was running this country I'd put a stop to that pansy-ansy disgusting habit. Looks bad. A man should act like a man. And if they want to show manly affection, they should do what real men do. Real men play football and pat asses after a good play. Or snap towels in the locker room. Or take up wrestling or hockey or any other contact sport. I don't trust the guy who takes a leak behind closed stalls. But this holding hands. Well, they look like little fairies, if you ask me."

There you go! It proves my point! Fact is fact: The grunts were just so totally uninformed about what was really going on in Nam. Like, no wonder we lost the war!

A SAIGON PARTY

Navy journalist Nick White, who talked his way through the war on his three-hour morning radio program at AFVN, American Forces Vietnam Network, was perched behind the bamboo bar, delighting four attractive nurses from Third Field Hospital with the anecdote of his interview with the Cambodian tap-dancing pig and her agent, Irving.

The husky-voiced disc jockey, a minor celebrity in Saigon, constantly invented outrageous skits to wake up his adoring listeners. Nick thrived on attention and continued his monologue by telling the modern day Florence Nightingales of Saigon's First Annual Cyclo Drivers' Contest that was aired on his program, "Dawn Buster."

The competition was arranged to see which cyclo (motorized rickshaw), or pedicab as they were called in Vietnam, could jump over the most barrels.

Using body language, he described how he had wedged himself between the barrels and bravely peered up at the flying Asian Evil Knivels.

The blonde-haired, blue-eyed sailor was reliving the imaginary moment of the revving and roaring of the engines, hoopla of the crowd, and the intensity of the action in a blow-by-blow account of the Olympian feat to thrill the fans at the bar who had been on R & R when the skit was aired on his program.

Sipping a gin and tonic and acting as urbane as a character right out of a Noel Coward play, he was enjoying the tender loving attention that he was presently receiving. Nick White basked in the limelight of stardom.

In a corner of the formal dining room, Marine Chaplain

Bernstein, in civvies, and a Buddhist monk, swathed in a saffron robe, were discussing papal infallibility.

Within earshot of these men of the cloth, Consuelo O'Keefe, ardent feminist, card-carrying member of the ACLU, and former freedom rider, was chatting coquettishly with correspondents from *Time, Stars & Stripes,* and *Playboy.*

The two news reporters lived in Saigon, whereas the photo-journalist from *Playboy* dropped by the city to check out possibilities for a layout featuring the girls from Saigon University.

All three of the writers were wearing what every journalist in Vietnam wore—correspondent suits, which looked exactly what anyone would expect a great white hunter to wear on safari. The only missing accessory was one of those bush hats that Stewart Granger donned to shoot elephants in jungle movies.

Consuelo was dressed in an Indian sari and had a dot on her forehead. The get-up had a purpose, even though jealous women claimed that her favorite holiday was Halloween.

Resourceful Consuelo was the creator of International Weeks at the Tan Son Nhut USO, where she was the program director. The outfit she had on this evening was to advertise India Week.

The recreation center, not far from the air base and formerly an elegant villa owned by a French plantation owner for weekend trysts in the city, was decorated appropriately each week.

This particular week, posters of the Taj Mahal and other scenes of Consuelo's favorite country were displayed, and the atmosphere was enhanced by travelogues and sitar music piped throughout the club. In addition, curried dishes were served free to the GIs by the male Vietnamese kitchen help who were dressed as Sikhs. They also wore turbans and brandished plastic swords. Consuelo and the female Vietnamese staff and junior volunteers—young girls who acted as hostesses during parties and dances—wore saris.

During Japanese Week, Consuelo paraded around Saigon in a kimono; and her Thanksgiving attire included an outfit that Pocahantas would have died for.

"Comrade" Consuelo, a nickname whispered behind her back

by conservative State Department wives, was a walking billboard for activities at her club, which was always mobbed by soldiers curious to see what in the world she would dream up next for their entertainment.

The German military attaché, his wife Helga, and their guests, the Italian deputy ambassador and his wife Marisa, were on the patio in a heated discussion with all four of the Sweet Adelines, a female barbershop quartet from Wichita, Kansas, in-country on a USO Show tour for two weeks.

Two C-130, one F-4, and three chopper pilots were engaged in animated conversation at the teak dining room table, outtelling tall tales of aerial and bedroom deeds of derring-do.

Four MPs, who usually guarded the American Embassy, had three giggling Vietnamese secretaries from USAID under, what appeared to be, house arrest.

Seventy friends of the hostess, friends of friends, or acquaintances of somebody there were milling around the Humphrey Bogart-like apartment with its languidly turning ceiling fans, cool tile floors, and dark green window shutters that served as a barricade against the afternoon tropical sun and seasonal monsoon downpours.

A Quaker humanitarian doctor and a young Korean general were feasting on the caviar and swapping dirty jokes.

Meanwhile, four French nuns from the Son Mai orphanage worked the crowd, as they always did at parties, finding volunteers and contributors for their worthwhile endeavors. They zeroed in on the Americans who they knew to be the most generous, especially while drinking. Similar to a squad of grunts on patrol, they kept alert and ambushed anyone holding an empty glass with a gracious offer to refill. The hostess, who invited the nuns often to her parties as a contribution to the orphanage, was pleased that they were accomplishing their mission.

Two teenage Amerasian pickpockets, who staked out the neighborhood and somehow befriended the hostess after trying to steal her wallet during her first week in Vietnam, were double-handily polishing off the tray of soft-shelled crabs, while keeping their promise of not plying their trade among the guests, at least while they were in her apartment.

The Indian brothers, owners of the International Newsstand on Tu Do, the next street over, were arguing with Mai Lon, a Vietnamese movie star and daughter of a senator. The popular beauty was defending her position that Ho Chi Minh was a nationalist before he was a communist.

The brown-skinned capitalists, and dear friends of Consuelo, began quacking at the end of their if-he-walked-like-a-duck argument. Mai saw that it was a useless discussion.

She politely excused herself and went into the bedroom to join the hostess and a group of Australians, three officers and a gorgeous redheaded night club singer. The Aussies, passing around a joint, were not exactly hiding in the room, but they were being somewhat discreet and respectful to the few guests who frowned on marijuana use.

Mai took a toke, held the smoke in her lungs and, as she exhaled, tried to recall any foreigner's party that she had been to where there was not someone someplace smoking pot. The hostess, Consuelo, and she had even shared some grass in a bathroom at the British Embassy, just to tell the story.

Enough food was scattered around the spacious apartment to feed a platoon of hungry soldiers, and there was sufficient liquor for another hundred guests. The hostess liked to be prepared when, as often happened, more people showed up than were expected.

After the 25 candles on the hostess's birthday cake were lit, the old standard sung in six languages, and the fire extinguished on the three-layered masterpiece created by the Chinese bakery shop next door, the living room coffee table was shifted to make room for dancing. Couples of various shades and sizes and political persuasions began to trip the light fantastic to Consuelo's favorite Motown records.

The crowd was a bit surprised, but nonetheless delighted, to watch Nicole, one of the Carmelite sisters, and the bald-headed

Buddhist monk move around the floor as adroitly as Ginger and Fred.

A separated (as he liked to regale his pilot friends, "well, if 9000 miles away from the old gal isn't separated, I don't know what the hell is") flight surgeon from Cam Ranh Bay in Saigon for a few days before jetting off to Hawaii on a secret (from his nurse girlfriends who believed him when he said he was single) wife-meeting R & R, was informing Consuelo that he had not eaten lettuce and grapes for a year in support of Cesar Chavez.

The Ivy League—Yale, class of '60—liar knew he had to talk fast. The handsome medical man had only 24 hours to seduce the enchanting, bleeding-heart Latina.

Without batting a wandering eye or missing a beat, he continued proclaiming his support for Huey Newton and Angela Davis if they decided to head up the Democratic ticket in the next presidential election against Nixon and Agnew in '72.

Before he even spoke to Consuelo, he had sized her up to a tee and had loudly donated $100 and a day of his medical services to the orphanage, all within earshot of Consuelo, who he knew was checking him out from the moment he walked through the door.

The suave sawbones was on a roll. He had her convinced ("liar, liar, pants on fire," kept running through his mind) that he was a staunch supporter of the Black power movement, women's liberation ("in your dreams," raced through his head), and the antiwar faction.

In her Elizabeth Taylor-violet, trusting, womanly eyes, this man was a tall, dark, and handsome doctor with all the right moves. She was also smart enough to know that a lot of his claims were bullshit, which did not matter to her. She wanted to sleep with him just because he turned her on. The grass she had been smoking since breakfast had enhanced her desire to spend a passionate night with the sexy gringo.

The philandering physician could almost read her thoughts, as he always did with women. Again, the signals were telling him that the chase was over, and she was his for the asking. He enjoyed the sport of the hunt and knew he had achieved his goal. Now the challenge was gone, along with the fun of this game he delighted in playing with women.

A bored expression crept over his face. He began searching the room for another target, someone who would give him a run for his money. The hostess was a possibility. Or perhaps the dancing nun. There was, after all, a woman under those layers of black cloth.

The Spanish spit-fire, who had escaped Cuba with her mother when Fidel overthrew Batista, knew a brush-off when directed at her in the form of a shrugged shoulder and quickly, too much so for her pride, found the hostess for an air-kiss before racing out the door.

The party that started at noon finally broke up at midnight. Leftovers were wrapped and taken to the orphanage. Business cards were exchanged, and rendezvous were arranged, openly and secretly. Cheeks were bussed, Rolex and Mickey Mouse watches were checked, and the guests drifted out to Nguyen Hue boulevard on their way home before the annoying war-time curfew at one.

THE PHILANTHROPIC EXECUTIVES

Immediately after finishing his third Vietnam tour as a second lieutenant assigned to Military Intelligence, civilian Lawrence T. Williams III, hankering to stay longer in the war zone, signed on with one of the organizations serving the military's off-duty needs. There were so many: Red Cross, USO, Special Services, to name but three. Automatically skipping the assistant slot, the ex-spook began his new civilian employment as the director of the recreation center in Chu Lai.

Within his four months of joining the nonprofit, philanthropic agency, there was an executive opening at headquarters in Saigon. George Cleveland, the personnel director, one of the five executives at the main office, had decided to head back to Philadelphia two months before his 18-month contract was complete.

"You can take this f_ _king war and shove it," was the only reason Afro-coiffured Brother George gave for resigning.

Three bright and conscientious women, each in-country for over a year with the charitable corporation, applied for the recently opened executive position.

Dick Wilson, a retired Navy captain and the head honcho of the organization in Vietnam, offered the prized job to Lawrence T. Williams III, even though he did not apply for it.

The women were "outraged at not even being considered."

Patronizingly, pipe-smoking Wilson calmly explained to the three females that men make better executives than women. Their loud and futile arguments after his justification not only irritated him, but the complaints also reinforced his decision.

Lawrence T. Williams III, former U.S. Army sleuth and now personnel director in Vietnam of the world-wide humanitarian organization, moved into an exquisite villa in Saigon. There, he kept a pet python that he draped around his neck while prowling the bars and brothels, hunting for prostitutes to beat up. He much preferred the ones younger than 16. Street boys also caught his fancy when he tired of the whimpering girls.

Lawrence T. Williams III went through unusual phases. Once, he refused to speak for a week, communicating by writing things down. Another week, he decided to come to work sporting a skin tone other than his natural white. After soaking for hours in a tub full of food dye, he breezed into the VIP office showing off his new complexion, a dark shade of purple.

The three women who had lost out to Lawrence T. Williams III for the rarefied position in the administrative office were flabbergasted that Wilson never said anything about his current personnel director's bizarre behavior.

The big boss had other, more pressing matters to concern himself with. For one thing, he felt that there were far too many Black soldiers frequenting the Cam Ranh Bay club. He wanted to know, "Why is that?" And he demanded to find out what the director there "was going to do about it, and how soon?"

For another thing, he did not want any more grumbling from women assistant directors, or "girls" as he called them, that they made less money than their male counterparts.

Furthermore, the female staffers were giving him ulcers by dating enlisted men instead of officers. A Black female program director was even dating a white soldier. What's more, a white "gal"—as his surrogate son, Lawrence (never Larry) T. Williams III, called women—was seen dining and dancing with a Korean war correspondent.

"God, please give me strength," Wilson loudly groaned.

Sitting in his comfortable leather chair with his feet propped on his large, uncluttered oak desk and puffing on his pipe, Dick Wilson blew smoke rings. The newly appointed, purple-colored personnel director, staring off into space, was perched across from him.

"I just can't get it into those girls' fluffy heads, even though, Lord knows, I've tried, that men make better executives than females. Always have. Always will," Wilson flatly stated with solid conviction.

Lawrence T. Williams III, who, if it had been Halloween, could have won first prize as a convincing plum, shook his head in total agreement.

THE WAR THROUGH PAMELA ROSE'S EYES

I was a USO program director for six months in sand-filled and cockroach-infested Cam Ranh Bay then, thank God, I was promoted to public relations director in Saigon. The new job, which was considered the female position in the executive office, included my being the host of a daily radio show at the main military station, American Forces Vietnam Network (AFVN).

The night before leaving Cam Ranh Bay, my gang, what was left of it, at the trailer park where I lived threw a going away party. Except for the band (a ragtag group of GIs newly arrived and stationed around Cam Ranh Bay playing USO instruments) and dancing on the deck, it was a rather subdued party. There was drinking, of course, but after the firing—for taking illegal flights—of my Red Cross pals, the trailer park had a new group of donut dollies, and they were keeping a very low profile. Pot-smoking rumors about Cam Ranh Bay dollies were flying all over Vietnam.

Since the arrival of Millie Noble, one of the very few Black women hired by USO in Vietnam, there were plenty of Black GIs showing up at parties—from the lowest privates to full bird colonels. Their choice of music was great, from jazz to blues and everything soulful in between.

Millie had arranged my send-off. The park was decked out with streamers, banners, balloons, and Vietnamese decorations. Sister Millie, my new best friend, had discovered an old Vietnamese widowed woman in the village who had recently lost a soldier son and set her up in a food catering business. The mamasan and her six unmarried daughters supplied the food, paid for by Millie, who had sweet-talked groups in Cam Ranh Bay into using the old woman's catering business for their hail and farewell parties. Millie was an early believer in workfare, not welfare.

Millie, always the romantic, despite her Black Power revolutionary, militant persona, had invited Bill Bailey to help patch things up between us. She, as everyone else, was appalled that he had slapped me in Hong Kong while we were on R & R but thought that it was an isolated incident, one that I had provoked. Thinking back now about how we thought then, it amazes me that any of us, including me, could blame the one slapped. But we did. I was so desperately in love with him that I would excuse anything he did, especially after his endearing apologies and promises that he never before had hit a woman nor would again do anything so awful to me, the first woman he "truly loved." I guess love is blind.

As I was sitting out a dance, perched on the top step of one of the Red Cross trailers, surveying the scene, and watching Bill and Millie dance, a man in one of those ludicrous safari suits strolled over. I knew who he was—the vice-president of one of the two airline companies that had the contract in Vietnam for charter flights back and forth to the States for GIs on leave.

There was so much money being made by both airlines, yet they both had a fierce competition, an Avis-Hertz battle raging constantly. They each had representatives signing up GIs in PX's, the civilian area of the Tan Son Nhut airport, and at some USO's; but, except for Stateside newspapers and magazines, they had nowhere to advertise in Vietnam. The *Stars & Stripes* and other military newspapers, bulletins, and magazines sold no advertising space. AFVN, the military television and radio station, had no commercials, and except for one Vietnamese radio and TV station, everyone in all of Vietnam tuned into AFVN. Very few GIs had a television set, but everyone had access to a radio, and AFVN was the only station that GIs from the Delta to the DMZ listened to—they had no choice. The disc jockeys had a very captive audience.

Molly Dew's show, soon to be mine, "USO Showtime," was

broadcast at 12:30 p.m., right after Paul Harvey finished with his trademark, "Good Day!"

Officers' and EM clubs, mess halls, and offices, were tuned in practically 24 hours a day to AFVN, making the Vietnam conflict a rock and roll war.

The airline executive and I were discussing the power of AFVN, estimated 500,000 listeners at any one time, and how few women broadcasters there were: "USO Showtime," a couple of nurses doing remotes occasionally, and some canned shows generating from Los Angeles during the night. "USO Showtime" was the only daytime show featuring a woman.

Before you can say, "There's no business like show business," the skinny guy in the tan Stewart Granger outfit sans the safari hat, made me an offer he thought I couldn't refuse: If I would mention his airline in a casual way a few times a week, he would give me an open ticket on another airline that flew everywhere in the world, and I (or my friends or family) could fly anywhere at anytime during the time I was host of "USO Showtime."

"Isn't that illegal as far as the military's concerned?" I rhetorically asked the bespectacled bush-hunter look-alike.

"Well, let's just say it would be our little secret," he said, putting his arm around my shoulder.

"Hey, Bill, come here a second," I yelled to that gorgeous Navy hunk surrounded by the flock of flirting donut dollies.

"This guy just offered me a bribe," I told the love of my life when he ran over. Without stopping for a breath, I repeated the offer, like a play back of a recording.

Mr. Vice-president denied it, stood up, and before walking away, turned and said, "You are a stupid little girl."

My knight in shining armor grabbed him by the shoulders. "Hey, pip-squeak, one more word out of your mouth and..." But before he could finish, Millie had joined us, to drag me off to cut the going-away cake.

Bill, no mental midget, later made the comment, "Christ, any idiot can make a fortune in this war." When I protested his reference to my mental capacity, he went on, "No, I didn't mean to call you an idiot, it's just that if all this money exchange, pilfering, black market shit is going on in backwater Cam Ranh Bay, think about the deals going down in Saigon."

As the doctor in charge of the dispensary at Naval Air Facilities (NAF), he was floored at how many medical supplies were stolen daily, later showing up on the black market stalls scattered along the roads not far from the bases.

The one item that aid stations and hospitals all over Vietnam couldn't keep from walking out the door were clamps, used by the legions of pot smokers as holders of roaches, the last bit of a smoked joint, and the most potent, that unless held by a surgical clamp, burned the fingertips. And, I might add, besides being bought up as far-out, groovy, way-cool drug paraphernalia by dope heads, these precious clamps made their way to VC underground hospitals. And "they" said that people in the antiwar movement were giving aid and comfort to the enemy.

"What a war," my prince lying next to me in the single bed remarked, exhaling a lungful of smoke, as he handed me a surgical clamp securely holding one of those potent roaches.

One of the most important parts of a USO director's job was called the door count, how many times soldiers walked through the door of a club in a month. There was not a turnstile or someone sitting out front actually counting. It was a guesstimate and, similar to body counts in Vietnam, door counts were a bit inflated. When I was doing my first report in Cam Ranh Bay and turned it into my boss Jenny, she looked at the numbers and asked how I came up with the door count number.

"To try to get an accurate number, I had two GIs sit outside all day, one day, and they counted every soldier who came in, then I multiplied that number by 30," I explained to her, proud of my ingenuity.

"Two soldiers volunteered to sit outside all day?" she asked.

"Yeah, after Derek promised them each $25 worth of anything in the psychedelic shop." (Derek was an Army cook by night and the manager of the USO gift shop during the day.)

"That's great and probably pretty accurate, but we can't send that number in."

"Why not?" I asked.

"It's too low."

"Six thousand is too low?" It seemed high to me.

"All the other clubs use the count of 9000 give or take," Jenny explained.

"Why send a made-up number?"

"Because then the New York headquarters will think we're doing a good job. And everyone else does it. If we don't, we'll look bad."

Jenny handed me back the report after adding 3023 more to the door count and, as I retyped the sheet with the new number, I thought about and understood how the body count in the Vietnam War worked. A platoon sergeant reports 10 enemy dead to a lieutenant, who reports 20 enemy dead to the captain, who reports 40 enemy dead to the major, who reports more to the colonel, who reports a higher number to the general, who reports a much higher one to MACV, who reports still a larger one to the Pentagon. That original 10 ends up in Washington as 283 (nobody at USO or in the field sent a round number), which was proof that we were winning the war. Everybody in Vietnam knew about it and talked about and joked about it. Of course, there were so many inflated stories that you could never be sure what was fact, hyperbole, or rumor.

After I began my new job as PR director in Saigon, I expected that the task of gathering the reports from the club directors and shipping them Stateside would be easy. Not so, I soon found out. The directors gave every excuse in the book why those reports were late.

"I was robbed on the way to the bank, and along with all the money the reports were stolen. I'll redo them and get them to you in a week."

"I had food poisoning for a week, but I'll get the report done as soon as I can get out of bed and eat again."

"The base was on red alert and when I ran to a bunker, the report, which I was carrying to the post office, fell in the mud and got ruined. Give me a few days to find my notes and do it again."

Then there was the constant excuse from the Danang clubs that I heard. "Jesus, Pamela, we're being rocketed. Can't you hear it in the background?" I could indeed hear the sounds of incoming.

"Well, okay, just make sure you get your report to me as soon as possible," I'd say, worried that I might look like I was not doing a good job to my bosses in New York.

Danang, known as Rocket City, was continuously being shelled, and the first time I heard the excuse about the late report, I was frantic for the USO staff's safety. However, I later discovered that sometimes the excuse was an honest one, Danang was being rocketed as we spoke, and at other times, whoever I was speaking with would put the phone next to a tape recording some clever director had made. I was never quite sure which it was. I was sure, though, that the new person doing the report was not privy to the door count game when the packet of statistics would finally arrive in my office and I would see a low number. I would simply inflate it, then retype the page before sending it off to New York headquarters.

Within a week of moving to Saigon and the new job, off I soared to Cam Ranh Bay to visit Bill. Before long, I knew every pilot who flew between Saigon and Cam Ranh Bay, most of them becoming frequent party guests at my apartment at 66 Nguyen Hue.

Mickey Mantle (not his real name, but a warrant officer with that famous nickname who looked exactly like the ball player) had called me during my first few days in Saigon to say that a bunch of the Crazy Cats, an Army unit, was planning a surprise birthday party for Bill.

After landing in Cam Ranh Bay and dropping off my stuff in

Bill's room, taking "a nap" as we called a quickie, and showering in the communal bathroom (when I was in it, there was a sign on the door announcing that it was off limits until I was through), we headed for the O (officers') club for the birthday dinner with his pilot pals. The place, as usual, was wall to wall men. The five Vietnamese waitresses and I were the only women there that evening.

Wendell Ridgeman, a fortyish warrant officer pilot from Arkansas, presented Bill with a gift for my new apartment. It was a wooden door knocker shaped like a penis. A penis belonging to King Kong, that is. Wendell had carved it himself and it took him a week.

When I asked with a straight face, "How come you made it so small?" Bill actually blushed.

When the slapping of Bill's back and the laughter died down, a hush came over the room. We were all frozen in our seats listening to the sirens, then turned to Andy Murdock, the XO (executive officer) on duty.

"It's not a drill," Andy shouted, surprised. "Shit, we're under attack."

Chairs were knocked over, guns were unholstered, and everyone ran for cover or for the doors. I sat there, still frozen in my seat. I did not know what to do or where to run.

Andy, an Annapolis grad, took charge. "Okay, everybody," he yelled, "get to a bunker. Bill, go find the dentist and get to the dispensary." I got up to go with Bill. "No, Pamela, you can't go with Bill. It's the first place that'll be blown up. And if it's overrun, well, you might get hurt."

"That's okay, I'll go with Bill."

"No you won't," the serious sounding doctor, who moments before was whispering silly sweet nothings in my ear, told me. "You'll be safe with Wendell and Mickey and the guys in a bunker."

Wendell and Mickey Mantle picked me up by both arms and carried me out of the O club. When we got outside, we could hear helicopters whirling by with that thump-thump-thump sound, machine gun fire, more sirens, whistles, and people yelling. Hundreds of men were running. And I do mean fast. I looked at Wendell and he appeared to be very worried.

"I don't want to be a sitting duck in that bunker over there," Wendell said, pointing straight ahead. "It's too damn close to the O club, and those VC really love to blow up O clubs." With that, he suggested to the other pilots that "we make a run to a bunker near the tennis court."

We ran, the party of 16. Wendell held my hand so tightly that it was becoming numb.

I am sure that if Wendell were telling this story, he could describe how many yards or meters it was, but I do not know measurements in those terms. It might have been the length of two football fields. I am not sure, but I am convinced that it was the fastest I ever ran in my life. And I was wearing sandals with two-inch heels.

Terrified of not only the enemy shooting me, I was also afraid of tripping and being trampled by the guys inches behind me. I guess I wasn't running fast enough, because Wendell picked me up, threw me over his shoulder, and speeded up. He held me like that with one hand, while brandishing a gun with the other. I started to worry that he would stumble, I would fall, and the gun would accidentally shoot me. So busy worrying about other things, I really never gave much thought to who was attacking the base. I have to point out here that Wendell was 6'5" and weighed about 230 to my 5'3" and 107 pounds.

It might look cool when someone does that in a movie, but let me assure you, my stomach and ribs hurt like hell, being pressed into his shoulder.

When we made it to the bunker, it would not open. It was bolted from the inside. Wendell, by now completely in charge, banged on the door with the butt of his gun.

"What's the password?" someone inside yelled.

Wendell turned around and asked, "Does anyone know what the password is?"

"No."

"No."

"I didn't even know there was such a thing."

Wendell, now realizing that someone inside the bunker was horsing around, calmly said, "The password is, if you do not open this f_ _king door by the time I count to f_ _king three, I will shoot and blow your f_ _king brains out."

The door was unbolted before the countdown began and we crawled in. It was like an igloo. Not that I have ever been in an igloo or anything, but like the ones you see in movies. Except it was hot and dark. I could tell as we crawled in that I was not the only one scared. There were five men already there sitting on a concrete floor.

Before we got there, one of the guys told us, they had shot a rat that was cowering in the back and had thrown it outside. There were rat droppings everywhere, and when Wendell flicked on his lighter, we witnessed an army of cockroaches scurrying for cover.

The bunker was made of concrete and reinforced with steel. The 20 men and I sat with our knees touching.

The smell of sweat was overpowering. We could still hear machine gun fire and helicopter blades whirling outside. For the first few minutes, there was total silence, except for heavy breathing, inside the sweltering bunker. The only sounds were the ones outside.

"Hey, we're safe in here," Wendell began, "the only thing we have to fear is a direct rocket attack. And what are the odds of that happening?"

"Twenty to one."

"Nah. A hundred to one."

"A thousand to one."

"Okay. Okay," Wendell stopped the guessing, "It's a long shot. But I'd sure as hell like to be out there seeing what's going on."

Mickey Mantle piped up with a twinkle in his voice, "You know, when I agreed to come to Vietnam on a handshaking tour, I never thought I would be sitting in a bunker while a base was under attack."

"Shit, I thought that was you sitting in the O club. Mickey Mantle, I'll be a son of a bitch. Let me shake your hand, man," the Air Force officer sitting in the back of the bunker said. "I don't f_ _king believe that I'm sitting in a bunker with a baseball star. Wait'll I write my wife. Jesus, man, can I have your autograph?"

"Sure. I'll even sign a baseball for you as soon as the attack's over," the fake Mickey Mantle answered, jabbing his elbow into my sore ribs.

The four other strangers, who also wanted autographed baseballs, included three naval officers from Navy Markettime and another Air Force pilot, stationed in Thailand, in Cam Ranh for two weeks on some kind of TDY (temporary duty), filling in for someone else on emergency leave.

When the guys heard that he was stationed in Thailand, they started to talk about NAF being shelled all the time. The old-timers went on and on about VC with dynamite strapped to them and American soldiers being skinned alive when caught and stuff that was so far fetched that I could not believe it when the young man from Thailand started to cry. I felt sorry for him when my buddies started to laugh and tease him.

"I can't believe you guys did that. It's so mean," I said, as though admonishing naughty school bullies. "Wendell, you owe Steve a drink after we get out of here."

"You're right, Pamela. I'm sorry, Steve. We were just horsing around. Nothing ever happens around here, it's boring as hell. What do you drink?" he asked the pilot blowing his nose in his sleeve in the back of the bunker.

"Scotch," is all he said. Then, regaining his pilot's cockiness and composure, "And not any of that bar shit. Chevas."

"Okay. Chevas Regal it is. Pamela, how about you?"

"I'll have whatever everybody else is having, if you're buying."

Wendell got on all fours and crawled to the door. "And Steve, to show you how safe it is, I'm going to run right now to the bar and get you that drink I owe you."

Nobody, but I, said anything. "Are you crazy? You can't go out there. You don't know what's going on. You might get shot, if not by some VC, maybe accidentally by one of our soldiers."

"Nah," he answered, "I'm wearing an American pilot's uniform and I'm 6'5" if I stand straight. Do you really reckon anyone would mistake me for a VC? Anyway, my dear, I was a long distance runner in high school, and I could use a libation myself."

Mickey and Garth started egging him on "You're a chicken shit Ridgeman. You don't have the balls."

I could not believe them. Then, I thought, that maybe he was joshing. "Okay," I said, patting his head, "if you are going, could you remember to bring back some cigarettes?"

He pulled the revolver from his holster, unbolted the door, turned around and ordered dramatically, "Cover me."

Four of the Crazy Cats pulled out their guns; and when Wendell opened the door, they crouched and peered outside. No one was in sight, but we could hear lots of ruckus in the distance, in the opposite direction of the O club.

Wendell got into a runner's stance, with one foot back as though perched on a starter's block and was bouncing, getting ready to shove off.

I yelled, "Wait!" And grabbed his shirt.

He turned to me, put his hand on my cheek, and said quietly, "Don't worry."

"Listen, if you're stupid enough to go out, could you also bring back some potato chips?"

He laughed. I tugged on his shirt tail. "And if it isn't too much trouble, could you also get some dip?"

He tipped his hat. "At your service, Mam."

Then he ran to the O club. The four officers covering him decided to shoot their guns in the air for effect. I had never been so close to a gun when it went off and thought my eardrums had burst. It's nothing like in the movies.

Wendell ran alongside the tennis court, past the pool, around a palm tree and a bed of flowers, then up the O club steps. He disappeared into the club as we watched, whispering.

Mickey decided that maybe we should close the door. "Let's not be reckless. Some VC could easily toss a grenade in here."

Garth, another Crazy Cat, added his concern. "Jesus, what if some VC is in the officers' club hiding. Wendell could have walked right into a trap. Some of the kitchen help could be VC. That cook always looked a little shifty-eyed. And how about that new waitress? I think I better go see if he's okay."

"I'm going with you," Steve, the crying pilot yelled from the back of the bunker. "I feel responsible."

Before you could say "Wendell Ridgeman," everyone in the bunker, except me, was planning on joining the posse to go forth and rescue Wendell from the battalion of VC in the O club. I didn't say anything while the mob was forming, but I was starting to get a little scared about being alone in the bunker. Not frightened about any enemy, I was terrified of sitting in there alone with all those cockroaches that were hiding and, I was sure, would appear and attack me once all the men raced off to save the former long distance runner from Little Rock, Arkansas.

While the men were trying to decide who should stay behind to protect me from insects, there was a knock on the bunker door. "Shh. Shh." Twenty people hissed in unison.

"Who's there?" yelled Garth, clutching his pistol.

"It's me. Let me in," the person standing outside the bunker answered. It sounded a little like Wendell, but not really. It sounded more like someone talking through clenched teeth.

"It could be a trap, some VC who speaks English," Mickey guessed. Then he screamed, "I've got a gun pointed right at your balls, now if it is you, Wendell, who won the World Series in 1947?"

We all held our breath waiting for the right response. Someone whispered, "I'm glad I'm not out there. I don't know the answer."

Through what again sounded like clenched teeth, the figure outside grunted, "If you do not open this door by the time I count to three, your ass is grass and I'm a f_ _king lawn mower."

"It's Wendell, quick, open the door," I screamed.

Wendell tumbled in, spitting out the bag of potato chips clenched between his teeth. He was holding three bottles of Scotch, an ice bucket, a table cloth fashioned like a hobo's backpack full of goodies from the restaurant, two cartons of Marlboros, glasses, plastic containers of dip (French onion and clam), and two candles.

The glasses of ice and Scotch were passed around, the chips opened, the table cloth was spread out, and the picnic in the bunker began. Booze flowed and cigarettes smoked and clusters of conversations started.

"Where you from?"

"When's your birthday?"

"What's your favorite childhood story?"

We took turns telling jokes. I promised to play everyone's favorite songs on my show. Wendell's was "Midnight Train to Georgia" and he wanted us all to sing it. We sang and drank, and sang it again, and drank some more, absolutely convinced we sounded as good as the recording. Ten, 15, 20 times, we sang "Midnight Train to Georgia."

"Do Wop Do Wop," the Pips yelped over and over.

We each took turns being Gladys Knight. Then, while Wendell was pouring the last of the Scotch into his glass, there was a loud banging at the door. You know what it sounds like when 21 tipsy people are trying to whisper? We were loud, but the banging at the door was louder. If there was danger that night, it was at that moment, when all the guys squatting in that bunker had their guns unholstered, waving them menacingly in the air. It was a miracle one of us did not get shot either point blank or by a ricocheting bullet. I was not frightened at the time, only later thinking about it.

"Open the door. It's me, Bill."

Mickey unbolted the door and pushed it open. Smoke from a

hundred cigarettes went rushing out, hitting Bill in the face. He started to cough. Hack, really. When he caught his breath, we could discern from his voice that he was quite angry.

"Christ, we've been looking all over the f_ _king place for you f_ _king guys. I stayed in the f_ _king infirmary an hour after the f_ _king all clear signal. Stubbed toes and shit like that." He didn't stop to take a breath, obviously not wanting to breath any more smoke. And he was a heavy smoker at the time. "Three sappers were killed. They were cornered at the air field. I assumed Pamela and the rest of you f_ _kers would be at the O club and when I got there and couldn't find you, I looked in the Crazy Cats' bar and along the way asked everyone if they had seen you. Didn't you hear the all f_ _king clear signal? Jesus, I was worried."

"Hit it gang," Wendell ordered us. When we broke into another rendition of "Midnight Train to Georgia," Bill started to walk away very mad and then turned around and joined us.

Later that night, Bill and I were at the Crazy Cats' bar a few minutes after curfew and were surprised to find the place empty. Within a short time, first Wendell, followed by the gang from the bunker, walked into the bar naked except for their boots and holsters and guns. I was waiting for the punch line and Mickey delivered it. The grown boys decided that being in a bunker was too hot for clothes and they wanted to be prepared for the next time. Also, Wendell had suggested that if they were going to die in a bunker, they better be ready and depart the earth like the cowboys of lore with their boots on. Wendell, too, was sporting a bow tie, because it was his turn to tend bar in their private club.

When I arrived at my friend Millie's USO club the next day to interview a couple of soldiers to justify my being in Cam Ranh Bay, everyone was discussing the attack on NAF.

"Yeah, man, 10 VC were killed."

"No. I heard it was 20."

"A friend of mine was there, and he swore it was 30."

I loved doing the radio show at AFVN. One day I arrived at

the station as usual around 11:30 and headed to the record room to select the requested songs.

As I walked down the hall, Nick White, the host of "Dawn Buster," the early morning show, passed me and patted my back, "Our heroine." Then he strolled on.

Danny, the country and western DJ, saw me as I passed a booth where he was making a tape and gave me the thumbs up sign.

Sgt. Malcolm, the anal-retentive lifer in charge of operations, came out of his office and shouted at me, "Way to go, Pamela!"

I popped my head into Colonel Grenada's office. "Hi. Chris, you busy?"

He stood up and came around the desk smiling.

"Was there an announcement today about my winning the Nobel Peace Prize? Everyone's congratulating me."

He laughed. "Better than that. You personally captured a squad of NVA soldiers in the Highlands."

"I did. I don't remember. Okay, I'm game. What's the joke?"

"Sit down. Do you have a few minutes?"

"Sure, I only have to get five records and I'll be ready for showtime. What's going on?"

He chortled again. "Oh, I'm not laughing at you. Christ, this is rich. Wait till you hear this one."

"Colonel, I'm listening."

"Well it seems that our boys were out on patrol yesterday afternoon, training an ARVN squad on how to patrol by actually marching around searching for the enemy as opposed to sitting around base camp drinking American beer."

"What does this have to do with me?"

"Well, anyway, our boys and the ARVN are hiking through the jungle, and all of a sudden they hear your theme song and then, in that friendly manner, shriek, "Hi. This is Pamela Rose for 'USO Showtime.'"

"I don't shriek. Do I?"

"No, no. Would you just shut the f_ _k up and listen. Anyway, our boys knew instantly that someone was listening to a radio, specifically some person or group of people was tuned into your show. So, one of our guys whispers for everyone to get down, and he crawls toward the sound. And what do you think he finds?"

"I give up. What?"

"A squad of NVA soldiers, pith helmets and all, AK-47's, the whole works, relaxing under a tree with the radio at full blast, listening to your show. So, the guy who crawled to check out what was happening crawled back, got the other American, and the two of them sauntered over to the NVA squad, and captured them. They didn't even have to fire their weapons. The enemy soldiers just raised their hands in surrender and yelled, 'Chieu hoi!' Is that rich; after they were caught with their pants down, so to speak, they decided to surrender."

"No kidding. They were listening to my show?"

"Yeah, and these guys were carrying real important documents, including maps on a few tunnel systems."

"Do I receive some sort of medal or something?" I was joking.

"No, the guys who captured them get the medals, but you get something even better. One of the captured AK-47's."

"What in the world am I going to do with an AK-47?"

"My suggestion is that you donate it to the radio station, and we can mount it and get a plaque relating the story of how the DJ's at AFVN are helping the war effort."

"Sure, that's a great idea."

"Also, since I am the commanding officer here, working hard for very little recognition, I know you'll want me to have it when I go home in four months. Please."

"Of course you can have it." I said. "Just remember when someone asks you back home how you got it, I better be mentioned in your war story."

"I promise, Scout's Honor!" He crossed his heart, made the sign of the cross, and flashed the V for either victory or peace, you never could tell what someone meant when they flashed it in Vietnam.

The reason I just didn't mention in a single sentence that a squad of NVA soldiers was captured in the Highlands while listening to my show is that I am fairly sure that Colonel Grenada, a wannabe raconteur, is somewhere in the Midwest proudly displaying that AK-47 in his den or library or playroom and telling the listener how he personally captured a battalion of NVA soldiers while he was in the Highlands on some secret mission. So, if you happen to be one of the people to whom he told the story, now you know the truth.

A few of the guys who congratulated me for weeks afterwards heard that it was a platoon; but the truth of the matter is, even though some jealous DJ's said that it was only one NVA soldier, it was actually a squad. Scout's Honor!

A SAIGON WARRIOR'S JOURNAL

February 10, 1971

Today was the first day of Tet, and I properly welcomed in the lunar new year, thanks to the staff at the Saigon USO. They hired a wispy-bearded old Vietnamese scholar to get down on paper soldiers' first writings for the coming year.

I should backtrack a bit and explain a few things about Tet. Most people in the States, when they hear the word "Tet," conjure up images of the 1968 surprise attack by the VC and NVA, which was basically the turning point in the Vietnam War.

In any case, Tet 1971 welcomes in the Year of the Hog. Each year of the 12-year cycle has a name of an animal with distinct characteristics passed along to people born during that time period.

Tet, a combination Christmas, Easter, Thanksgiving, and New Year's Eve rolled into one, lasts for three days. During this celebration it is important to avoid anything unpleasant, such as sickness, for fear that it will be repeated throughout the year. Also, this is the time when all debts must be paid and ancestral graves be visited and tended.

The Vietnamese have many customs commemorating this, their most important holiday. For instance, the first visitor of the new year is important.

Since Tet is the renewing of spirit and body, ancestral family altars, found in every home—villas, as well as shacks—receive special attention with incense, prayers, food and flower offerings. The homes are also decorated with bright colors and "banh chung," a special rice cake, is prepared.

One week before the celebration, families erect a bamboo pole, called a "cay neu," in front of their homes to protect them.

Tet is also the time to buy new clothes for the family.

To these ancient people, the first visitor of the new year is significant, and fireworks and explosives are used to drive away evil and dangerous spirits.

The Tet celebration continues for three days, ending the evening of the third day, when all ancestral souls who have returned to the family for feasting and celebrating must depart for their world. It's then that artificial silver and gold paper money are burned by the family. This allows the departing relatives to hire sampans to transport them across the river that divides spirit Heaven from the world of the living.

Soldiers from all over Vietnam on R & R or with a few days' passes, plus Saigon clerks—REMF's—like me, were huddled around Mr. Tran in the USO, waiting for him to translate their "noble and enriching thoughts" into Chinese characters and record them on the scarlet red "Hong Dieu" paper, which symbolizes cheerfulness and luck.

The old man, who looked 90 but was probably in his late fifties, had a new brush pen of sable that is used for cleanliness and purity. He also explained to the audience, who wasn't really paying much attention, that the fresh slab of stark black ink symbolizes stability.

Mr. Tran patiently went on to explain that the first writing of the new year is always the most important, because each year is a completely new phase of life, a circle of destiny. What happened last year is forgotten and a new period is begun, which is different, vital, and promising.

The origins of first writing go back thousands of years to ancient China, where "the beauties of graceful calligraphy prompted men to seek in the written word not only the moral worth of the author but also the external symbolization of his character within the disciplined beauty of his penmanship," to quote Mr. Tran.

"Senseful ideas, beautiful handwriting," is an old Vietnamese saying. And to think that so many GIs look at the Vietnamese and believe they are either stupid gooks or prostitutes to be bought.

Before Mr. Tran arrived at the USO, he told us, his military audience, who were taking his picture from every conceivable angle, that he had lit an aloe wood fire to chase away the wicked atmosphere of yesteryear, and then he washed his hands in perfumed water. A few of the guys laughed and winked at each other when he said he used perfume; but I was standing right next to him, and he smelled fresh and clean, and there was just a hint of the smell of gardenias.

Any GI can buy red calligraphy posters on just about any corner in Saigon from fortune tellers but, as the poster said at the information desk, "it will be more personal and more meaningful for a GI to actually take part in the custom of First Writing and cast his own fortune with his own sayings."

The GIs were getting a little bored as Mr. Tran pointed out in precise and flawless English sentences that the first writing must be elegant, noble, and beautiful. It must be precise, clear, and the strokes should be bold yet delicate, full-bodied, yet sharply defined.

He went on to say that it "must be a work of art, jet black written on crimson red, and kept throughout the year in order to set the mode of one's life for the year ahead."

The guys were getting rowdy, thinking up short sayings they wanted as their first writing, graffiti they had spotted on helmets, jeeps, and latrine walls.

Two guys decided on "F_ _k Communism."

Another one chose, "Vietnam, Love It or Leave It."

Other sayings included: "Texas Hippie," "Ho Chi Minh Sucks," "Number One GI," and "Kill Slopes For Peace."

I thought of using a quotation from the Bible, or from a Beatles' song, or even a favorite poem from childhood, but I was afraid that the other guys would laugh at me. They were all having a good time being irreverent.

"Saigon Warrior" is the phrase I picked.

Mr. Tran looked so dignified and distinguished, even as he translated our stupid phrases into Chinese on the "Hong Dieu" paper. The one word that comes to mind when I think of him penning those words is "stoic."

But he smiled when he read aloud the poem on the piece of paper that a baby-faced GI, stationed in the Delta and in Saigon waiting for his R & R flight to Hong Kong, handed him. It's funny, but of all of us soldiers standing there in front of Mr. Tran, that poetry-writing GI was the only one with a CIB, Combat Infantry Badge, on his uniform.

I looked closely at the cluster of fruit salad on his chest. Sure enough, the only one of us brave enough to write a poem to Mr. Tran had won a Purple Heart and a Bronze Star.

I asked that soldier for a copy after the crowd broke up and most of the guys headed to Mimi's Bar on Tu Do Street.

I wish I had written what he had: "Eyes filled with yesterday knowingly stare at the present blank faces, but cannot tell what only time can tell."

ROB CLAWSON, SOLDIER OF FORTUNE

If Rob Clawson had been a Japanese man walking down the street of the Ginza, he would have been mistaken for a revered sumo wrestler. His countrymen would have bowed deeply with respect as he waddled by. In reality, he was a grossly overweight American civilian working in Vietnam for a highly respected non-profit organization.

The "little" dictator was an aggressive, hard-nosed manager who was extremely unpopular with his subordinates (all women, whom he called "girls") but thought of by his boss (a retired Navy captain) in Saigon as such a competent administrator that he received three promotions within a year in-country and rapidly rose to control the organization's entire northern operation in the war zone. If you looked at a military map, you could see that his domain was I Corps, which was nicknamed "Eye" Corps by everyone who ever set foot in Vietnam during the American conflict.

After obtaining his 4-F draft notice and diploma from the University of Maryland, after six gentlemanly years, the only son of a prominent Washington attorney signed up for an 18-month hitch with USRO and requested to be sent to Vietnam. USRO was a civilian organization similar to USO.

By 1968, when Rob headed for the war, there were 14 USRO centers, from the Delta to the DMZ. They were staffed by executive directors (mostly men) and program directors (mostly women).

Essentially, the personnel were young, enthusiastic, daring, and fearless. Some went to the war zone for the adventure. Some went because of patriotism. Some went just to see what the hell was going on over there. Some were against the war, but in support of the boys fighting it. Rob went for the money.

He realized there was a lot of dough to be made. After reading *Our Own Worst Enemy*, a scathing indictment of the open corruption in Vietnam, he knew his destiny lay East.

On a salary of $9,800, he resided in a villa in Danang with a household staff of 12 and lavished his beautiful Vietnamese mistress, the former mistress of a CIA agent, with jewelry and monthly shopping trips to Hong Kong. By the end of his first tour—he signed on for two—he had stashed away a few dollars shy of a million in a Swiss bank account. Most of this was accomplished by exchanging money on the black market.

It did not take an economist from Wharton to figure out how the black market money exchange worked. Everyone knew about it. Everyone was approached with a deal. Everyone was tempted to make a fast buck. Not everyone did, even though it was as casual an occurrence as smoking pot in Vietnam.

Here's how it worked. The American military, in its infinite wisdom, issued script called Military Payment Certificate, affectionately and simply called MPC, to avoid flooding the South Vietnamese economy with American dollars. So many GIs; so much cash to spend.

Upon arriving in Vietnam, every American, military and civilian, whether there for a day or 365 or 18 months, was required by law to exchange all of his or her American dollars, a.k.a. greenbacks, into piaster or MPC through official money exchanges.

MPC, also nicknamed "funny money" or "Monopoly money," was used as cash in military and American civilian installations—PX's, commissaries, service clubs, movie theaters.

Piaster, the South Vietnamese currency, was used on the local economy. If you wanted to buy a beer at the EM (enlisted men's) club, you used MPC. To pay for a meal at a local restaurant, you used piasters. This system of payments made the greenback, the mighty American dollar, a prized commodity.

MPC and the piaster had value only in South Vietnam. As far

as the piaster was concerned, nobody really knew how many of those things were being printed, since the South Vietnamese government was allegedly corrupt and devious with everything else it handled. Even the Vietnamese preferred just about any currency to their own. Therefore, the American dollar bills were most sought after. The U.S. dollar was king everywhere on Earth, especially in Vietnam.

With the valuable green paper in hand, a Vietnamese could bribe officials to leave the country for safer ground, pay off a particular general to keep a son or nephew out of the military, or stash it away in a bank in Hong Kong or Paris or Switzerland for a rainy day.

Black market goods, drugs, prostitutes, practically anything could be acquired for a lot less if the payment was in American dollars. MPC, which could be exchanged for American dollars, was also desired by the Vietnamese.

The process was rather simple. If a person exchanged MPC into piaster or vice versa through legal channels controlled by the United States government and its authorized agents, he received the official rate of exchange that fluctuated erratically day by day. If the same person took the MPC and exchanged it on the black market for piaster, he got double the piaster he would have received from the official exchange.

If he used American dollars on the black market money exchange, he received four or five times the going rate. Then he could turn around, go to an official money exchange booth, and turn all that piaster back into MPC. Then he would have at least double the buying power at the PX. There he could buy stereos, TV's, refrigerators, cigarettes, booze at ridiculously low prices.

He could either enjoy these PX purchases in Vietnam, ship them home, or, as some enterprising individuals did, walk out of the PX and sell them on the black market for 10 times what he paid for them. Of course, he would be paid in piasters, which he could either spend on the local economy or go to another official money exchange and trade for MPC.

It was relatively easy for an American to exchange piasters into MPC that would eventually, upon departure, be traded for American dollars without any trouble. That is, unless a person with a $6000 annual salary was trying to exchange $50,000 in MPC for greens.

To prevent someone from amassing a healthy nest egg of MPC, the military, without warning, would announce that new MPC's were being issued; and every authorized American in Vietnam had a matter of hours to change the old for the new. Red flags went up if someone tried to change too much at one time. Once new MPC was issued, the old stuff was worthless.

Let us return, back to Rob and the other big-time crooks who never had any difficulty dumping their MPC at any time, including during a surprise MPC changeover.

The only way to do a really large—over $10,000 at one time—exchange was through an organization, approved by the American military, that had a legitimate bank account that could accept MPC, piasters, and American dollars. USRO was just that sort of organization.

Each of the 14 USRO clubs had restaurants, money exchanges, travel agencies for GIs' R & R's, and concession stands selling gifts, jewelry, posters, and other trinkets. The clubs generated millions of dollars. Soldiers paid for goods at USRO clubs mostly with MPC, which was deposited in an account and counted as American dollars. Rob had absolute rule over five clubs and its five million dollars in all the various currencies.

Repeatedly he would "borrow" a few thousand in greenbacks or MPC, visit one of the leading Vietnamese or Chinese black market money exchangers—a general or district chief or mayor—and do a fast exchange. Then he would take his profit of piaster, change it at the USRO for MPC, deposit it in the USRO's MPC account, then write a check, in the exact amount he deposited, to Star Enterprises (his personal bank account) in Hong Kong for nonexistent products.

Nobody ever questioned the merchandise not arriving, because no one except Rob ever saw what checks were drawn. There were never any audits. There was never any problem, because the clubs in Vietnam were making so much money that the 14 clubs in the war zone were supporting activities and programs for USRO centers in Europe that were strapped for cash.

Rob loved when there was a surprise MPC change. He made even more money, because Vietnamese frantically tried to dump the funny money before it became useless. He gladly took it off their hands. For quite a hefty profit for himself. He simply rode it through the USRO account and it came out the other side in his hefty bank account in Hong Kong that siphoned it, as more time went by, to his account in Switzerland.

Rob saw nothing wrong with his activities during the Vietnam War. After all, he explained to himself, no one got hurt and no USRO funds were stolen, merely borrowed for a few hours at a time.

The only thing, he believed, that the currency manipulation hurt was a complicated, convoluted, and artificial Vietnamese economic system created by the U.S. government and run by stupid bureaucrats.

He scoffed at the idea that the VC were involved in the black market money exchange in order to ship American dollars to Hanoi, where the enemy then could use them to buy bullets and guns from China and neutral countries to kill American soldiers. Rob thought of himself as a patriot, a capitalist, and certainly no lover of Commies. He hated them almost as much as he hated those bureaucrats.

Hell, he had met plenty of pencil-pushers in Washington. All showoffs with their Ivy League diplomas hanging arrogantly on State Department walls.

Rob hated to see their Phi Beta Kappa keys swinging during doubles on tennis courts with snobby girls who went to Miss Porters or some other finishing school before heading off to Radcliffe and, he just knew it to be true, not shaving their legs. That really galled him.

Rob knew he was extraordinary, like the adventurers who panned for gold in the Klondike, or dug wells in Saudi Arabia with Getty, or plundered for treasures in the jungle with Cortez. He knew he was an important man who could buy and sell, 20 times over, all those frat boys in college who laughed at him.

When he left Vietnam, he would be on easy street. However, it was still too early to leave. It was becoming easier and easier to make bigger and bigger profits as more and more troops left. The Vietnamese were frantic to leave with them, and American dollars were becoming more and more valuable. Bribes were becoming more expensive.

No. Not yet; 1972 was still too soon to leave. Rob would stay longer. He would remain as long as the Ambassador. As long as Old Glory flew over the American Embassy in Saigon, he would stick around.

After that, well, Phoung and he could live quite comfortably in Hong Kong. Perhaps buy a bar like Rick's in *Casablanca*, one of his favorite movies. If that got boring after time, maybe the two of them could head off to another war. Rob knew for sure there would always be another war. Another war somewhere. Another golden opportunity for a smart guy like Rob Clawson.

THE VC COLONEL, A.K.A. HANNAH

It is quite amusing the recollections one has of war. Take for instance the time Jane Fonda came to Hanoi in 1971. Or was it 1972? No matter. During her visit, I was her personal guide. Oh, my word, let me assure you, I was surely honored to be chosen to squire her hither and yon around the capital.

You see, dear friends, I wore two hats, as most of us did, during the Revolution. One as a North Vietnamese high ranking official, escorting VIP's, that sort of thing. And the other as a Viet Cong Colonel to ascertain if our brothers and sisters in the South were performing their duties. Those Southerners, even our compatriots, did have a tendency to be a tad lazy, and it was my assignment to keep them on their toes, so to speak.

By the way, I usually introduce myself to journalists as a former VC—Americans do so love initials—Colonel. Much more romantic than being referred to as a former North Vietnamese high ranking official, which, frankly, gives the impression that I merely shuffled papers during the war of liberation. N'est pas? Do you not agree?

Where was I? I lost my train of thought. Oh, yes. Each person was most eager to show Miss Fonda every last piece of propaganda that we had painstakingly created. I was anticipating her shocked reaction at the "bombed baby milk factory," which before the B-52's dropped their loads was actually an ammunitions' foundry.

However, her mind kept drifting to other things besides the quote unquote destruction caused by you evil Americans.

The first day she arrived, she inquired as to how it was that most of the people she observed were in such tip-top shape. I believe, if memory serves me correctly, her exact word was "toned."

I turned on the television set in my office to let her view the exercise show that we broadcast for the civilians in North Vietnam who had desk occupations and scant time for exercise.

On the subject of work environments, I additionally had an office in the jungle, one in a rice paddy, and another in Saigon.

What was I speaking of? You know what they always say? The mind is the first go. Let me see. Ahhh! The exercise show! Voila!

The program had commenced in the mid-sixties when an unnamed nincompoop bureaucrat in Moscow had become drunk on entirely too, too much vodka and misread a requisition order form from the Bolshoi Ballet.

Incredibly, the troop of 50 dancers was sent 10,000 tights instead of the 100 it had requested. In fact, the ballerinas wanted 50 but, being well aware of how bureaucrats cogitate, decided to double the request, knowing full well that that is how the game is played. You never get what you petition, so ask for more and you will get what you really want. Quite simple, in fact.

Be that as it may, there was the Bolshoi Ballet with 10,000 tights and no storage space. There were many closets, but they were packed with male dancers. Ha! Ha! Please forgive an old man for a very naughty wisecrack.

Closet? Dancers? It is on the tip of my tongue. Tea? Tie? Tights! Yes! Yes! Tights! The ballerinas could not very well toss them in the rubbish can; consequently, they sent them to us, their poor cousins in North Vietnam.

When the Aeroflot plane landed in Hanoi with crates of supplies from our Russian benefactors, I breathed a sigh of relief. At the time, we were in desperate need of bullets, guns, grenades, plasma, bandages, toilet paper, the basic essentials to conduct a war.

When I personally opened the crates and discovered that they were ballet tights, I wept. Not only were we being undersupplied and missupplied by our allies, the Soviet Union and China, but I also knew for a certainty that on the other side of the country in Saigon big ships were being unloaded with unlimited supplies from America for our enemy, the corrupt South Vietnamese puppets.

Not only were those running dog simpletons receiving millions of dollars worth of military hardware, they were also being sent each and every luxury known to man and woman from that giant PX across the ocean, the U.S. of A. Perfume, televisions, refrigerators, fondue sets, you name it, they received it from their ally. It just was not fair, I thought, as I stared at those ridiculous ballet tights stacked in my office.

For a brief moment, I contemplated quitting and procuring a seat on the first plane to Paris and opening a restaurant. I certainly had enough leave time accumulated. In fact, I had not taken any time off since 1945 and there it was 1971.

Yet, mon cheri, as Edith Piaf, the little sparrow, and I both say, "Je Ne Regrette Rien." Absolutely none. The reunification of my country was my life, but ahhh! how marvelous it would have been to sip a cognac at an outdoor cafe on the Champs Elysees and observe the world strolling by.

Paris! To be away from the war and the heavy burdens of leadership. Oh, dear. I have once again lost my train of thought. I was verbalizing about 1971 and wishing to flee to Paree. Yes! Yes! Those damn ballet tights! Merde!

In any event, to make a lengthy story short, somebody, I do believe it was the Xerox repairman, who spent so much time in my offices that we were as close as brothers, came up with an idea to produce an exercise show and distribute the tights to all the office workers to wear as they drilled.

He noticed during his very busy war days that the desk warriors were becoming flabby, similar to the ones in Saigon that his cousin—an interpreter at the *Newsweek* office and one of our agents, a VC major, actually—noticed.

Of course, the difference between us in the North and our brothers and sisters in the South, patriots as well as traitors to the cause, was that we Northerners were not exercising enough. The Southerners were not getting any exercise and they were becoming addicted to American trash food.

There is an ancient Vietnamese saying: If someone hands you a mango, you should make mangoade. Needless to report, the TV exercise show was a resounding success.

In fact, I have to be honest and state that the star of the show was drop-dead gorgeous. I love that American colloquialism. Incidentally, if you ever visit Dallas tune into her program there. It is on the NBC affiliate. She was the reason our exercise show was such a hit. The music she selected was pure Motown and she insisted it be shown at the same time as the censored news, which nobody watched, on the American Forces Network, the only other station at the time in Vietnam.

I recollect as though it were only yesterday how Miss Fonda kept gushing over and over about what a marvelous idea the exercise program was.

She spent hours conversing with the film crew and our exercise star, Mai Lon, who at the time was using the Canadian Air Force high impact aerobics. On a side note, she had a cousin living in Saigon who was a cinema star. Her name, too, was Mai Lon. Since they could pass as twins, the girls loved trading places from time to time and having a little fun. They even mislead me, a trained intelligence officer, several times.

Frankly, I was rather annoyed at Miss Fonda for wasting my valuable propaganda time on the set of the exercise show. I had strict orders from General Giap, detailing what to divulge and what not to reveal to the famous American film star who, by the way, was not his favorite thespian.

General Giap preferred the splendid performances of John Wayne, a World War II draft dodger, who through exceptional acting convinced Americans that he was a war hero and a great patriot. Marvelous acting.

Mon generale and I adored all his movies, with the exception of his performance in the *Green Berets*. Mr. Wayne was definitely not suited for comedy.

However, I digress, as old men often do. Movie stars? Let me see? Let me see? I was speaking about the war, was I not?

Ahhh! There it is. Jane Fonda and her social call to Hanoi!

General Giap gave explicit instructions to show her bombed schools, damaged orphanages, and decimated hospitals that our student architects had built solely for her visitation.

Now that I contemplate it, perhaps her interest in the exercise show was a blessing in masquerade. She was so distracted that she never in effect looked closely at those hastily built props.

Be that as it may, after I literally dragged her away from the TV studio, I then escorted her to a cooperative food store to reveal to her how the typical North Vietnamese shops. Not the one for colonels and generals, but the one for the "nuye young," the man in the street.

My, my, my, the oh so serious actress, to use that quaint American phrase, went bananas over the nuoc mam bottles with Uncle Ho's picture on them. It was his family's recipe, and he carried the secret to the tomb with him.

I was pleased when she procured two cases of the substance. Most Americans despise nuoc mam, which is a delightfully pungent fish sauce used as a condiment to flavor rice dishes. It is truly scrumptious.

Yet, I became perplexed when she poured out the nuoc mam and mailed the empty bottles to friends in the States. I personally drove her the Hanoi post office. One carton of vacant containers bearing Ho's likeness was sent to Paul Newman, another to her uncle Orville, and two more to her distant cousins on her mother's side, Ben and Jerry in Vermont. Need I spell it out?

Oh, now that I recall, I never in a hundred lifetimes would have dreamt that Janie was such a clever business woman. Capitalist! I really thought she was merely a little fluff actress who had a funny hairdo—remember that foolish shag cut she wore back then?

Dreadful. Absolutely dreadful. I believed that all her energy was given to our cause. Live and learn, I always declare.

Enough about Miss Fonda. I have to chuckle when I read accounts of how devious we North Vietnamese and Viet Cong were depicted during the American war. I believe a more appropriate word would be "ingenious" or perhaps "flexible." Let me present you with some examples.

Once it was established by the American military and the international press that the Viet Cong wore black pajamas, we ceased sporting them altogether. Ahhh, yes, we desisted donning them, however, we continued manufacturing them and had black pajamas' stalls set up all over South Vietnam. In Danang, Cam Ranh, Chu Lai, everywhere.

There were even black pajamas' boutiques in Saigon and at the American military PX's. I would not be surprised if Miss Our-Good-Friend Fonda did not ship a few cases to boutiques in Beverly Hills, where they were regarded as radical chic. Similar to those belts constructed of cartridges worn at most of Truman Capote's parties back then.

You Americans are so, so strange. During the war, you were so absurdly capricious. Now, after these many years, you are so, so serious about that period. When speaking of the Vietnam War, Americans tend to whisper in hushed tones as though it were a sacred subject. As though there never existed any levity at all.

All that angst and beating of one's chest, intoning one mea culpa after another is not healthy for a nation such as yours. Dear, dear, people, you must learn to, as Confucius once said, lighten up. Oh, forgive an old man. I wander off the subject from time to time and wax philosophical.

As I was remarking, our side stopped wearing black pajamas but continued producing them. Why? you may ask. Quite simply, so that those cowardly devils, the South Vietnamese, would wear them and resemble us, the quote unquote enemy. The American military intelligence—an oxymoron if I ever heard one—ordered your brainwashed troops to shoot anyone in black pajamas.

We marketed with wild abandon around South Vietnam. If one bought an ice cream cone, one received a free pair of black pajamas. We sold hammocks at cost and then pitched in a free pair of black pajamas. There were inferno sales, pavement sales, going out of commerce sales, buy one receive one free sales.

Within a short time period, everyone all over South Vietnam was wearing black pajamas. Everybody, that is, but our people, the Viet Cong.

We wore American clothes that we ordered from the Sears and Roebuck catalogs when we could not steal enough from the PX's.

As a matter of fact, I still have my favorite ensemble—bell bottom pants, tie-dye shirt, and color coordinated headband—that I wore from time to time when I made my monthly visits to Saigon to check up on our agents.

Oh, yes, there you had the American military orders from the very top sent down to the GIs in the bush to shoot everybody wearing black pajamas because they were obviously the VC, the dreaded foe.

Please keep in mind that the brilliant General Westmoreland was in charge of the complete show. I jest about his intelligence, though, and cannot for the life of me deduce why dear Westy was put in charge. The only logical reason I can hypothesize is that the Pentagon desired, and planned, to lose the war. For what possible reason? Search me.

I hope God, Allah, whomever, forgives me someday for so many innocent lives wasted. Yet, I swear on Buddha's stomach that I never for one minute believed that such an imbecilic idea such as the "Ebony P.J.'s Operation" (the official code name) could actually succeed. But then again, we Hanoi planners invariably overestimated you Americans after viewing your World War II films. No offense intended.

The innocent, basically nonpolitical villagers in black pajamas were repeatedly fired upon, and their villages were burned to the ground. The ones who were not wearing black pajamas, because perchance they were being washed or mended, were relocated at gunpoint to strategic hamlets. And bam, bam, bam, un, deus, trois, before you can declare Winning Hearts and Minds, the villagers, who rarely supported the VC, began hating the Americans. Consequently, we indirectly won them over to our side. That which, of course, was the correct side, the noble faction.

My cousin Tran supervised the PR for the Ebony P.J.'s Operation. He was a scholar of advertising at Berkeley at the time we were fighting the French. As a matter of fact, his college chum was Bob Haldeman. You may remember him, even though most Americans believe that history is something that transpired five minutes ago.

Haldeman, as a few of the informed may recollect, was Nixon's pit bull in the White House. A deranged SS officer would have trembled in his presence. A formidable man, yet, Tran indisputably loved him as a brother. They spent so much time together that, well, there were some nasty rumors floating around campus.

During those idyllic college days, the two of them would sit up late at night, many nights, articulating their dreams and aspirations. Bob was actually the foremost influence in Tran's life, the inspiration for multitudinous campaigns we utilized in the war against you Americans. Jocular, is it not, how events transpire.

Bob instructed Tran innumerable times that by employing advertising and public relations' techniques, one could change the course of history. In case the event had already occurred, an inventive individual could merely put a different spin on it—what a picturesque phrase!—and revise and virtually change history.

What a skilled and diabolical man. Moreover, he is one of my favorite Republicans, next to Lee Atwater, of course. Now there was a genius. A classic American.

Indubitably, even back then in those pre-hippie college days at Berkeley, Haldeman maintained that by practicing the proper PR methodology he could even assist an ignoramus in being elected president.

Tran registered Bob's every word, each idea. They thoroughly deliberated how it was feasible to win a war without firing many shots or engaging in many battles. Haldeman tutored Tran that anything was feasible by applying adroit public relations and creative advertising.

Accordingly, all I can declare after these numerous years is: Thank you, Mr. Bob Haldeman. Thank you for dispatching Tran back to us with such efficacious skills to triumph in the American Vietnam War.

Wherever you are, and I do hope it is not exceedingly hot, you were worth a thousand Jane Fondas to our majestic Revolution.

I apologize once again for tottering off the topic. Now, where was I? Tran, was it? Clever, crafty Tran.

Tran was the PR specialist who also hatched the Coca Cola stand idea to assist in subsidizing our war effort.

The South Vietnamese, your allies I might add, by that time had Coca Cola stands in the bush, located where American patrols frequently passed.

Hence, we VC resolved to vault in with both feet when we surmised that there was a necessity. Quite simply, we charged normal Coca Cola stand prices, because your allies were extorting 10 times the average soda fountain cost.

It was outrageous. The VC soft drink stalls even gave away free popcorn with each six-pack sold. And, I hasten to amplify, besides overcharging the American grunts, the South Vietnamese Coca Cola stand merchants were not very polite to the GIs. Truly shameful business practice.

Imagine, if you might, a squad of miserable soldiers, marching for hours in insufferable heat in the jungle, attempting to avoid land mines and serpents, being nibbled by mosquitoes the size of birds, in essence being distressed. Then, out of the blue, these wretched boy warriors stumble upon a South Vietnamese Coca Cola stand in the midpoint of nowhere.

Picture six anguished, dying-of-thirst kid GIs holding M-16 rifles, grenade and rocket launchers, and hearing some hoodlum in stolen American clothes, informing them, "No five dollah, no Coca Cola, Joe."

Yet, under those grueling circumstances, the American boys, for the most part, were honorable enough to actually pay for a refreshment that they could have merely taken by force.

Usually, the grunts guffawed and sauntered away. However, more times than not, the Americans tossed a dollar's worth of piaster or MPC down and grabbed a Coke. Even by doing so, they were nevertheless overpaying by at least 75 cents.

Ahh, and the South Vietnamese, those rip-off artists, wondered why the American soldiers hated them so much.

Here and now, you are doubtless questioning why our side decided to get into the Coca Cola stand business and be moderately fair to the GIs. In fact, it is quite simple to explain, really.

It is true that we desired the Americans to turn against the South Vietnamese. However, we did not want them to abhor all Vietnamese. Aware that the war would eventually end, we established our own Coca Cola stands to neutralize the bad, and getting worse, situation in the jungle.

I am not attempting to give you the impression that it was all for altruistic reasons. On the contrary, we made a bloody fortune merchandising pop to soldiers in the bush and at fair market prices, I might add.

Tran's idea was to earn money without gouging, then to casually eavesdrop on conversations for our military advantage.

Beaucoup money we did earn. Cool hot tempers in the jungle, we certainly did. However, we not ever acquired any serious intelligence information while, to employ a delightful American colloquialism, shooting the breeze with the customers. The only subjects the GIs conversed about were music and broads. Broads and music.

Oh, I forgot, we moreover charged a penny deposit. The soldiers habitually walked away drinking the Coca Cola and then, when finished, tossed the container away a few feet from the stand. Cadres collected them later.

As a matter of historical fact, do you know of those Vietnamese old ladies who collect bottles and cans in American cities? In fact, most of them in their youth were VC who gathered them in the jungle. Back then, during the war, we had platoons of girls collecting cans. That was their sole assignment as patriots. Each empty was a penny more for the revolution.

Furthermore, I might add, the Coca Colas were pilfered from the PX by VC clerks who labored there or by our agents who unloaded ships at the docks in Saigon.

Also, a few enterprising GIs, who toiled at the docks and on the ships, stole them then sold them to the black market dealers. We controlled nearly all of the black market operations in South Vietnam, too. So you see, one does not have to be a swine to earn a good profit.

To be perfectly honest, I unceasingly felt slightly sorry for those young soldiers who, after seeing their comrades step on land mines and punji sticks, would come upon a South Vietnamese, supposedly their ally, trying to extort $5 for sugared water.

Our cowardly brothers in the South were a bit too avaricious for my blood. Everything to them was the short term profit, whereas, we in the North and our VC agents had more patience and viewed the long range effect for all Vietnamese.

To our side, it was a war to reunify Vietnam. I do not know what the war meant to the South Vietnamese.

Regardless, enough about those stupid Southerners. Let me see? I was vocalizing about how intelligent our side was. Yes. There is no doubt you Americans picked the incorrect horse to bet on. But enough gloating. Truly, it is so impolite of me.

Oh, yes, yes, I must relate to you of the time I was watching a John Wayne cowboy movie with my staff and noticed trading posts. I do not remember whose idea it was, but I decided it was an excellent notion to establish trading posts throughout South Vietnam to earn money for our cause. The American GIs treasured VC souvenirs—flags, sandals, pith helmets, ears, well, dried apricots soaked in ketchup.

Combat soldiers would stumble upon our trading posts while on patrol. They would trade part of their 50 pounds of supplies for a VC souvenir. Afterwards, they would barter with the soldiers in the rear for articles much more valuable, such as hot meals and clean socks. There were also GI friends that we used as sales representatives. We discovered rather early that noncombat soldiers just loved war souvenirs. Much more so than the fighting men.

We traded for blankets, food, ponchos, insect repellent, snake bite medicine, periodicals, Coca Cola, materials that our side required desperately. The Coca Cola we resold at our jungle stands. For what it is worth, our soldiers adored reading *Playboy* and *Mad Magazine*.

What other remembrances are there with regards to the war? Oh, yes. Bob Hope. I had tickets to all the Bob Hope shows in Vietnam, from the initial one to the last. I acquired them through barters at the jungle trading posts. I never attended, because I would trade them with my superiors. We did do personal barters, too, you must be aware.

I will share a little known fact, something that never is recorded in history books, since historians obtain their information from articles written by reporters. Inasmuch as the journalists rarely relate the truth, history is distended with falsehoods. Nevertheless, I am digressing.

The beforehand discussion concerned Bob Hope. Quite so, we were going to release 500 POW pilots if Bob Hope would do a show at the Hanoi Hilton. However, we insisted on employing our own stage hands and lighting people and best boys and first grips. Our theater people required the practice for after the war when our movie and television industries could function again.

But alas, the American stage hands', electricians', and best boys' unions vehemently refused to allow us to use nonunion workers. Consequently, the show did not go on.

Repeatedly we sent offer after offer for a production in exchange for prisoners, but negotiations kept breaking down. Because of those damn unions.

By Jove, if Reagan did anything right, it was attempting to bust those unions.

Judiciously, we caved in and applied for union cards; but, by the time they arrived from Hollywood, the Paris Peace Accords were signed. Authentic story.

You must understand, my friends, even in a war there are many light moments. Take for instance that evening, one I shall never forget, when I was sitting alone in my jungle office, or was it my rice paddy one, no matter. Nevertheless, there I was pondering how much I missed my loving wife in Hanoi and my dutiful son in Saigon and my smart-as-a-whip nephew at Harvard when the phone rang.

"Merde!" I groaned. I was sure it was war business as usual and almost did not answer it. After about 20 rings, I surmised it had to be important. With trepidation and weariness, I picked up the phone.

Aware I am that this is going to sound farfetched, but I swear on Lenin's grave that it was Martha Mitchell, the American attorney general's spouse telephoning from Washington, D.C.

Difficult to believe, but she was striving to get through to a journalist friend of hers who was in Vietnam on a fact-finding trip. The wires somehow became crossed and there I was, not far from the DMZ, conversing with the wife of a member of President Nixon's cabinet.

Initially, I thought it was a practical joke and someone on my staff was pulling my leg. I am just mad about American phrases, as you must be able to ascertain. Nonetheless, in war there are so many, many pranks and highjinks.

There was a loony-tunes disc jockey on Hanoi Radio who would call people while he was on the air and pretend he was someone famous. The fellow was a card, a real joker, and I listened to his program all the time. He did remarkable impressions—the Duke, Lyndon Johnson, Bette Davis, Nixon. If you are ever lucky enough to be in Cleveland, check out his program. He does the early morning commute on the FM band.

Where was I? Yes! I remember so vividly. I was being attentive and going along with the gag, but the more I listened, the more I realized it truly was Martha Mitchell. I can not recall what she said precisely that made me think it was she, but after 40 years in North Vietnamese, Viet Minh, and Viet Cong intelligence, I suppose a few smarts sunk in, so to speak in your vernacular.

I am aware that sounds arrogant, and please do forgive an old man's pride. But, to be accurate, compared to the Russian and American intelligence communities, a village of monkeys would appear to be geniuses. I do not intend to be rude, merely honest.

Nevertheless, I am rambling on again, exactly as Martha Mitchell did that first time well over 20-odd years ago. The more she chirped on and on and on, the more I liked her. What a sweetheart and funny, too. Delightful without even knowing how enchanting she was. What a gal, to employ one of Ho's best-admired phrases.

Double M was calling from her bathroom phone, and I could indeed hear the water running in the tub. She had informed her husband John that she was going to be in the bathroom awhile, because she desired to take a long soak.

For the initial few minutes, after I realized it was not a practical joke being broadcast on "Hanoi Antics Live" and it really was the American attorney general's wife, I took notes. What a marvelous windfall that she accidentally reached me, a North Vietnamese official and VC Colonel. It was similar to dongs from Heaven.

However, and you are not going to believe this, after a while I discontinued jotting in my notebook and decided to divulge the truth of who I was. She seemed so innocent and so, I do not know, so unRepublican, with nary a despicable, vicious bone in her body.

I did not want her to get into trouble for giving any information to her government's enemy. Not that she was, mind you.

Of what intelligence significance is the knowledge that John thought she had the cutest bum in Washington and that he could not wait until she grew older and reached her sexual peak?

People have frequently said that I have a soft spot in my heart for women. Go ahead, call me an incurable romantic, I do not care. I am guilty as charged of being a sentimental old fool. Consequently, I tried to explain to her, as clearly as I could, that she had accidentally phoned a Hanoi area code and not Saigon.

Then, she began rattling on about her dearly departed, but not forgotten by one and all, Aunt Hannah, who, by the way, was a saint. Martha reminisced about her aunt's fabulous and "yummy to the tummy" chocolate chip cookies. Her exact words, I assure you. She kept remarking that it was too, too funny that "Hannah" was a man's name in Vietnam.

I swear on each of my ancestors' graves that I attempted to explain the truth. Yet, I could barely get a word in edgewise. Moreover, I was chuckling most of the time. She was more humorous than Thuy Ky Dangerfield, the host of "Hanoi Antics Live."

Be that as it may, we chatted for well over two hours about a hundred little things—those yucky Democrats, Wayne Newton, miniskirts, how Alexander Graham Bell should be canonized, you know, typical small talk between strangers becoming fast friends. I would have hated to see her phone bills.

Before long, I heard quite a racket on her end of the line. It turns out it was John banging on the bathroom door, bellowing that she was going to shrivel up like a prune if she lingered in the tub any longer.

She whispered that she thought John was getting suspicious—he forbade her to talk on the phone without his approval, the Fascist, so she had better ring off. And, she added, when I was in D.C. to "please, please, pretty please stop by for some tea and a chat."

Ahh, she was as a tonic for my soul and spirit, a weary and very tired old war horse. I slept like an infant that night and recalled the phone conversation upon waking. Truly, I could not stop grinning.

I thought about how much my wife would also enjoy Martha, so I phoned my better half that morning and related to her the previous night's conversation.

The Mrs. was thrilled because she knew all about Martha Mitchell from reading *Time* and *Newsweek* articles. My sweetie was excited that I was acquainted with someone in Washington with a heart, as well as a little pizzazz, ever since the Republicans assumed control.

As I dwell on the past, I remember it was my spouse who predicted that the war would last as long as it did. She concluded that the Pentagon officials, the arms' dealers, and war profiteers were all Republicans. War was business, big business, and only a fool would want to stop the profits from flowing into their coffers. Smart woman, my wife.

When, playing the Devil's Advocate, I countered her argument with, "Do you not think those people care about the soldiers who are dying and being wounded?"

Her retort was, "Oh, Honey, grow up. Do you honestly think those big shots even know any family or friend with a child fighting in Vietnam or even care about them. No, it will go on until the cash cow runs dry."

Wise woman, my wife.

Where was I before I digressed? Oh, yes, my wife suggested that we send a little present to Martha, a small token of friendship, as she put it.

"We'll need all the friends we can muster after the war ends, and anyway," she added, "Martha boosted your morale more than I have seen it raised in ages."

I requested that she find something nice from the both of us and send it as soon as possible.

As luck would have it, it just so happened she was on her way to Saigon with certain Russian wives who were vacationing in Hanoi—really freeloading if the truth be known. They were surprised to learn that my wife journeyed to Saigon frequently.

My missus sent Martha a lovely vase from the Cham Dynasty that she acquired from a Saigon auction house owned by one of our agents. He let her have it for a carton of American cigarettes and a promise from me of a medal and a promotion. She signed the card "From Hannah and His Wife" and affixed our son's Saigon address.

A few weeks later, Martha posted a beautiful handwritten six-page thank you letter to me in care of my son.

Alas, instead of tarrying for the letter to reach me through the American military postal system, the APO, in Danang as I invariably received my mail, I resolved to mix business with indulgence and to take a swift mid-week trip to Saigon.

I donned a South Vietnamese colonel's uniform and gathered the proper identification supplied to me by an American friend of mine, a private, actually an actor in civilian life, who worked in an Army printing office in Saigon.

He did not know my true identity. He believed I was an actor in Saigon who enjoyed playing practical jokes, as he did.

Some of you reading this, who may have spent time in Saigon during the war, may remember the famous American General Gutenberg. I may be disappointing you, but the illustrious General Gutenberg was none other than my young friend playing a part. Has he related his story in any publications yet? I venture to guess that he has many unique adventures to recount.

Dear me, dear me. What in the world was I reminiscing about? It will come. Cameron Mitchell? Thomas Mitchell? I am merely being silly. As I was mentioning, I was on my way to Saigon to retrieve the letter from Martha Mitchell.

Dressed appropriately in a South Vietnamese colonel's uniform and armed with enough identification to choke a water buffalo, I drove to Danang, via the Ho Chi Minh Trail.

I departed early, before commuter traffic.

In any event, I have to chuckle when I hear New Yorkers complain about five o'clock traffic jams. You have not seen clogged highways unless you have traveled the Ho Chi Minh Trail on a holiday weekend. Unbelievable.

That is why I always launched my trips down the Trail mid-week.

Then, I cut across to Danang and caught an American C-130 headed for Tan Son Nhut airport.

Nearly every single Vietnamese who toiled at the Danang and

the Tan Son Nhut airports worked for me. In which case, we could have destroyed the terminals in a second.

However, it would have been similar to murdering the goose that laid the golden eggs. Assuredly, it would have been a hassle for us North Vietnamese and VC to move around Vietnam without the aid of American planes and terminals.

In addition, we were aware that once we won the war, we would have marvelous airports in place for the tourist trade that was sure to come flocking in. We were counting on the radical chic crowd who would covet a destination off the beaten track. I would not be surprised to learn that our good friend Jane Fonda, and I am being facetious, has tours departing Kennedy as I speak. Oh my, I do digress. Where was I? Oh, yes, on a flight to Saigon to retrieve that letter from Martha Mitchell.

The minute the plane landed and I was outside the terminal, one of my best agents in Saigon was curbside with his pedicab waiting to whisk me to Mimi's Bar downtown.

I recall that ride as though it were only yesterday. I resembled James Bond, as we passed my colleagues on the way to Mimi's that day. I was self-satisfied as a peacock that we had infiltrated Saigon as well as we did.

As a matter of fact, 2034 VC agents did nothing else throughout the day but cruise around Saigon on motor scooters, tying up traffic. That is all they were ordered to do, merely gum up the works and slow down the American tanks and jeeps.

Sometimes, though, they felt obliged to make citizen's arrests of the South Vietnamese cowboys who rode the streets stealing cameras from GIs. Those little juvenile delinquents were messing up everything.

Our agents were under orders to annoy the Americans, not to make them hate the Vietnamese people, North or South.

The South Vietnamese were so utterly contemptuous of Americans that it was giving the whole country a bad name. Please remember, I informed you, our side was deeply concerned for the long range effect. When the war ended, we desired to be in the same situation as the Japanese and Germans were after World War II.

If only the Southerners had been a tad more courteous, that annoying embargo would have been lifted earlier. Still and all, I suppose it is too late to weep over spilt milk.

Be that as it may, when I arrived at Mimi's Bar those many years ago, which, by the way, was a VC way station and a haunt for American print journalists, who did not have an inkling of its true purpose, I tore open the letter and read with delight about all the gossip in Washington.

Martha, the gracious dear, also sent along her bathroom phone number in case I ever had the desire to phone and ignore the war for a moment.

To this day, I am not even certain if she was aware which side was which. During our initial conversation, I asked her something about the North and the South and she poo pooed it with, "Oh, Hannah, I've always been such a ninny with directions."

I reread the letter and on a whim decided to ring up and say hello. Mimi guided me to her private office, dialed the number that allowed her into the American military phone system, the autovan, and the GI operator—her favorite one was Teddy—patched me through to Washington.

Mimi, by the way, was not only a damn good soldier, a highly decorated VC major, but she was also remarkable at pinching pennies. And, I venture to add, she concocted one mean Singapore Sling that she had learned from one of the American generals she dated.

Martha was engaging in a bubble bath when I got through to her, after attempting for well over three hours and four Singapore Slings. War can be hell on a liver.

During those busy-signal hours, Teddy, the GI operator that Mimi adored, a Polish kid from Wisconsin, and I became acquainted. Say hello for me if you ever see him. And please do relate to him that Mimi would send her best, too, I am sure. She is still spunky Mimi. After marrying one of her generals, she moved to Fiji and opened a Club Med there. I receive an occasional Tet card.

When I finally got through (and thank God I did when I did, because one more of Mimi's specialties and I would have been three pillowcases to the wind), I informed Martha that I was phoning from Mimi's Bar, a place that she would most assuredly love. So Bohemian. So laid-back. So groovy.

I close my eyes and view and hear it all now: bath water running, Martha chirping, a *Playboy* photographer sizing up one of the waitresses (a VC lieutenant), two *Washington Post* reporters tossing darts at a Spiro Agnew dart board, Edwin Starr belting out my favorite song, "War," on the juke box, and Mimi attempting to yank the phone from me with pleas of, "Let me talk, please let me talk to her, Hannah,"

Yes, that is correct. Mimi began referring to me as Hannah, and the nickname stuck. Imagine, there she was, my best agent, stomping her feet and pouting to speak with Martha.

I detested it when Mimi became petulant, hence, I gave her the phone.

Surprise, surprise. Martha charmed Mimi right out of her Nancy Sinatra boots and even invited my best agent to Washington.

Truly, I must admit that I was a tiny bit jealous. After all, I was the one who had discovered Martha, and I suppose, well, yes, I was as a little kid who wanted her all to myself.

Before I had another chance to speak with Martha, Mimi rang off with promises of visiting "real soon."

It seems that the Mitchell's maid was banging at the door, screaming that Martha had a call from Helen Thomas of UPI on her bedroom phone and a call from Pat Nixon on the one in the kitchen and John was fuming in the foyer because they were an hour late for a reception at the White House honoring South Vietnam's President Thieu.

That explained Mimi's comment of "Oh, yeah, I know him,

and Martha, between you and me and the lamppost, he's a real dick."

The next week Mimi rang me in the rice paddy to inform me about the packages Martha had sent us.

Mimi was ecstatic with the purple psychedelic princess phone for her private office in the pub, and I was tickled pink with my present, a photograph of another famous dick.

The picture was inscribed, "To Hannah, Martha Mitchell's cherished and dear friend. Good luck in all your endeavors and may God always be on your side. With sincere sincerity, Richard Milhouse Nixon." I keep it on the wall next to the signed *Barbarella* poster.

So I suppose, my dear friends, after these many years, I could sum up my feelings about the American Vietnam War quite simply. And that is to declare: You Americans are the best enemy any country could ask for. Buddha bless you all.

THE AMERICAN JOURNALIST'S DEATHBED CONFESSION

I would not be telling these stories, but since I am dying, well, I regard this time in my life, what is left of it, as a deathbed confession. Similar to Lee Atwater's apology to Mike Dukakis for dirty campaigning. Oh, God, what I would not have given to have been around during Nixon's last minutes on this earth. But then I guess I'm rambling, aren't I? That's what happens with brain tumors, you know.

Let me see, the subject was Vietnam. Oh, how I wish I had written the truth instead of what everyone expected a war correspondent to write. But we cannot turn back the clock, and what is past is past. All water under the bridge.

To sum it up, almost everything was a lie. Westy lied to LBJ, who lied to the American people. The lieutenants lied to the captains, who lied to the majors, who lied to the colonels, who lied to the generals, who lied to the Pentagon. Well, you get the picture. But I'm sad to confess that the biggest pack of liars was us journalists. Or is it we journalists? Never could get that right.

Considering what I just said, nonetheless, I have a hell of a lot of fond memories of my assignment in the combat zone.

Like every other reporter, I wanted to see the "real war" right away. You know, bombs bursting in air and all that red-blooded macho stuff. For that reason, my first week in country I arranged to go out on patrol with a bunch of grunts.

The night before the search and destroy mission, I stayed up late with the squad and smoked pot. Cambodian Gold, actually. In between tokes and uncontrollable giggles, the guys tried to explain to me how things really were in the bush, but I kept interrupting with John Wayne-type questions.

"How many of the enemy did you kill?"

"What's it feel like to slit a man's throat?"

They listened to my questions, but never answered the blood and guts' ones. What they did get across to me, though, was that no matter what their mission was, all they wanted to do was stay alive.

Before falling asleep, they promised that when I went out with them the next morning I would see things I never dreamed about. Things I never read about, too.

"F_ _king A!" they bellowed in unison.

Great! Pulitzer, here I come! I imagined severed VC ears, wounded men writhing in pain, unbelievable heroics, you know, John Wayne stuff.

Even though I was excited, I was terrified of having nightmares throughout the night and confided my fears to Digger, the squad leader.

Digger. What can I say about Digger? Let's put it this way: If you had a daughter, Digger would be your worst nightmare of a son-in-law. The guy was scary as hell. Yeah, mean as a rattlesnake, I thought, until we shotgunned some more weed as a nightcap.

It was late and the other guys were sprawled all over the hootch. Music was blaring, some Hendrix tape. Empty potato chip bags were scattered helter-skelter. Black lights were adding to the surreal scene. And there I was, bonding with the meanest son of a bitch in all of Nam, my John the Baptist, the guy who was going to christen me into the horrors of war. Grass has a way of exaggerating a thought and turning mismatched strangers into intimate friends.

Exhaling a barrelful of smoke, Digger explained that he was as cherry as they come once and followed orders like a good soldier, an obedient robot.

His C.O. at base, a real dickhead by the name of Major Holloway, would order his men out on patrol without an objective except to look for the enemy, anyone wearing black pajamas.

All they found in the areas Major Holloway sent them to were punji sticks and land mines and old villagers too weak to even pick up a BB gun.

Digger had seen over 20 men die during his two tours in Vietnam. He forgot their names once they bought the farm, and he became so hardened that it even scared him.

Then, while listening to Jon Lennon sing "Give Peace a Chance" one night, he decided to smarten up, because that was the only way to keep his men and himself alive.

I wasn't sure what he was trying to tell me. By then, I was so stoned that all my concentration was focused on searching the hootch for junk food. I had the munchies something fierce.

After finding, and finishing, four bags of M & M's, a jar of pimento-stuffed olives, a sent-from-home tin of chocolate chip cookies, and 10 cans of cold C-rations, I asked him to remind me what we had been talking about.

He finally remembered himself that it was about staying alive on patrols. After polishing off the crumbs in the scattered potato chip bags and being reminded again of the topic at hand, I asked for an explanation of such a cryptic comment.

His answer was solemn. "Wait till tomorrow. You'll see how squads stay alive."

The next morning we trooped out of base camp. Digger, walking point, was followed by Red, Smitty, Junior, Horseface, Shimmy, and me, Ink, the nickname the guys gave me.

We ventured out about two klicks and stopped in a clearing that sort of appeared out of nowhere. I quickly glanced around and spotted a makeshift latrine and shower near a small stream.

There was a storage hut that I went into and inspected. It

contained a bookcase filled with the complete *Encyclopedia Britannic*, most of Shakespeare's plays, over 200 paperback novels—ranging from *The Canterbury Tales* to *Love Story*. There were chess and checker boards, Monopoly, Clue, canned peaches, comic books, cleaning supplies, soap powder, and an old French iron, the kind you put hot charcoals in.

Next to the storage hut there was a tiny thatched-roofed hootch. When I opened the door to see what in the world could be in it, an old Vietnamese lady started screaming at me for waking her up. It turns out she was a mamasan the guys hired during patrols to do their laundry.

For every three-day patrol, the guys paid her what other mamasans made in a month, plus free room and board. It was a sweet gesture, but I was somewhat surprised when Junior explained why the guys felt sorry for the old hag.

She was alone and penniless—they found her begging near the base—since her sons had gone off to war. Touching, right? Yeah, well, her six sons were fighting for the VC.

"Shit, man," Horseface explained, "it don't matter which side they're on, they're still soldiers. And soldiers is soldiers and we needs to take care of each other."

I could not believe my ears and asked, "Who informed you that her sons were VC?"

"She did, when we offered her the job," he shot back with a hurt look. Then added, "Since she's been with us, nobody, but nobody has surprised us. Think that's a coincidence, or what, smart guy?" He had a point there.

I looked around at the guys, who just a moment ago I thought of as very, very stupid. Their collective IQ had shot up hundreds of points in a few minutes.

And there, over there near the shed, was the dame that Diogenes was searching for, the old toothless mamasan pressing khaki pants with a rusty iron left over from the last occupying force. I realized then and there: the more you know, the more you realize how little you know.

While I was examining the well-stocked camp site, the grunts were setting up two large tents that had been stacked in the storage hut. There were also pillows, sheets, blankets, and cots.

I could not believe my eyes.

Shimmy came over to me with an outstretched hand holding a J and gave me the skinny on what was going on. First of all, he reminded me of the plush apartments the civilians had in Saigon and of the great restaurants we all went to. He was right, they were first class by anyone's standards and heavenly compared to what the guys had in the bush.

I felt like an ignorant schoolboy as he rattled on, trying to explain how things really were in the bush and not how the journalists wanted them to be.

Grunts like them had to go out into the jungle to search for the invisible enemy. They had to walk in unbearable heat, all the while terrified of every step they took for fear of being blown to bits, or worse, surviving the land mines but minus limbs. And then there were the snipers who fired at them from tree limbs and tunnel entrances.

"No sir," Shimmy said, "it just doesn't make sense to patrol this late in the war."

It was 1971 and just about everybody with half a brain knew what a waste the whole thing was.

Shimmy went on to explain how the guys felt that it made better sense to go on patrol and stop at a safe distance from the firebase and set up camp.

"Plus," as Red, who wanted to study accounting after his tour, pointed out, "it's patriotic not to waste taxpayers' money by needlessly firing bullets."

The way they saw it, they could set up camp, then go back to base after three days with clean uniforms, spit polished boots, and alive.

To kill time and not people while out in the field, they played cards, honed their chess skills, wrote letters home to their buddies, telling them of the hell of war and making them green with envy for getting deferments.

Smitty, especially, liked to rub it in to his right-wing college pals back home who supported the Vietnam War but found convenient ways of staying out of it themselves. He peppered his letters to them with quotes about the summer soldiers and the sunshine patriots and excerpts of Henry V's speech to his men on St. Crispin's Day. You know, "We few, we happy few, we band of brothers...And gentlemen... now a-bed shall think themselves accursed they were not here, and hold their manhoods cheap whiles any speaks that fought with us..."

Smitty, who had flunked out of high school, had been in-country for nine months and had read most of Tolstoy, Ibsen, and Shakespeare while out on patrol.

Horseface taught himself crocheting and was on his seventh afghan.

Junior from Brooklyn had quite an impressive fauna collection.

The squad just wanted to develop their hobbies and roast a few marshmallows, then go back to base camp, make up an enemy body count, and keep Major Holloway happy and off their backs while they crossed off dates on their short-timers' calendars.

Digger explained it well, "If we actually did the job we were ordered to do, we'd get ourselves injured or killed and still maybe, just maybe, kill one VC when our quota was 20. And who's to say it wouldn't be an innocent gook farmer or other civilian that we wasted. Christ, only an idiot could believe the VC actually wore black pajamas.

"No sir, this is the best thing all around. Like summer camp, except the tall tales we bring back are better than truth. No one gets hurt, the Vietnamese stay happy and safe, we stay happy and safe, the major sends the colonel our fake body count, who doubles it when he sends it to the general, who doubles it before he sends it to Washington. The major is thrilled with 20 confirmed dead, the colonel is thrilled with 40 confirmed dead, the general is thrilled with 80 confirmed dead, and the Pentagon analysts, seeing that one squad on a three-day patrol killed 160 enemy soldiers, is convinced that we're winning the war."

As a journalist I felt it was my duty to the Fourth Estate to write the truth but, hell, those smart bastards would have been court-marshaled and the major would have been replaced by one with a higher IQ and the next set of grunts would have to pay the price with their blood.

Yet, I could not very well get back to Saigon and tell anyone the truth about what actually happened on patrol. I didn't want to get the grunts in trouble, and besides it was tres chic to out-war story other journalists.

I did not have a clue what I was going to write and frankly was a bit disappointed at not dodging bullets and all that other stuff I imagined while sipping gin and tonics on the Continental Palace's outdoor verandah in safe Saigon.

After the guys and I polished off a great meal of beans and franks, spam, and canned peaches, and were passing around a joint, waiting for Smitty to finish toasting the s'mores, the guys told me war stories of patrols and firefights before Major Holloway showed up to shape them into a better fighting unit.

Under their previous C.O., who didn't give three shits for counting bodies, they each had experienced real jungle fighting and hand-to-hand combat. Their objective back then was protecting the base and surrounding villages.

I was mesmerized by their accounts of sneaking up and slashing throats of VC cadre who were spraying AK-47 bullets into villages, being surrounded by a company of North Vietnamese regulars, then narrowly escaping by calling in air strikes. Back then, they could do their job of fighting a war without worrying about arithmetic.

My bladder was practically exploding before I could finally excuse myself and get up to find relief at the latrine near the stream.

At last, after crossing and recrossing my legs for an hour, I went to take a piss. On the way there, I tripped over a banyan tree root and cut my foot. Red, the medic, bandaged it and suggested that I explain the foot injury in a more manly way. He suggested I say that a VC surprised me. Reacting with lightning speed, I wrestled him to the ground, took away his AK 47 and broke his neck, thereby saving the squad who were still asleep.

The guys to a man agreed that it was a pretty good story, and Digger added that I should include that I got the knife wound when the VC knifed me in the last moments of his life.

I looked around at all the guys hovering over me as I rested against that damn banyon tree. I felt as if I was in a writers' conference creating a John Wayne movie. But it did sound like a pretty damn good story to me, too.

And the icing on the cake was supplied by Mamasan, who after listening to us make up the story, ran into the storage shed and came out with a bag of dried apricots. I was stuffed from dessert and declined her offer.

The guys started laughing and then told me that the dried apricots looked like VC ears, and that they wore necklaces of them to scare the FNG's—the f_ _kin' new guys, the cherries, the newbies.

Horseface got out his needle and thread and made me a necklace of one dried apricot. Honest to God, it even looked like a shriveled ear to me and I had seen Mamasan tear open the bag of apricots with my own eyes.

After three fun-filled days—sort of like summer camp—we made it back to base camp, with me hobbling on one foot, supported by Digger. I was filthy since I had no change of clothes as the squad had stored in the shed.

I asked Mamasan if she would mind washing my clothes, but her loyalty was to the squad and she made it very clear that their gear came first. By the time she finished their laundry, they would be back for more. She was up to her slanted eyeballs with enough dirty skivvies.

We reported the enemy killed at 21 and repeated the story of how I was injured. The major puked when he saw the apricot soaked in ketchup hanging around my neck.

"Christ," I thought, "this is going to work after all!"

The guys, God bless them, played up the fake story of my saving them while they slept. I almost started to believe it myself, especially when the cherries walked by me with stars in their eyes like I was John F_ _king Wayne.

To tell you the truth, I felt exactly like John Wayne.

You know, of course, that the only war heroics that the Duke ever experienced was in the movies. He had a deferment during World War II and never went into the service. He made films in Hollywood during the Big One.

And yet, when young men during the Vietnam War thought of war heroes they thought of John Wayne, a reel celluloid hero, a made-up hero, just like I was. So, yes, you can say, I was just like John Wayne and not be misstating the truth.

My standing in the eyes of the major was raised a bit after he upchucked his lunch over the dried apricot, but he kept shaking his head, claiming how surprised he was at my bravery, me being Jewish and everything. I'm telling you, the guy was a prince, with not one prejudiced bone in his Wonder bread-fed body. The lifer prick.

Major Holloway may have been surprised at my bravery, but he was not surprised that I was dirty after getting in from a patrol. He said I was not cut out to be a soldier and would never be able to cut the mustard in his man's clean and orderly and disciplined army.

After another slow motion and munchie-filled night with the squad, the next morning I caught a chopper back to Saigon, went straight to the newsroom—dirty, smelly—and filed my story gleaned from the real war stuff the guys had told me around the camp fire.

Of course, I included the item about my killing the VC and saving the squad. Smitty had made up some great quotes and plagiarized a few from Shakespeare to add a little spice to the news story.

"Hell, no one reads the Bard, anyway. So no one will notice," Smitty convinced me.

That story, which was picked up by the wire services, ran in every major newspaper in the country. Jesus H. Christ, it almost won me a Pulitzer; and I was besieged by offers to turn it into a novel, you know, Norman Mailerish or Hemingwayish.

I tossed it around for a few years and even discussed collaborating with Smitty, but you know how it goes, there was always another war for me to cover and Smitty was too busy as a history professor at Yale.

As a matter of fact, I learned from Digger not long ago that Smitty may turn his Vietnam War lectures into a PBS documentary. He will no doubt win a Peabody for what will be perceived as facts, when he should be awarded the Pulitzer for fiction.

But to quote Smitty, "History is fiction and fiction is history."

I guess his John Wayne explanation is apt. "John Wayne pretends to be a war hero. John Wayne is believed to be a war hero. War heroes are patriots. John Wayne is big. Therefore, John Wayne is a big patriot." Smitty, if you're reading this now, did I get it right?

Well, anyway, back to 1971 in Vietnam.

During those weeks and months after my story hit the newsstand, I promenaded around Saigon, proud as a rooster, limping on a cane, even after my foot was as good as new.

Journalists on fact-finding trips to Vietnam sought me out for the truth about patrolling in the bush.

Young journalism students sent me fan letters, gushing about how much they wanted to be just like me. It was a heady time. I almost started to believe my own stories about my courage.

Still, I was somewhat relieved when Vietnamese maids pulled me aside and whispered, "I give you real VC ear for bag of dried apricots."

I do not know what got into me, maybe it was Smitty, who

used to visit me in Saigon, telling me that he would bet everything he owned that the NVA and VC were patrolling just like his squad.

I argued till I was blue in the face and finally took up the challenge, mainly because Smitty would not stop badgering me with taunts of "Ink, you're a chicken-shit phony."

I decided to prove my bravery, as well as my point, and cast my fate to the wind and go out on a North Vietnamese patrol. First thing I had to do, of course, was to make contact with the enemy in some way.

Smitty suggested that I ask the people who always knew where the action was whether it was in New York, London, or Hong Kong. A cab driver.

He was right on beam, but the person I always asked for anything—a good barbershop, a great prostitute, potent marijuana, what illegal money exchanges were giving the best deals at any given hour of the day, anything at all—was a cyclo driver.

In case you don't know, a cyclo is a motorized pedicab or rickshaw. Like a motorcycle, being driven by Evil Knivel, pulling a chair built for two.

My favorite cyclo driver was a guy by the name of Tran. Tran seemed to know everything there was to know in Saigon.

I found him at his regular parking spot in front of the Caravelle Hotel, screaming at a fat sergeant getting out of his souped up pedicab. The lifer was handing him a lousy tip.

I'm relatively sure, now that I think back, that Tran could have told me outright who the VC were in Saigon, but I think he just wanted to play me along since I was an American and the Vietnamese were sure that all Americans were stupid.

During my explanation of why I wanted to speak with a VC, he pointed out six guys at six different tables on the verandah of the Continental Palace—one of my haunts—across the street having drinks. He said they were CIA agents.

I could not believe my eyes. The six guys he pointed out were all wearing belted trench coats and fedoras. The temperature at the time had to be 102 degrees. In the shade.

After handing him $20, he directed me to Mimi's Bar and told me to ask any bar girl there what I wanted and to tell them Tran sent me. I did as ordered and handed over another $20 to a bar girl with my request. She directed me to the bartender and for another $20 he directed me to Mimi herself, who was sitting in her plush office talking on a lavender psychedelic phone.

When she saw me at the door, she smiled from ear to ear and waved me in. Pointing with three-inch bloodred polished fingernails at the wicker chair across from her, she motioned for me to take a seat.

Pretending not to listen to her conversation, I slowly surveyed the room.

The wall behind the desk where she was sitting was covered from floor to ceiling with autographed photographs of Mimi and various celebrities.

Mimi receiving Holy Communion from Cardinal Cooke.

Mimi, in a strapless ball gown, dancing cheek to cheek with Ambassador Ellsworth Bunker.

Mimi, with her head thrown back in laughter at something General Westmoreland, who was pouring champagne into her glass, was whispering in her ear.

I was more than impressed.

Mimi and Mamie golfing.

Mimi and Imelda trying on shoes.

I glanced around the rest of the mauve and pink office.

In one corner, there rested a surf board next to a scuba tank.

In another, a baby grand piano held up a giant candelabra next to a framed photo of Mimi and Liberace playing a duet.

I looked back at Mimi, and she winked and gave me a signal that the conversation was about over.

"Teddy, you smooth operator, listen I've got to run. I've got a good-looking hunk in my office. Keep trying and call me back when you get through. Even Martha Mitchell can't stay on the phone forever. Chou."

She hung up the phone, slinked over to me, and shook my

hand.

"I read your piece about the patrol. Marvelous writing, but was it kosher to plagiarize so much of the Bard?" Then she laughed and ordered two Singapore Slings.

After a few hours and many drinks, she told me that even though she hated the VC (me thinks she doth protested too much) and was herself a true believer in Democracy, she thought she could make a few calls and arrange for me to go out on an NVA patrol. She added, that when I got back to make sure to stop by her villa for a cocktail party that she and her American general boyfriend were planning for some Pentagon officials in-country on a fact-finding trip.

She blew me a kiss good-bye after answering the phone with, "Martha, darling, who in the hell have you been gabbing with for the last four hours? Listen, I'm going to put you on hold while I make a quick call. It will only take a few seconds."

I raced back to my apartment to wait for the call. I assumed I would be sitting by the phone for days.

But the phone was ringing as I turned the key to my apartment. I was surprised to hear General Giap on the phone calling from Hanoi.

General Giap was the top banana, the general in charge of the whole war, on the enemy's side, of course. Anyway, he said he loved my story and thought it was the best piece of fiction he had read since *Catch 22*. I protested vehemently and proclaimed that it was all true, every word of it.

There was a pause. Then he condescendingly said, "Of course it is, dear boy. Now back to facts. I hear through the grapevine that you want to go out on an NVA patrol."

My adrenaline was pumping when he directed me to fly to Danang the next morning and wait in the terminal next to the ice cream stand.

He added, "And do not forget to wear a white carnation in your handsome blue correspondent's suit."

When I asked him how he knew I had a blue correspondent's

suit, he said that I also had a gray and tan one. He chuckled as he explained that for years he thought it was a sort of journalist's uniform for lounging in Saigon.

Smitty had said the same thing not a week earlier, and even I had to laugh at myself and my byline brothers reporting the war, all looking so natty. Rumor had it that Dan Rather wore a pearl-handled pistol to accessorize.

I caught a C-130 at six the next morning and landed at Danang with the word "fag" still ringing in my ears from the GIs aboard the flight. The carnation was a bit much, even for this clandestine mission I was on.

After signing autographs for a group of donut dollies in cute blue uniforms on their way to a Kool-aid run, I was approached by a baggage handler who asked me to follow him. I wasn't sure if he was my contact or part of some gang out to rip me off, but I threw caution to the wind and trailed him outside the terminal.

There waiting was a South Vietnamese four-star general's jeep. In the driver's seat was a guy dressed in a South Vietnamese major's uniform. He looked like the bartender at Mimi's Bar.

When I told him of the resemblance he said, "We all look alike, don't you think?"

He motioned me to get in the back seat, and he drove outside the compound. The American MP guards waved us through without stopping us. Then the driver braked the jeep and blindfolded me.

We drove for about an hour in what seemed like circles.

The jeep came to a stop and the blindfold was removed. There we were in front of a pagoda. Two saffron-robed Buddhist monks came out and ordered me to climb into a coffin in the back of an ox cart. I did as instructed.

And that's how I got over the DMZ and into North Vietnam. It was explained to me along the way that we had to go that route because lunchtime traffic on the Ho Chi Minh Trail was impossible, especially during the tourist season.

When the coffin was finally opened, I found myself in a North Vietnamese Army camp. An NVA colonel—"Just call me

Hannah"—greeted me by bussing both my cheeks. He was also a VC Colonel when he went South on business, he explained.

"Your story was most entertaining," he said over tea. "Was any part of it true?"

I asserted that it was all true.

"My dear young man, do you imagine that I was born yesterday?" He stared at me with hate-filled eyes.

I surveyed the well-armed camp of hard-core fighting men. I did not want to anger him. As I looked around at the predicament I was in, I started sweating profusely.

"Well, okay, I did exaggerate a bit, Colonel," I recanted quickly.

Colonel Hannah smiled and said, "Good. Now we understand each other. More cookies? My dear fellow, I will give you a chance to write an even more thrilling story by going out with our men on patrol. But in this story, I would like you to write from the point of view of our prisoner. It could mean a Pulitzer. Do I make myself clear?" I shook my head. He continued, "Good. And by the way, you will be a hero in this story, too. Make it up as you go along. I'm sure you can do that."

He explained that as a youngster he strongly believed the truth was important, but after so many years of fighting the Americans, and hearing our lies, his side, too, had to put a little spin on events to be believed.

My God, I was thinking then, could Smitty have been right? Was everything going on during the war bullshit?

The Colonel, I could see, wanted to talk and continued, "Unlike the Americans, we do not go out looking for the enemy. We wait for them to come to us. I know it is not John Wayneish, but, you see, he is not a war hero to us. He is just a movie actor and a bad one at that. This war with you Americans is a reality and we fight to win, not to look macho. With that strategy in mind, we order our troops to go out about two kilometers from base camp, and they are ordered to sit and wait. Until now, they would wait to kill the American patrol but now, well, they are ordered merely to sit and wait. And they are under strict orders not to get dirty, because the laundry bills are crippling the economy of North Vietnam. You see, the mamasans have become spoiled by you Americans and your inflated salaries. We truly cannot compete. You look perplexed, dear boy. Really it's quite logical at this point in time. Our soldiers and leaders are merely waiting for the Americans to become weary and return home where they belong. The South Vietnamese will never fight without foreign aid. And the moment the Americans pack up and depart on the last chopper, we will take over all the cities and towns and roll into Saigon and win the war. We merely have to wait and be patient and not get dirty in the process."

Hannah sure was a wind-bag.

That night, I went out on patrol with an NVA squad, as a prisoner, of course. Or, to be more accurate, I should say nonpatrol.

The squad leader, a wily guy by the name of Nguyen, bitched to me that he did not become a soldier to sit and wait. But orders were orders. He did not have to like it, though, and wanted so badly to see some action.

You see, he had read American comic books since he was a kid and wanted to be just like his hero Sgt. Rock. He even referred to American soldiers as "Japs" and "Krauts."

When we got to their camp in the jungle, I could see from the light of the full moon that it was quite an established set up. Tents, cots, books, typewriters, Japanese lanterns. There was even an oven for baking French bread.

Nguyen allowed the men to tune into the American military station, AFVN radio network. "Soul Train" was on, and the guys started dancing.

It seemed odd to me that they were making so much noise in the jungle at night with American patrols still searching and destroying. I warned Nguyen that they could easily be giving their position away and that maybe they should pipe down a bit.

Nguyen's answer to me was, "No sweat, GI," and continued dancing with the medic, who happened to be one of the best dancers outside of Harlem.

Hell, I thought, if they weren't worried, why should I be? I decided to join the fun. I tapped Nguyen's shoulder to cut in and the medic and I danced to the next three songs. Even though I was the "prisoner," I insisted on leading during the slow songs. After all, I was taller by a foot.

I got a chance to talk to all the guys on patrol who, by the way, spoke a spattering of English and fluent French.

One of the men, who had been patrolling for four years, had finished the complete works of Harold Robbins and had actually read from cover to cover Marcel Proust's *Remembrance of Things Past*, *War and Peace*, and every book written by every Nobel literature winner.

Another NVA grunt was completing a correspondence course in "How to Write Children's Books" from the Famous Writers School in Wisconsin. He banged away at the typewriter during the party, because he had an assignment due and, like students everywhere, put it off till the last moment. He claimed—and haven't we all heard this ole chestnut—he worked best under pressure.

I taught the guys how to make s'mores, and they proudly showed me a fine collection of sandals made from tires. The snow tires were the most durable, and the whitewalls were a work of art. The radials were quite nice, too.

We spent the long hours grouped around the campfire. But I thought it strange that we had a fire going and were still being quite noisy. I figured that we could be easy targets for American patrols. By the time the hollering and shouting was over, I would be deader than a doorknob and good-bye story. Jesus, my editor would shit if I did not get my quota in on time.

"Relax, Ink," Nguyen assured me. "If there is an American squad within six kilometers, we will hear them and have plenty of time to die out the fire and be quiet." He added, I guess to calm me down, "Chill out, Dude."

While we were singing the "French National Anthem" and enjoying water buffalo wings dipped in nuoc mam, I heard in a distance what sounded like a herd of elephants stampeding our way.

I remembered watching Tarzan movies and realized that we were in a jungle and almost wet my pants imagining being trampled to death. The fire was quickly doused and the men began whispering.

"What's happening, Nguyen?" I pleaded for assurance of my safety.

"An American patrol about a half an hour away," he whispered back.

We sat frozen in our spots as the noise got louder and closer.

Then I heard an American voice yell, "Hey, Ralph, where the hell you goin'. There ain't no VC out here. Charlie's back at his base camp catching some f_ _kin' Z's."

Another voice shouted, "Jesus H. Christ, I just stepped on some gum. Oh, f_ _k, it's dog shit."

It sounded as if we were surrounded, and I whispered to Nguyen, "What are you going to do?"

But he and the other enemy grunts were giggling so hard that they had both hands across their mouths to suppress their laughs.

One guy was trying to control his hiccups. And another whispered that he was about to pee his pants from laughing so hard.

Another voice from the American patrol shouted, "Hey, man, why should I kill VC. None of them dumb mother f_ _kers ever called me a nigger."

Another voice responded just as loudly, "Since you're a white boy from South Boston, why should they, you stupid f_ _kin' Mick?"

The noise and loud conversations went on for well over an hour and then just as quickly as they had arrived, they moved on. They were even louder than a herd of elephants in any Tarzan movie I had ever seen.

Soon things died down. And after that close call, nothing happened the rest of the night and for the next few days.

Three days later, we got back to base camp and Nguyen reported enemy activity in the bush. I asked Colonel Hannah why his men did not shoot them. They were like sitting ducks, trampling around and making enough noise to wake the dead.

Looking amused, he answered, "Ahh, yes, why indeed? To be truthful, it is really not necessary for us to fire another bullet. There are land mines, booby traps, bouncing betty's, animal traps. Then there are fraggings by your own troops against hated officers and lifers. The American soldiers become drunk and have auto accidents. They get malaria. And then, of course, your friendly fire takes its toll. Search and destroy missions dreamed up by your Pentagon analysts, who by the way probably never saw any combat themselves, were the stupidest thing in military history. Ahh, yes, why indeed?"

He was pretty smug, which angered me. I mean, after all I am an American. I angrily asked, "What about the damage from our bombs?"

He smiled. "The bomb damage in the South has turned your allies against you, and the bomb craters in the North have become fishing ponds and swimming holes. We have built R & R centers around them. They will be glamorous resorts after the war is over and the tourist trade picks up."

"Tourist trade? Are you serious, Colonel?" I could not believe my ears.

The Colonel smiled again and went into one of his monologues.

"Hannah, please call me Hannah. Please understand, we do not desire to come face to face with you Americans anymore. I mean to say on the battlefield, that is. We do not want to antagonize the foot soldiers since they will be gone soon. But even though the American GIs will go away thinking that they survived the worst year of their life in a hellhole, they will become nostalgic and mellow as they get older and will begin daydreaming of returning as tourists. They will forget the ugly and only remember the beautiful beaches and women and how exciting it all was. You will see, mark my words. Nostalgia will take over."

Hannah continued to explain that the North had only one problem: Once they won the war it would be difficult to establish diplomatic relations with America, a country that had never lost a war. It would become a macho thing led by the biggest machos in America, the guys who did not fight in Vietnam but yelled the loudest about fighting Communists. I knew plenty of them.

The Colonel went on to explain that there was much discussion among the Hanoi leadership that they should surrender as the Japanese and Germans and other losers of wars, take all the money that losers get, wait a few years, and then take over the whole country quietly through fair elections, as Ho Chi Minh could have won in 1956.

"Simple really. We let you win, you go home, then we win. But the hard-liners in Moscow are truly as stupid as the hard-liners in America. As a matter of fact, they are cut from the same cloth and I cannot see any difference. Both sides of hard-liners want to crush the other. We moderates wanted to surrender as early as 1965, but then you Americans started pumping so much money into Vietnam and we Communists were getting so much of it that it was stupid to stop the war. Our coffers were bulging with money siphoned to us through the black market, money exchanges, and the selling of drugs to your troops. Unbelievable how much of your money came our way. Mind you, that was after the South Vietnamese generals and American business owners got filthy rich. Everyone but the peasants and the soldiers benefited, and yet they are the ones who suffered the most. Life, my dear boy, is one big cosmic chess game."

Hannah stared down at his desk and I thought I detected a tear in the corner of his eye. But before I could say anything, he looked up and smiled.

"I am being rude to a guest by pointing out the stupidity of your government. Let us not have any more serious talk."

The rest of the day was delightful. We discussed movies and books and things not pertaining to the war.

The guy loved American comedies, politics, and collecting stories for the memoir he wanted to pen in his old age.

I asked him about Marx and he answered that Groucho was highly overrated and thought the Three Stooges were much funnier.

Then I asked about Lenin and he answered that John was so so, but that Yoko had a great set of tits. Davy Jones from the Monkees was much more talented in his humble opinion. He added that he loved joking around and was just pulling my leg to see how I would respond.

My time with him was drawing to a close, and I began gathering my things.

He stopped me and said, "but before you depart, let me share with you one of my most prized possessions."

We walked into his sleeping quarters. The room was bare except for a sleeping mat on the floor, a kerosene lamp, and a poster of *Barbarella*. Autographed.

"This is from my favorite movie. I even told Jane to drop the protesting and get back to making sexy movies. And for goodness sake, 'let your hair grow back,' I advised her."

As we were shaking hands when I was leaving, I asked him why he trusted me enough to show me what their side was really doing.

He answered quickly, "I don't want to be rude again but you are new to Vietnam and if you ever tried relating the truth, you would surely be laughed right out of the country. No, you will have to play the game and write just as other correspondents if you ever want to get ahead in the news business."

Before I headed back South, Hannah asked me for a small favor. He wanted me to write a letter of recommendation for his son who was applying to my alma mater, Yale. I asked him to tell me a little about the boy and was surprised to learn that I had already met him. He was the guy who picked me up at the airport, the one who looked like the bartender at Mimi's Bar. In fact, I learned that he was the bartender at Mimi's.

All through my time in Vietnam, after that, Mimi's bartender became one of my best reliable sources, since he was invited to all of Mimi's parties at her villa. Plus, he hung out at the USO and shot pool with the GIs. Thank God he did, or else he would have judged all Americans by the journalists who hung out at Mimi's Bar and the embassy staffers and high ranking military honchos who went to Mimi's villa. Talk about the Ugly Americans, the wannabe Colonialists. Including me, I am sad to confess.

Hannah hugged me good-bye and advised me to write a great story about my time as a prisoner of the VC. Smitty helped on that one, in exchange for use of my apartment and favorite prostitute while I was in Hong Kong on R & R.

I have to laugh. After that story came out. I was treated like a God by the press corps. Hannah was right. Writing the truth was completely out of the question. No one would have believed me, and my reputation would have been ruined.

Oh, yeah, after I left North Vietnam, I was driven back to Danang without a blindfold via the Ho Chi Minh Trail.

Now I know this is going to be hard to believe, but did you know there was a McDonald's on it? Have I ever lied? There were Dairy Queens, Texaco stations, Holiday Inns, and toll booths as well. I swear on my rusty Smith Corona. It was just like a major turnpike in America except Howard Johnson's wasn't allowed on it. Bad food was the reason I heard from Tran, the bartender.

When Tran and I reached Danang, he suggested we have dinner at the American officers' club. He wanted to introduce me to other reliable sources.

The manager of the officers' club warmly welcomed Tran and me. Tran explained how I was to be told the truth and the manager, who was also a VC major named Tran, called the manager of the barbershop concessions on base, who was also a VC major named Tran, and he called the off-base brothel owner, who also was a VC major named Tran, to dine with us.

There I was, supping with the VC who had infiltrated the Danang base. Infiltrated hell. They ran the base and told me that all the VC in Danang either worked for or with the American military, press, and CIA. It was too unbelievable and so far-fetched that it would not have been believed if I had written it as fiction.

I know I sound crazy or like Oliver Stone, but it's all the truth, so help me God. Now that I think about it, Oliver Stone is probably the only one telling the truth.

And I know, I know, I will be criticized by my colleagues in the media for either lying in my stories or telling the truth about lying. I am not too sure either they or I would know the difference anyway. But all I can tell them and you is, he who is free of sin may cast the first stone.

And as my good buddy, Professor Smitty, once wrote, "They say the tongues of dying men enforce attention, like deep harmony. Where words are scarce, they're seldom spent in vain."

DAN QUAYLE'S DOUBLE

Nowadays, people say Dan Quayle and I look so much alike that we could pass as twins. But years ago, when we were at college in Indiana together, folks then claimed that we both resembled Robert Redford. Yep, that's right, I knew ole Dan in college. We even played pick-up basketball together.

Back in those days, during the sixties, Dan was gung-ho the Vietnam War and believed that it was vitally important to fight Communism in Southeast Asia.. However, he was convinced that he was more valuable in the National Guard than on the front lines in Vietnam. Oh, he used to declare that he wasn't afraid to fight, it was just that he wanted to make darn sure Indiana was safe from Communist infiltration.

J. Danforth saw the bigger picture and was being groomed to take over his father's newspapers. The duo—daddy and sonny—felt that the pen was mightier than the sword. As Dan used to proclaim, he would honorably serve on the home front where decisions were made, on the golf courses and in the board rooms.

Dan affirmed loudly that the United States had to stop Communism by using the little people, who wouldn't amount to much anyway, as cannon fodder. It was imperative that young men, such as he, had to remain at home in order to prepare to become the future leaders of America. Besides, he was concerned about the possible contamination of his precious bodily fluids and sperms that were needed to carry on the Quayle name. You see, his father's friends did not want him exposed to Agent Orange, although they wholeheartedly approved its use in the war that less important boys fought in.

Frankly, I didn't want to go to Vietnam either. Not that I was from an important family or being prepared for greatness or anything. It's simply that I did not want to die. To be honest, I didn't care a hill of beans about fighting Communism.

But my grades were lousy; and I was just drifting along, not sure where I belonged.

The more I watched the news of the war on television, the more I hated staring in the mirror and seeing not only me but also Danny boy. I kept thinking, who the hell were we to let other guys fight while we stayed safe in Indiana?

Oh, I guess to be fair, Dan saw some kind of bigger picture, but my father wasn't a mogul or anything and I didn't have a legacy to fulfill. Sure, Dad was a Republican who wanted to stop Communism everywhere, but I was just plain apolitical.

Now and again, I dreamed about how cool it would be to have a war experience like Ernest Hemingway, but I didn't have the guts to march over to the recruiting office and enlist. What I did instead was decide to do nothing. Before you could say, "Hell No We Won't Go," I flunked out of college and got drafted. A decision was made for me.

Without a chance to take a big breath, I whizzed through basic training. Completely brainwashed within six weeks, I was eager to ship out to Vietnam and kill gooks. Christ, I was revving to kill, kill, kill. For peace, of course.

Man, I was so pumped up that I even seriously considered volunteering for a combat assignment. Then again, I pondered, maybe I should let fate take its course and go with the flow. Robot-like, I floated along with the Army agenda, which included filling out hundreds of forms.

The day I received my Vietnam assignment, I threw my body across the bunk bed and wept. I'm not sure if the tears were for joy or for sorrow.

One of the guys in my barracks, one of the ones who seemed to do many things late or wrong, definitely not a happy camper about going to Vietnam, spotted me sniveling and came over to cheer me up. Ben assumed from the sobbing that I had gotten a combat assignment.

When I showed him what my war job would be, he stared at me as though I had three heads.

"What's the problem?"

I blurted out, "I'm gung-ho and geared up to go kill slopes, and this official document proclaims that I'm on my way to a cushy job."

Ben became real excited. "How in the world did you land this cake slot?"

I couldn't for the life of me figure out how. After going over every possibility, I speculated how it surely did happen.

This is rich: there was a form the Army wanted soldiers to fill out. It's called a "Close Relationship To VIP" sheet. If you're related in any way to a politician or some other famous person, you're supposed to inform the Army in case anything bad happens to you.

What it really meant was, if you did have some mucky muck relative, you were going to be sent somewhere safe. The military machine didn't mind nobodies getting killed and maimed, because relatives of nobodies don't make much noise.

Now on the other hand, famous and influential people sure as hell can cause the green machine plenty of trouble; hence, it was a lot smarter just to place relatives of VIP's somewhere safe, like a million light years from combat. Far, far away from danger, somewhere real safe, like Saigon.

Ben, who hadn't done any of his paper work as of yet, asked, "Who did you put down as a VIP relative?"

"No shit!" he screamed, when I whispered that my aunt was Gypsy Rose Lee. At that point, Ben got that look, as if a light bulb had just gone on in his head.

That night, he burned the midnight oils filling out all his paperwork.

On his VIP sheet, he wrote in large block letters that he was a direct descendent of Benjamin Franklin. Shrewdly choosing a long-deceased personage, he didn't want there being any chance some wise lifer could check it out, considering that Ben was Jewish with the last name of Schwartz. Talk about chutzpah.

As it turned out, there were only the two of us out of hundreds of guys who put any names down on the VIP list.

Ben Schwartz, who began referring to himself as Benjamin Franklin Schwartz, was quickly assigned to a military printing office in Saigon.

While there, we became great friends and even shared an apartment on Tu Do Street, directly above Mimi's Bar. It was a wonderful tour of duty for both of us. My job took me out of town most of the time and he was gone a lot, too.

What was my job? If you can believe this, I was attached to Army Special Services, and my military responsibility was to escort USO Show groups and other visiting celebrities all over Vietnam. Is that too much, or what? I know what a plum assignment I had, but there were some hairy moments during my 365 days in the war zone.

Take for instance, one time a female barbershop quartet was in-country for a few weeks. The women were in their forties and were unbelievably excited to be there to entertain the troops.

Dear Lord, I was hoping and praying that we could fly to a firebase, let them sing a couple of tunes, and dart out before we got booed and hissed and harangued by the GI turnout, mostly teenagers, who demanded rock and roll and young beauties to oogle at.

I worried: where in the world am I going to take these old broads and not have them embarrass themselves or, for that matter, me?

While I was striving to figure out where in the hell these menopausal women could put on their preposterous production without too much hostility from the audience, my roommate Ben suggested that I mull it over with some grunts who were spending the night in our apartment. His new pals were part of a squad from a firebase where my roomy, ole Benjamin Franklin Schwartz, had cut himself orders and gone TDY.

These combat veterans explained that on their firebase whenever a USO Show or any celebrities visited, the lifer major sent all the enlisted men out on patrol and the only ones left to catch the act were the officers.

The brightest one, Smitty, added, "Those lifers would really dig the female barbershop quartet. Big time."

The next morning, I met my antiquated wards at the helicopter pad at Tan Son Nhut airport. Cheerfully, we flew out to the firebase. I had phoned ahead and talked to Major Holloway, who predictably sent the peons out on a search and destroy mission. When our chopper landed, sure enough, the audience consisted of only officers.

The show lasted a very, very long time. There were so many curtain calls and standing ovations that by the time we were ready to leave, it was too dark to fly back to Saigon. The major suggested—practically ordered—that we should spend the night, then escorted the ladies to a room next to the officers' club to freshen up for the party that he and his "fine officers" had planned. The old gals were bubbling over with excitement.

It was well past four in the morning before we practically crawled back to the room after the soiree. The four women never had so much fun in their entire lives.

The major and his lifer cronies, all 19 of them, took turns dancing with the women. Besides tripping the light fantastic for hours, the boys and the girls drank and drank and drank and played "Wales Tails" and every other college drinking game you could possibly name.

When we finally made it back to the room for some shut-eye, I spent the rest of the night, what was left of it, answering the knocks at the door. I didn't sleep a wink. I was busy as a bee accepting gifts for the women and arranging rendezvous, whispered outside the bedroom door:

"Tell Mona to meet me near the mess hall."

"Tell Rhoda I love her and to meet me near the motor pool."

"Tell Mildred I think she's swell and to meet me beside the flagpole."

"Tell Matilda I'm separated from my wife and to meet me in the officers' bunker."

Geez, I felt like a dorm mother or something.

Hell, I even had to be careful for my own safety. Two or three of the West Point guys kept gawking at me in a strange way and asking if I'd like to take a shower. I became even more suspicious when they wanted to know what my birth sign was. And the creepy thing was that they were the most macho of the bunch.

By the next morning, I was sleep-deprived and relieved when I jumped on the helicopter and headed toward Saigon. The women, on the other hand, who I thought would be appalled at the highjinks of the major and his boys, were gushy and thrilled that they could show their patriotic support for the men fighting the war.

Yeah, right. The only combat those fellows ever saw was the battle of the stomach bulge from all the rot gut they poured down their gullets.

Here and there, I wrote to my old college pal, Dan Quayle, while I served in Vietnam. I'm telling you, his letters were filled with more danger than mine, including plenty of sandtraps and gopher holes on the greens and rowdy peace rallies he had to help break up.

As I said before, Ben Schwartz, who claimed Benjamin Franklin as a relative, worked in a military printing office. At first, he was just happy to be in a safe slot, then decided to take advantage of his position, which was designing invitations to officers' parties and dinners. Thanks to some captains' uniforms we bought off the black market and the extra invitations he brought home from the office, we attended quite a few parties. After a while, we just didn't have enough time to go to them all. There were so many.

Now, I'm going to tell you a story about Ben, who by the way changed his name while in Vietnam. Well, he didn't change it legally or anything. What he did, actually, was change all his military records, which he had access to where he worked. In which case, I'm not going to cause him any trouble because Ben Schwartz doesn't exist anymore. He was killed off by Ben Schwartz in Saigon. And the reason for that? You'll soon see.

Let me provide some background information on my good buddy. Ben was an actor in civilian life. Small stuff. Dinner theaters and community playhouses. While in Nam, he decided he'd like to hone his craft, so he created a hero. All on paper, through the printing office, that is.

The first thing he had to do was get rid of Ben Schwartz. That was fairly easy. He cut himself orders to be attached to the firebase where I took my female barbershop quartet and where his pal Smitty was stationed. Immediately upon arrival, he went out on patrol with the grunts there—Smitty, Red, Horseface, and the rest of that squad. While out in the bush, Ben dyed his hair, grew a mustache, and acquired a Boston accent. What emerged was Captain Benjamin Franklin Gutenberg, who strolled into base camp and caught the first chopper back to Saigon.

Ben had already printed up TDY orders for his new persona before he left the printing office. People were always coming and going. Nobody paid attention to who was who or where anybody was at any given time.

Before officially assuming his new role, he had to get rid of the old one, Private Ben Schwartz. That was easy. When Smitty and the squad got back to the firebase, they reported that Private Ben Schwartz had been killed by Friendly Fire and the only thing left was his dog tag. Since Ben had been a foster kid, he had no living relatives. There were no remains, no family, and the Army automatically added Ben Schwartz's name to the KIA list.

Thinking ahead, he had assigned Smitty as his beneficiary on his $10,000 life insurance policy and they split it. As a matter of fact, Ben planned the whole charade as though he were writing a play.

Before he left for that fake final patrol, he had created a complete file on Captain Gutenberg and entered all the information in the computers at MACV and the Pentagon. If it's in an Army file or computer, then it's authentic.

Thereafter, his new persona, Captain Gutenberg, supposedly attached to MACV, just showed up whenever and wherever he felt like it. He had carte blanche of everything in the printing office, and nobody bothered with him, because they all assumed he was CIA. And nobody—lifers or enlisted guys or generals—messed with the CIA.

Gleefully, Ben printed up TDY orders for his new persona to go here and there and everywhere around Vietnam. At various times, Captain Benjamin Franklin Gutenberg led or fought alongside tunnel rats, search and destroy patrols, and marine detachments. He battled from the Delta to the DMZ with the Army, Navy, Air Force, and Marines. On paper, that is.

Before you knew it, Major Gutenberg got really creative about his TDY assignments and sometimes couldn't resist actually going on them. Oh, not to do any actual fighting or anything, though that crossed his mind for a few insane moments.

When he went to the Highlands, he'd hang out playing poker with the Montagnards for a couple of days, then head back to Saigon after the unit he was supposed to be with finished fighting whatever battle they were waging.

After a while, he began writing himself up for medals and, of course, putting the paperwork officially in his official files at the printing office, which made their way to the official files at MACV, which sent those files to the Pentagon. He kept promoting himself. With each advancement, he got cockier. It was as though I was living with a person with a split personality.

Lt. Colonel Ben Gutenberg wanted to experience it all while he was in Vietnam. He'd cut those orders for a week with the Navy Seals and then head off to go tiger hunting near Dalat or go on another R & R. He took one R & R a month during his tour.

I couldn't believe that a guy could actually get away with everything that he got away with. I truly believed, many times, that his number was up, especially when he got carried away.

Like that night he, by now Colonel Gutenberg, was telling his fake stories about his heroics—real whoppers—one night in Mimi's Bar, below our digs. Sitting nearby and recently back from the bush, a journalist overheard him shoveling the shit to the bar girls. The whole time ole Ben was winking to his buddy Hannah, dressed in a South Vietnamese colonel's uniform.

Anyway, this journalist, who bought every word Ben was shouting about fighting for democracy, my country right or wrong, ad nausea, begged Ben to let him do a story on him. I thought, man the jig is up if any of this hits the papers. But Ben just went on and on in glorious terms about how he had won each medal on his colonel's uniform—he leaped from PFC to full bird in five months while working in the printing office.

His buddy Hannah, who always wore a South Vietnamese colonel's uniform or a hippie outfit, wasn't in the military. He was an actor that Ben somehow met at Mimi's Bar, and the two of them hit it off.

Ben supplied all of Mimi's friends with uniforms and any kind of identification they needed. Why you ask?

Well simple, really. Ben and Hannah (odd name for a Vietnamese man, but that's what it was) decided to start a theater person's network. Hannah had friends, he claimed, who were in show business all over the Far East; and Mimi, who had a French passport, had connections with the film industry in Paris, London, and Hollywood.

I'm not sure for a fact, but my guess is they used the fake uniforms for parties they wanted to attend like the ones that Ben and I did. Ben, Mimi, and Hannah planned to start a Vietnamese theater group, too.

One time, I remember Ben and Hannah were trying to dream up more exploits for Colonel Gutenberg and decided it would be really cool if Ben were captured, sent to a POW camp, and then escape. I don't know how Hannah managed it, but he arranged for

Colonel B. F. Gutenberg to be captured by the enemy and to escape.

Jesus, the story of that escapade made every paper in the States. Afterwards, there was no living with the guy for a while. He got a little weird and started to take on new roles.

One time I was escorting Martha Raye around a Green Beret camp, and I swear Ben was our cyclo driver or else he has a Vietnamese twin.

When he'd come back to earth and just be actor Ben playing the part of war hero, I used to love watching him parade around Saigon wearing that damn eye patch and hobbling with his cane.

By his sixth month in-country, he had awarded himself three Silver Stars, five Bronze Stars, and 10 Purple Hearts. Then, he received a call from General Westmoreland, who by this time was Army Chief of Staff.

Westy had read about him. Yet, when he phoned his general friends in Saigon to ask about this heroic officer, nobody knew anything about the mysterious and courageous Colonel Benjamin Franklin Gutenberg.

Be assured, heads rolled; and before you can say military intelligence, Ben's alter ego was given his first star, for real, and put in charge of the JUSPAO office, where all the war news was gathered and passed out to the civilian press. JUSPAO stands for Joint United States Public Affairs Office.

What a perfect place for the biggest fraud that ever passed through Vietnam.

There he was, in the JUSPAO office, the locale where all the war information was disseminated. General War Hero, actor, and master forger, proceeded to churn out the biggest whoppers about the war.

His pal, the Vietnamese actor Hannah, helped him compose the reports. I always felt like I was sitting in on a writing session for "Laugh-in" because of the way those two carried on, chortling and making up stories that were handed out to journalists of the free press.

"Man, it's all a big joke anyway, so chill out, Dude," Ben would say, when I complained about the harm they could cause with the bogus reports.

By the end of his tour, there was plenty of talk about how he was destined to be chairman of the Joint Chiefs, how he was definitely presidential timber, and how he was the greatest war hero since John Wayne. Everything just seemed to escalate in Vietnam. It must have been the heat.

Oh, yeah, I almost forgot to mention this, the reason he made himself a colonel in the first place was so that he could eat in the high-ranking officers' dining room at Long Binh, where there were crystal chandeliers and the waiters had master's degrees in hotel management from Cornell.

Not surprisingly, Ben became the most reliable source for journalists and visiting members of Congress on fact-finding junkets. Also, after a while, there was no way anyone could expose him. The lifers in charge of the places he said he had been to were too afraid to admit that they had never met the famous General Gutenberg. Everyone claimed to know Ben, or that he had saved their lives, or that they were in a battle with him. Everyone wanted to meet the hero and have a picture taken with him. Hannah, Mimi, and I were the only people who kept him in his place when he started to believe his own outlandish stories.

And check this out. General Gutenberg went to the Paris Peace Talks, but I never heard any anecdotes from that escapade, because by then I was already back in the States, working as a casting agent in Hollywood, thanks to Mimi and Hannah. No shit, GI, they sure as hell had some heavy-duty and important contacts in L.A.

I really have to look up ole Ben someday and hear about how his life was after we parted ways when I left Vietnam. I do know that he eventually retired as a four-star general with a different name.

His official records said he was in his early forties, yet I know for a fact that he retired six years after Vietnam, which would have made him 26 by my count. Anyway, it would be fun to get together with him and to hear some of his tales.

Besides feathering his own nest, Ben sure as hell helped other GIs in Vietnam. For instance, we spent time at 22nd Replacement Battalion and shot the shit with newly arrived GIs who did not want to play war games. Pulling a few strings, Ben put them in slots, thanks to his printing office maneuvers, more to their liking.

Two of those lucky soldiers were assigned to guard the USO Saigon from midnight till 8:00 a.m. They spent the war watching movies inside the recreation center. Those two bastards, supposedly protecting the USO, had favorite movies that they watched with the sound turned off. They knew all the lines by heart and took turns doing actors' parts in *King Kong* and *Casablanca*.

Ben, Hannah, Mimi, and I joined them some nights after curfew. Not that we had to abide by any silly time restrictions. Our special papers said that we four could be out and around any damn time we chose.

Ben assigned another guy to drive the Red Cross girls around Danang. Another soldier he assigned to MACV, where the only thing that GI did was read the *Encyclopedia*. He reupped, because at the end of his first tour he was only up to the M's.

Then there's my favorite Ben-good-deed story, and I have to be careful because the soldier he helped is pretty important now and I don't want to spill the beans and ruin his career.

While Ben was Colonel War Hero supposedly leading some Marine battle, he heard about a soldier who was in a hell of a lot of trouble in Danang. The fellow noticed that anytime the German hospital ship anchored there left Danang harbor for open seas, the base got hit. Before long, he put two and two together and went to the general in charge to report this great piece of information. Truly, the concerned GI wanted to save lives. He saw the ship leave and the base attacked at least 10 times before he was sure of what he saw.

The General's response to the worried GI's report was, "So?"

The soldier was not in the least bit surprised. Slowly, he continued, "Don't you think, General, there might be a connection between the ship's leaving and the base's being attacked?"

The General answered, I heard this from Ben's own mouth, I swear to God, the General said, "A connection between what? The Germans are our allies. If I hear any more talk like that, I'll have you brought up on charges."

The GI just walked away shaking his head, knowing he was right and knowing that the General was a complete idiot. Instead of dropping the whole matter, he began to make bets on when the base was going to be hit. He never took into account the military grapevine. Before long, word leaked out about his winning bets and the CID, the military equivalent of the CIA, got involved and did a massive investigation on the guy.

Not long after the military sleuths began investigating the poor shmuck, the IRS, FBI, and the CIA started an inquisition on not only the GI but also all of his family and friends. There were audits, background checks, talk of treason charges being leveled at him and everyone he knew, including his grade school teachers.

Repeatedly, he kept telling them the simple truth of his "just accidentally figuring out the connection between the German hospital ship's leaving and the base's being attacked."

It wasn't a good enough explanation for the legions of investigators, who I guess had nothing better to do but make the guy's life miserable.

"Don't be smart with us, wise guy. We know you're working for the enemy as a Soviet spy," the inquisitors warned.

So, this is where Ben came into the picture. Like a fox, he cut some orders for himself to head up another investigation through some made-up office he created and went to talk to the kid, who by that time was ready to crack and say anything anybody wanted him to confess. Feeling terrible about the young soldier's predicament, ole heart-of-gold Ben told the kid that he knew of a way to get him off the hook.

The youngster followed Ben's orders, pretending to go into a trance. When he came out, he did as Ben had advised and claimed that he talked to trees and rocks by order of the Virgin Mary who spoke to him, and only him.

Ben and Hannah came up with this one together. It seems that Hannah also had some friends at the Vatican and knew the truth about the whole hospital ship escapade.

Now, I'm relating this second hand, and I might get some of the facts screwed up, but I'll tell it the way I remember it being told to me by Ben as he heard it from Hannah.

Hannah learned that word reached Rome about a GI in Danang, Vietnam who claimed that the German hospital ship's leaving and the base's being attacked were somehow connected. (You have to understand one important thing: The Pope at the time, Paul VI, had been very close to the Germans during World War II.) Immediately, the Pontiff called Helmut Schmidt, Minister of Defense at the time, and found out that the German ship was in fact warned by the VC before an attack so that it could get to safety in open sea.

The Pope couldn't very well squeal on the Germans because Germany's a large Catholic country and well, it's tough at the top and the Pope has to make some rough calls, so he sent a Devil's Advocate to Danang to see if there was (wink wink) any truth to the story of the Blessed Virgin Mary appearing to the GI.

Ben handled the Vatican visit and strongly advised the soldier to just sit on the beach each night. When the German ship left the harbor, he was to report that the Blessed Virgin Mary had appeared to him, warning him that the base was going to be attacked. After three "visions," the Devil's Advocate reported to Rome that it was a miracle, and the Pontiff officially named the GI "The Danang Mystic."

With Ben and Hannah's help, one thing led to another and before not too many years, The Danang Mystic, who now has a different name, nationality, and race, thanks to Ben and his printing office and acting expertise, is now a cardinal at the Vatican. His Eminence is secretly in charge of miracles, UFOs, and extraterrestrial visits.

Throughout his clerical career, from PFC to cardinal in a blink, The Danang Mystic has declared that Our Lady of China Beach has appeared to him in his sleep and informed him that the Americans would lose the war in Vietnam, Ronald Reagan would become president, Mick Jagger and Bianca would split, and that the Edsel would never, even though many wished it would, have a comeback. The former GI and former The Danang Mystic is considered next in line for St. Peter's Seat. So help me God, it's the truth.

For years, after being involved in the production of Vietnam movies like *Platoon* and *Full Metal Jacket* and a number of others, I've retold plenty of noncombat Vietnam War stories to my Hollywood colleagues. I've even tried to get someone interested in making a movie based on them, or at least based on Ben.

But the response I always get, especially from guys who never were there, is: "That's not what war is all about."

The only thing can I do now is stare at them and ask, "Really?"

ACKNOWLEDGMENTS

Many friends were helpful to me while writing these stories. David McPherson and Carol Dingle helped with the editing. As always, my sister Barbara was generous to a fault. I am also grateful for many kindnesses to the following people: Ruth Dell, Linda Estes, Paula Mahan, Christine Guido, Kay Kavanaugh Zarif, Mai Pham, Millie Majette Smith, Mame Dimock, Mick Smith, Susan and Andrew Reardon, Donald Hamilton, Heather Butts, Donna Alger, Mary Brodie, Gerard Leahy, George Sommers, Debbie Marshall, Jimmy Oscar Dell, Richard Ott, Jim Dell, Laura Beck Poskus, Rick Dell, Paige Dempsey Rockett, Pamela Reed, Maryann Hurley, Jacques Bargiel, Linda Kerr, Eddirland Duncan, Leigh Mason, Lore Fields, and my son Mark Clark.